Vampire League

Book V

Nemesis

Vampire League

Book V

Nemesis

by Luiza Dobrzynska

Part 1

God has entrusted us with this mission

When they found Gladiator's burned body, Gerard almost passed out. Even though he had seen many things, it shook him deeply. He was still, deep down, the same Gerard, ethical and sensitive, and such a sight might shock even someone much stronger than him.

"Get a grip." Fronda shouted at him, but hesitantly and quite weakly.

Oggy was crying completely openly, unable to contain herself, and Theo clenched a reassuring hand on her frail shoulder, unable to find any words of comfort.

Never, the most resilient of them all, examined his friend's remains with unbelievable concentration. In the silence of the post-Nazi bunker, only Oggy's heavy breathing and sobbing could be heard.

"His heart was pierced with stake, then his head was cut off and he was poured over with some kind of napalm," Never said at last, rising from his knees. "Probably in that order, so... it seems he didn't suffer very much. However, it makes me wonder. IVH doesn't work that way, much less Nuntia. I don't like it."

"What we do?" Fronda asked.

"First of all, we're getting out of here. We need to get in touch with Nuntia as soon as possible."

"And he?"

"We'll bury him, of course."

The Indian vampire's cold calm seemed inhuman, but it had a sobering effect on the other three. With a concerted effort, they wrapped the half-burned corpse in a blanket and carried it to a rented van. Far from the bunker, in the woods, they dug a grave and buried the Gladiator, masking the place as best they could. They preferred not to risk the vampire's body falling into the hands of forensic pathologists, after all, it is not known if they would find something essential. This has always been the case - vampires from all over the world took particular care that the bodies of their kinsmen did not end up on the autopsy table, because the anomalies that formed in them over time could give scientists too much food for thought.

Dea was waiting at the motel where they had rented rooms.

"Where's Janek?" She asked sharply, looking at her friends with anxious eyes.

"He's dead," Never replied shortly. "What did you find out?"

"It will be unpleasant when Stasiek hears about it," the girl muttered gloomily. "I'd rather not be there...

But to tell you the truth, I was expecting something like that. Jurgen said he lost almost the entire group. He is scared to death, he is out of his mind. All Nazi pride escaped from him like from a pierced balloon."

Jurgen was the leader of Nuntia. It was difficult to track him down when, furious with this internal struggle, they finally decided to talk seriously with the leadership of this organization and came to Berlin. Since they had learned from rumors that Jurgen had a soft spot for go-getting women, they were not afraid to send Dea to him when the Gladiator was missing and he had to be looked for. But if they knew what would turn out, they would never let her go alone.

"Where is he now?" Never asked.

"Here," Dea replied calmly. "He's in the bathroom, afraid to go out."

"My word."

Never opened the door to the tiny bathroom. Huddled in a corner by the sink, the fair-haired man in sweatpants shuddered and instinctively covered himself with his arm.

"Relax, hero, it's just me," said the Indian and sat down on a white stool. "Is it that bad?"

The German looked at him with dark circles under his red eyes. Though he was undoubtedly a strong and fit man, judging from his build, he was now a waste of a human being.

"Ask those who died," he replied hoarsely. "They find us in an unknown way. They are armed with machetes and flamethrowers. There is no escaping them once they track you."

"Slowly, from the beginning and clearly. Who they are?"

The German vampire took a moment to think before he replied:

"They say about themselves that they are the Rast Order. They dress in black and dark brown, wear large crosses on thongs and give the impression of religious fanatics. Men have long dreadlocks, girls shave their heads to the skin, probably for contrast. They're a cult to me, not like Vanhelsingers. They are extremely effective. I saw them murder three of my team with those blasters of theirs."

He sobbed suddenly and bit his fingers.

"I saw one of them run after Karl, who was burning like a torch, and then cut his head off with a machete," he blurted out. "I couldn't help him. I couldn't do anything."

"Calm down. Hysteria won't help you. We also lost one of us here, which means there must be a confrontation."

"Confrontation? Are you mad? Run, and it's best to the end of the world! Nuntia doesn't exist anymore and other organizations will cease to exist soon, you will see."

It was obvious that Dea was not exaggerating. Jurgen was in a state of shock, and there was little to learn from him other than what he had already said. Never looked at his friends standing outside the bathroom door and shrugged.

"I'll give him some sedatives," muttered the doctor, and went to look for a suitable medication in her bag.

"It won't help much. More like anesthesia, I think. We are losing the ground under our feet," Theo pointed out. "Nuntia was organized like a paramilitary unit, if they didn't manage to some Order, then we are already grilled."

"Where's your fighting spirit, knight?"

"I traded for Jen's peanuts last week."

Oggy shuddered miserably and snuggled close to Fronda, who embraced her reflexively.

It was the first time she was so afraid, and for the first time it occurred to her that she would find herself in a situation where her friends would not be able to protect her and she would not be able to help them. Never looked at Jurgen again.

"Are any of your people still alive?" He asked.

"Hermann's squad, I think. I haven't contacted them since it all started, there are still chances they haven't tracked them down."

The German's voice was not very confident. It was evident that he was at the end of his tether and that he had lost all hope of rescue, so he was merely trying to postpone the inevitable. He received the injection by Dea indifferently, hardly noticing it.

"We must go to them immediately," Never said after a short thought. "Immediately. If Jurgen is right and they have no trouble locating someone like us, then we can't stay in one place as much as we have been up to now. Why are you standing there, fools?! Pack up now!"

The friends did not have many personal belongings, so "packing" in their edition meant simply grabbing the handy knick-knacks left on the table or bed, and it took no more than five minutes. Now, chased by the fear and shouting of their leader, they wrapped themselves up even faster, and soon they were in their recreational vehicle. They felt a little more confident in it, even Jurgen regained some courage, though he was most likely helped by the injection given by Dea. Seeing that their forced ally looked a little more awake, Never ordered Oggy to take his seat at the wheel, and he shifted backwards himself.

"Tell me more about this order," he demanded.

"What else would you like to know?"

"Are they human? Are you sure they are human?"

"Sure, just crazy! They call themselves the Order of Saint Obadiah, or Rast, of your choice. RAST is an acronym, but I don't know what it means. They have nothing to do with the Rastamans[1], much less the Rastafarians[2]."

"Do they have any common features?"

---

[1] Rastamen - youth subcultures, generally composed of white teenagers fascinated by Rastafarianism.

[2] Rastafari Movement - a millenarian-messianic syncretic religious movement originated in Christian cultural circles in Jamaica in the 1930s and started by Marcus Garvey. Rastafarians believe that Jah who is God created the world and takes care of it. They also believe that it manifested, inter alia, in in royal majesty the race of Tafari Makkonen, from the time of his coronation as Emperor of Ethiopia known as Haile Selassie I, motivated by veneration for him as the Victorious Lion of the Tribe of Judah, God's Chosen One, Lord of Lords and King of Kings, or recognizing him only as vicar of divine majesty on Earth.

"They're mostly dark-skinned, though probably not African, but rather Hawaiian or Latino. They are led by a woman, Akheela, an Egyptian, as far as I know. They suddenly appear as if they sprouted from under the ground, and once they see you, you are dead. We tried to fight them, but it's for nothing, they're like... wraiths. They have extremely sensitive senses, but they don't find us with them. I'm sure of this one."

"Where do you get that confidence?"

"I don't know. Call it intuition if you like." Jurgen spread his hands helplessly.

Never thought to underestimate his gut. Vampires know things, often failing to explain how they acquired it, and over the years they learn to use this puzzling quality of their minds. But it complicated things in an unforeseen manner. It seemed someone had devised an objective way of detecting the undead, which could mean the beginning of the end of the entire clan.

The recreational vehicle jumped on some bump, and Jurgen immediately covered his head with his hands.

"Take control, hero, nobody is shooting at us, it was only a bump," Never admonished him with disgust. "Fronda, how are we with weapons?"

"Bad. Three Glocks and two clips for each. Such an armament is laughable."

"Laughter is good for health. That's the only thing we have permission to do, so don't fret. That's good, too. We must be careful and trust no one from now on."

Theo remembered something and reached for the phone from his bag.

"I have to call Lilka."

"Later. Now we'll try to warn that Hermann's squad, and then... and then we must seriously consider what to do next. I don't like using big words, but we're probably cornered and we'll have to get out of it somehow."

"He rediscovered America!" Dea snorted.

"Only India. Jurgen, try to remember something else, every detail counts."

"Do you have a plan? Gerard asked hopefully. Until now, Never has always supported them, was the mainstay, the first and last instance they turned to. Like a ship's captain. Now they also hoped that he would find a way out of this situation.

Naver returned Gerard's gaze with a reassuring smile. He, too, was aware of what he was to his "bunch" and did not show that he was, in fact, no less afraid than his friends.

The problems so far were stupid compared to the present ones, since a new group of Hunters had managed to terrify Jurgen, tough and experienced, to death and wipe out his paramilitary organization.

In addition, it was terrifying to know that the Rasts did not spare humans either. They dispersed and partially killed the Hunters of the Van Helsing Institute, considering them... collaborators, for a basically trivial reason - because they used the services of "bloodhounds", dragged vampires to their side. They did not cooperate with anyone outside their circle, and it seemed they even severed contacts with their families. They really looked like a kind of cult.

Such a picture emerged from the words of Jurgen, who, under the influence of the medications administered to him, seemed to regain his memory and began to be ashamed of his unmanly breakdown. Following his directions, they finally drove to the headquarters of the only surviving Nuntia branch.

Hermann's branch was based in the basement of the Berlin casino. The entrance led through several lockable bulkheads, and in every hallway, as Jurgen said, there were cameras and wiretaps in case the vision was damaged. The last corridor ended with a door to a beautifully decorated general hall, from which several doors led to further, probably sleeping rooms. The Order hadn't gotten here yet, but the squad - five young vampires and six older vampires who must have been over a hundred years old - must have known what was going on.

"We're not going anywhere from here," Hermann announced sternly, the typical blond-haired Nordic man with strongly modeled jaws and blue-gray eyes. "If they try to come for us, they will regret it."

"May you be right. But I advise you to get out of here as soon as possible and get as far as possible," said Jurgen.

His behavior made Gerard think that he was the commander of Nuntia only nominally, and he shared this observation with Never. The latter nodded slightly. He also got that impression. The structure of Nuntia had to be less uniform than it appeared at first glance.

Hermann, meanwhile, regarded Never with obvious disgust.

"Well, are we working with the enemies now?" He asked ironically.

"Don't be an idiot," the Indian replied contemptuously. "What enemy am I? At the moment only those lunatics are the enemies, and if we start eating each other instead of working together, it will be really bad. Besides, I would like to remind you that it was not us who started the enmity between our groups."

"You've entered our premises," interjected a girl in a denim set.

"SUPPOSEDLY your territory," Dea corrected dryly. "Nobody has designated areas of action for anyone and so far, there has been no friction against this background. You started to blur the water, quote "Mein Kampf", and you can only blame yourself if you got owned."

The German woman bristled and immediately launched a counterattack. For a moment, nothing was heard in the hideout except the raised voices of the two girls, who twittered like machine guns, speaking both at once, and they were probably the only ones who understood something of the exchange, because the rest could barely tell a single word in the stream from time to time their pronunciation.

"Maul halten, Sie verdammte Frauen[3]!" Hermann finally boomed as he saw the vision technician on duty at the monitors enter the room.

Both women were speechless with indignation what Hermann had used to address the technician:

"What's up? Why did you quit your post?"

---

[3] Zip your lip, damned women (German).

"Just for a moment," the man looked at the newcomers as if he were counting them, then scratched his head and shrugged. "Nothing, nothing... I would have sworn there were more... but it's probably a temporary fault."

Hermnann looked worried.

"Fault? Have you checked if there is anyone unwanted here?"

"Who do you think I am, Otto? Of course I checked. It is not there and it has not been. Only when they were walking through the third lock, I thought there was someone else with them. A fault, or I imagined it because of fatigue."

"Yeah, you've been sitting there for almost twelve hours. Gruber, replace him. And you have a drink and go to sleep."

"Yes, Herr Kommendante."

The technician walked over to the huge cooler with apparent relief, took out a bottle of tinned blood, and walked into one of the further rooms, closing the door behind him.

"Listen up," Dea said as he left. "You'll shout at me again and you'll lose all your teeth. Got it?"

"Calm down, fury. This isn't the time for a personal rumble. So you don't run away, do you?" Never asked Hermann.

"Do you have hearing problems? No, we're not running away. Here is our den and we are well protected. When Jurgen recovers, he'll admit it himself."

He looked at his friend who nodded uncertainly. Never shrugged in resignation.

"Well, as you like. We warned you and now we wash our hands of it."

"There is never too much hygiene. Goodbye coldly with a hint of irony."

"What a jerk," Fronda hissed through his teeth, giving Hermann an unfriendly glance. It was obvious that he really wanted to talk to him in private, but Never kicked him slightly in the ankle and pushed him towards the door. His patience was running out. Since those hard-lined Germans did not want help, there was no point in persuading them.

After a brief deliberation, they decided to rent a room in a nearby mid-range hotel and wait a few days. If their predictions were to come true, during those few days the Rasts - whoever they were - should track down the casino and attempt to assassinate there. They had a good view of the illuminated front of the casino from their hotel room and could chat, almost certainly safe in this security guarded, always crowded place.

"And how do we arrange the order of the guards?" Dea asked, continuing her routine check of the room and the adjoining bathroom.

"We will establish by the conventional roll of the dice. There are five of us. I take points one and six, Theo two, Oggy three, Gerard four, and you five."

"I've always been a solid five woman."

Theo smiled approvingly at the words. Although he generally preferred gentle and demanding ladies (he was a flesh-and-blood knight, after all), he greatly admired strong, resourceful, and energetic women like Dea. They have never formed a band with any "fixed" ones - in their world men kept them together and the fair sex with them. Oggy did not change this pattern, because she was a werewolf. But Dea had a peculiarity: she seemed to prefer the company of men.

"And if they will come?" Asked Gerard, who had dropped out of first watch at that impromptu "vantage point."

"Then, of course, we'll get them from behind," Never replied calmly. "And I don't want to hear the word that you're against violence or something stupid like that. They are cold-blooded killers, and we must be as ruthless with them as they are with us if we are to survive."

Oggy growled softly to indicate that she agreed with the previous speaker. Fronda released Jen from the carrier and placed water on the table and a bowl of dried fruit and nuts. The monkey eagerly began to eat.

"Who will take care of her if something happens to me..." He sighed.

"Can you hear yourself...? Daddy..." Never snorted angrily. "Don't be afraid, more people will take care of her than of us. Dea, do we have anything else to eat?"

"One bottle left per head. And a piece of tenderloin for Oggy," the doctor reported, looking into the thermo bag.

"Come on. We all need recovery. Then we'll worry about where to get the supplies," Never decided, and the friends took care of the meal.

Then they washed the empty bottles well, scraped the labels off them and put them back in the bag. It was better not to dump them on the hotel premises after all. The precautions taken by the undead might have seemed exaggerated, but they guaranteed them greater safety... if anything could be safe in their complicated lives.

They cheated life and they cheated death. This was what it looked like. It would be absurd to add any ideology to what they were doing. Probably, the only one was... just to survive the next day. Never's group was probably the only one that went beyond their own needs, helping what they needed, the rest focused solely on themselves and their circle, not even out of selfishness, but out of a pure self-preservation instinct. They wanted to survive, therefore they did not get involved in anything, and yet they perished. They did not want to fight people, but they were forced to do so against their will. Yes, it is not easy being a vampire in the human world, and it is impossible to exist outside of it.

After the meal, Gerard returned to his seat by the window, which had a perfect view of the casino and part of the area. Never, an expert in such matters, arranged the curtain and curtain in such a way that the guard could observe the entire "foreground", being practically invisible to anyone from the outside. After two hours, Gerard changed Fronda and the actor was finally able to enjoy a bit of rest. He felt very tired and fell asleep, barely resting his head against the hotel pillow. Jen curled up beside him, for whom it was far too cold in Berlin and was still looking for someone's warmth.

He slept with a heavy sleep with a fluffy monkey hugging his neck until he was awakened by a shaking on his shoulder.

"Get up," Oggy whispered in his ear, "I think it's starting."

The Frenchman sprang to his feet and fell to the window where others were already present. He saw a group of dark-skinned people dressed in camouflage leopards gathering near the casino.

They didn't seem like guys wanting to play games. In their hands they were holding what looked like sticks from this distance, and they wore a kind of small backpacks on their backs. Never handed Gerard the binoculars. In several dozen close-ups, he saw their Polynesian hairstyles, as well as a few shortly cut to the skin of their shaven heads - he already knew they were women.

"Is that them?" He asked, his voice lowering involuntarily.

"It looks like it, Cheetah" Never answered him. "Fronda, put Jen in the baby carrier. We're going now."

"And if we don't come back, what will happen to her?" Theo asked uncertainly.

"Nothing. Some maid will definitely be interested in her. Don't be an idiot."

Fronda grimaced with dissatisfaction but obeyed. He checked to see if the small water bottle mounted inside was filled with clean water, then ran after his friends.

In the street, they broke into a line to attack the Rasts from all sides, but they were no longer in the place they remembered. Oggy, who had taken her doggy form as soon as she had left the hotel, growled anxiously, sniffing as if she had been hired. Finally, she barked and ran forward, circling the building until she reached the back door. They were open. Cautiously, looking in all directions, they stepped inside, trying to step as quietly as possible. Oggy squealed anxiously, and after a while, not only she, but everyone else, smelled smoke.

"Dea, Cheetah, go to the casino, warn the people!" Never cried. "Fronda and Oggy with me!"

Gerard followed the doctor to the main entrance, where they were stopped by security.

"Get out of the way, jerk! A fire in the basement!" Dea yelled to the bouncer's face, struggling to put words together in German. She knew the language very badly. The only thing that came easily to her was the term "Dummer Esel."

"Where's the fire?" The man was surprised, forgetting even to be offended, and looked at the smoke detectors. Dea bypassed him and caught the devices. As she had supposed, they didn't work.

"They're locked!" She screamed. "Get the people out of here, you idiots, it's gonna be hell in here!"

Security didn't seem very convinced, but as soon as they turned to look at the room, Gerard slipped inside, jumped on the black-jack table, and shouted a fire warning in German. Most of the players didn't even look at him, they were so busy betting the next numbers. Only the dealers froze, looking at him with indignation rather than amazement. After a while, some players started looking around, and security moved towards the intruder.

One of the inner doors burst open and a sooty, coughing back office worker burst in. Black smoke billowed behind him, and in almost the same second the hell Dean had foretold broke loose. People rushed to the exit, suffocating and trampling each other, screams and squeal of terror echoed around them. Many took the opportunity to call in someone else's winnings, and Gerard and Dea, who were no longer paying attention, began pushing their way into the back room, squeezing through the walls.

It was almost black in the back and they literally couldn't breathe. The heat increased as it got closer to the descent to the underground. Dea smashed the glass in the fire cupboard, pulled out two fireproof blankets, and tossed one to Gerard. Wrapped in protective sheets, they reached the stairs, but failed to go down to the cellars. The fire expanded so quickly that they finally had to flee.

They barely managed to open one of the supplier's side doors and jumped out of the casino, looking for their friends. Fire trucks screamed and in the blink of an eye Dea and her companion were drenched from head to foot with icy water. Swearing noiselessly they left the threatened area and stopped at a distance from the burning casino. Neither the Rasts, nor the Nuntia branch, nor their friends were anywhere to be seen. On the other hand, police cars, ambulances and ordinary onlookers came from everywhere.

"What a mess," Dea muttered, relieved to abandon the soaked blanket. "Let's get out of here before they arrest us for complicity."

"Let's go, but where to?"

"Silly question. To the hotel, we need to change. I don't know about you, but I'm not going to take part in the Wet Jacket contest."

"T-shirt I think..."

"Neither am I going to."

In the hotel, no one noticed the guests soaked in water, not even the receptionist. She handed them the key without taking her eyes from the view from the window where the crowd swirled around the burning casino. Taking advantage of this auspicious circumstance, they quickly went to the rented room, took a shower and changed into dry clothes.

Dea was just drying her hair with a hotel towel when her cell phone beeped.

"Where are you?" Never's voice asked.

"At the hotel, and you?"

"Doesn't matter. Listen up, collect our stuff, put it in the van, check us out and take the E-4 toll, direction to Dresden. Go and look for us."

"Whatever you want. Did you get them?"

"Hell no. I'll tell you when we're together. Follow the instructions and be careful."

Dea didn't add what she thought about such instructions, but, as you can guess, they were the worst things. Almost all of Never's ad hoc plans gave her a headache, and if she didn't protest, it was only because she didn't have a better idea now.

"Pack those madmen's things, I'll go check us out," she instructed Gerard, and left.

The actor quickly got the job done - they never had much with each other, so it was easy. Jen, watching him from her carrier, realized that they were going on a journey again and, as Fronda had been laboriously teaching her, she curled up instantly so that she began to resemble a sleeping cat.

"Good monkey," muttered Gerard, grabbing the baby carrier.

He ran down the stairs to the reception desk, where Dea was just finishing the paperwork. Her expression did not bode well, so he was silent just in case, until they got into the recreational vehicles cab and started driving. Only then did he dare to ask:

"Where are we going?"

"By the highway to Dresden," Dea replied glumly. "Apparently, they will be waiting for us at some kilometer. May it be true, because only now something has occurred to me."

She fell silent.

"What?" Gerard looked at her urgently as the silence dragged on.

"A mobile phone is a very clever invention. The only problem is that, it's fucking easy to track. No, I'm not saying they find us that way, but carrying cells with us is an unnecessary risk for us."

The actor shook slightly.

"What do you think Hermann's squad managed to escape?" he asked softly. "And if the "others" got them?"

"Well, if they got them, we can't help it anyway," Dea replied mercilessly. "You saw what happened there. Besides, we warned them, even though they did not deserve it, so they had a choice. They are to blame themselves. Whoever does not listen to his father or mother will listen to the dog's knocker."

"Kind of right..." he admitted.

"Oh, yeah. Kind of right. Instead of tormenting yourself, better unfold the map and tell me how to get to the E-4 road. This is the toll highway to Dresden."

Dutifully, he switched on the flashlight and spread the city map on his lap which he had bought at a gas station.

"Third block to the right and straight ahead to the entrance," he said after a moment. "I'll prepare a change for a fee. I hope our people will indeed be waiting for us there."

"Me too," Dea gripped the steering wheel tighter in her hands, staring at the windshield at the same time.

The atmosphere of danger had an effect on her, though, true to her character, she was more angry than terrified. It wasn't easy to scare her, but she was very easy to "freak out", which in Never's eyes was an advantage, not a disadvantage. He loved the vixens and marveled at men who preferred the docile hens.

Turning onto the highway, Dea slowed down and began to look around urgently. Finally, at some kilometer, she saw a few shadows under the trees and stepped on the brake. Shadows ran to the recreational vehicle and jumped inside.

"At last." Fronda grunted, sitting on a bundle of rolled blankets.

His shirt hung in tatters, and his left eye was so black he couldn't see anything on it. Oggy, still in doggy form, curled up at his feet, panting, and mouth wide open.

"It was hot?" Gerard asked, looking back.

"Don't even ask. That was a nightmare. Happy when they set fire to the carpet, so much smoke was produced that the Germanic people probably managed to run. They fought a good deal, they were sure those Rasts wouldn't risk a raid in a casino full of people, but they miscalculated."

"They are more dangerous than we thought so far," Never added.

He didn't look too well either - he was sooty and battered, but that wasn't why his expression was rare enough. It seemed he had discovered something really bad. He sat for a moment gasping for breath, then looked up at the window.

"They have some extra support," he said. "They are ordinary people, and they seem to have supernatural abilities. I was able to try the blood of one of them, and I swear I tasted some medicine that I couldn't identify."

"You think they drug themselves?" Dea asked, slowing down a bit as she realized that she had exceeded the speed limit on the German motorway.

"Drug themselve... I wouldn't go that far. However, I think that they are taking some substance that intensifies the sensitivity of the human senses. Otherwise, they wouldn't be able to work so effectively."

He took a deep breath and groaned involuntarily. The hot air in the casino vaults had irritated his airways, so badly that he felt as if his lungs were covered with open wounds.

"Wash and change your clothes," Dea said harshly. "There's a water bubble in the corner, in this checkered bag you have towels and washing gel. You can't look like two slugs when some kind of control stops us. Oggy, turn into a human, because we don't have any German dog papers, and this is a law-abiding nation. They can take you to a pound."

Oggy barked indignantly but obediently, though with great difficulty, assumed her human form and put on her dress. Then she took a brush from her bag and tried to tidy up her tousled, reddish black hair.

"Oggy gave two of these chocolate guys a healthy bite," Fronda said, continuing to follow Dea's hygiene routines. "She is a brave girl and an even brave wolf. Nev, what are we doing?"

"We're going to Dresden," replied the Indian. He, too, washed himself as carefully as possible under these conditions. "I have a plan, but I will need your help. And your captivating charm."

"Cool."

Fronda's love dilemmas sometimes got friends into trouble, but sometimes they turned out to be unexpectedly helpful.

His friend, a policewoman from Dresden, easily let herself be persuaded to a loving meeting years later.

During the date, Fronda received from her the address of a corrupt engineer from the Volksvagen plant, Udo Leihar, who could mediate the acquisition of the mannequins.

The next day Dea went to him and after a long conversation she made a deal with him. She didn't know what Never's plan was, and didn't quite believe him, but she had done her part of the job flawlessly.

Returning to the hideout, she told Never about her mission, but barely finished speaking when Oggy burst into the small room, hair on her back.

"Alarm!" Fronda exclaimed, leaping up from his seat.

"Let's go," Never ordered.

The friends rushed out of the warehouse through a cautiously open emergency exit. They managed to confuse the Rasts, but only for a moment - they literally ran into them soon, as if these peculiar people had the ability to move in any direction in the blink of an eye. Luckily, their blasters were useless in direct combat and it was a melee fight.

It was the first time when friends could test the Rast skills in this area, and found to their relief that they were no better than the other Hunters' skills. Yet for all their training, they were only humans. Vampires, whose strength and agility are always higher than those of an ordinary human, can even deal with an outnumbered opponent, although of course they are helpless against weapons that strike at a distance. This clash ended with a victory for Never and his squad, although it was not without some injuries - Dea had a dislocated arm and Gerard had his head cut, although he did not remember who had made him so at what point. This time, he too succumbed to the amok of battle, in which aggression prevailed over his innate gentleness.

The other two suffered only minor injuries, such as bruises or scrapes, but the Rasts lost three-quarters of their group, almost all their equipment, and had to withdraw in the end.

"What now?" Gerard asked, wiping away the blood that flooded his eyes.

"How's what now? We pick up our order, and then I fly to Poland, and you wherever you want," Never replied, looking at Dea's hand.

"Why to Poland?" Fronda asked.

"So that I have to warn everyone, take what's in the vault and confuse these lunatics. I will contact you when I can."

"How will you contact us, unfortunate, when you don't know where we are?" Dea hissed.

"Don't worry about that. I'll track you down."

Never, with a sudden movement, jerked the girl's wrist, who cursed and immediately breathed a sigh of relief.

"Thanks, better now," she said. "But wouldn't it be better for me to make this maneuver? I know Warsaw better than you do."

"Maybe, but I know a job like this better. You have a different task. Choose a safe hideout and get these three lunatics there in one piece. It is hard enough work, believe me."

She huffed contemptuously, but said nothing more. Once she acknowledged Never's leadership, she had no intention of arguing with him, though she hated that he wanted to play the role of bait on pathological killers. It could have ended completely badly, but on the other hand, how could she be sure that this maneuver would be successful at all? Or maybe the Rasts will not let themselves be catch out and will follow them in order to catch them at the next stop? They will die and Never will survive, or vice versa?

Guessing her thoughts, he patted her shoulder lightly and smiled fondly.

"Cheer up, I haven't been in such trouble before," he said. "Now let's get together and rush to the hangars, because Leihar will think we double-cross him."

"If he's ever there."

However, Udo Leiher kept his word. He delivered the four crash test dummies made entirely of ballistic gel to the designated location quietly and discreetly. The engineer did not care that anyone found out about his undercover earnings and made efforts to keep everything secret. Never handed him a bundle of bills and opened the chests lined with sawdust. Inside each of them lay a yellowish, translucent figure of what felt like not very hard rubber.

"I don't understand what these puppets are for. Do you think anyone will dupe?" Dea asked skeptically.

"You don't have to understand. Let each of you drop a little blood into the center of your chosen mannequin," he ordered.

Everyone seemed to understand now and hastily obeyed. If, as it was supposed, the Order had some kind of mechanical detector, it might have worked.

"Now watch out: I will provoke the Rasts and drag them with me. During this time, you must leave Germany as quickly as possible and go... wherever. Just in case, I don't want to know where to."

"Why?" Gerard asked, pressing the handkerchief to his still bleeding forehead.

"The basic principle of an interview: you don't know what you don't know. If they crouch me, which is possible, I don't want them to get from me where you are. Dea, you are in charge and you are in charge until I contact you."

The doctor tore open the sterile bandage, washed Gerard's forehead with hydrogen peroxide and wrapped his head expertly.

"I know where I'm going to take you," she said after a moment. "And you, do you know what you're doing?"

"In fact, yes."

He wasn't as sure as it appeared. The plan he developed was risky, but there was no way out, he had to try.

Without hiding, he arranged for the shipment of three large crates with mannequins bought "to the left" on the same plane he was supposed to use to return to Poland.

He knew that as long as he was in sight, among the humans, the Rasts would not dare to attack, so he tried not to stay aloof for a moment.

He was a bit concerned that these fanatics might try to plant a bomb on the plane, but luckily they weren't that fanatical. They knew certain limits. The flight went smoothly, save for the fact that one of the engines choked every now and then.

After getting off at Okecie Airport, Never first of all paid for the transport of the chests to one of the nearby warehouses and only then started the implementation of the second part of the plan. If, as he suspected, the Rasts were following him, it would be necessary to somehow get them to reveal their presence.

Confrontation, though very dangerous, might have helped establish the targeting they were using, and now that was a priority. He hoped his group was on their way to a safer region, just in case he preferred not to know which - if he managed to confuse the pursuers he would find them. If not, well, from now on they will have to fend for themselves. He did what he could to let them escape.

He drove straight from the airport to the main post office, from where he sent a dozen postcards with short greetings, which were a long-agreed slogan to remain in combat readiness, paid for an advertisement in several capital newspapers, and, after a moment of hesitation, called Octavia di Mauro.

"I need to talk to you. We are in serious trouble," he said, "can I visit you in a few days?"

"Come over," said Octavio shortly. "We are in Denmark, the town of Sro, an old guesthouse at the South East tollgates. Hurry up, because we're changing headquarters."

"I'll be there as soon as I can," Never promised him and hung up the phone.

As he left the crowded building, he looked around carefully and saw two dark-skinned men with dreadlocks nearby. He only saw them for a blink of an eye, then they were gone, but that was enough to make him sure they were on his trail. He felt his hands go cold. The situation was becoming very dire. He only hoped the pursuit group hadn't split up and that they all followed him, giving his friends time to escape. He thought less about himself - he always managed somehow in the end. If something was bothering him, it was caring for others and thinking that he would probably be forced to fight to the death.

He disgusted killing, a loathing which he carefully concealed so as not to become a laughing stock. It is true that not one was like that, but he had a reputation for being a tough guy and did not want to lose it. Maybe it was childish, but that was how he felt it, and therefore he did not tell anyone how much he disgusted him with killing someone, even if that someone was his enemy. The conviction, taken from his native country, also played a role here - that if someone has an assigned number of enemies, the more he kills, the more they multiply. The Zen priests who instilled this belief in him tolerated his otherness for very similar reasons...

After walking a bit through the streets, Never went down to the canal and hid in one of the branches. Such a hiding place had at least two advantages - it was easy to miss and it was so acoustic that he would hear the Rasts, they would barely come in - and one powerful drawback: if there was a sudden downpour, he would not have been able to get out of there.

Under other circumstances, he wouldn't have risked so much, but now it was an acceptable risk. Finding a relatively dry place, he huddled against the wall in the hideous-smelling darkness. Rats flited around him, and he could see their curious eyes glowing red nearby.

They were not afraid of him, they knew very well that in this place they ruled, besides, they sensed with animal instinct that this strange intruder did not threaten them in any way.

At one point the big rat carrying her cubs treated Never's arm as a comfortable ladder that she could get where she wanted to go - to the pipe above. In fact, these furry creatures, not necessarily favored by people, were now giving Never a spirit.

He didn't feel so lonely as they bustled around him about their affairs, sometimes rubbing against him or even taking a shortcut through his legs.

Most of them would feel nauseous in disgust in this situation, but luckily Never had ever detested any creature.

Even though he promised himself to stay awake, he fell asleep several times, lulled by the steady sound of the sewage, the stench of which finally ceased to bother him.

It took a long time, over a day, before he decided to come to the surface. It was just dusk, and he saw no danger anywhere. He hoped the Rasts had lost his trail, though that might not have been the case.

The first thing he did was check the nearest Empik shop and browse the latest newspapers, looking for his advertisement. It was wherever he ordered it to be posted, so the coded message went to Poland. As he flipped through the press, he saw a short message with a suggestive photo of a raging fire. Someone set a fire in this warehouse where he rented a box for his mannequin chests and all night firefighters fought the element to prevent it from moving to nearby buildings. The Rasts acted with ruthless precision... and they were obviously fooled by their trickery. It was reassuring, but it also indicated that they did indeed have an excellent targeting system.

Well, of course they had. Before he looked back, he had them on his neck - they pressed him against a wall in an alley, between old tenement houses to be demolished. There were only three of them, you can see the squad split up to chase him - here were two dark-skinned men with dreadlocks (they looked Polynesian) and a white girl with a shaved head. He sensed more than guessed who she was.

"You are Akheela," he said, grasping her wrists so that she could not reach for the pitcher, and at the same time shielding himself with her body from the men.

"And you're a dead," she replied, trying to tear her hands out of his grasp. "We will cleanse the world of creatures like you."

"And who gave you such a right?" Never asked, slightly assuming a position suitable for the attack-retreat action.

"We have a mission from God to get rid of the devil's envoys." Akheela with a sudden twist freed herself from him and reached for her weapon. He pushed her so that she ran into her friends and threw himself between the old walls. He now had to use all his skill and experience to confuse the chase.

He ran into the bus stop at full speed and jumped into the overcrowded Icarus bus at the last moment.

He didn't care where he was taken - he just hoped the Rasts wouldn't track him down, wherever he was. But it miscalculated, because when the bus stopped at a loop somewhere on the outskirts of the city, they arrived shortly after it. For a moment he was inclined to believe in extrasensory perception, but then he concluded that most likely one of them noticed which bus he had jumped on and they organized a chase. It was enough to know the timetable to know what to observe.

He cursed in helpless anger. The game of cat and mouse began anew, this time in an area he did not know at all.

*****

"And we'll live like stray cats again, I'm not having fun like that," Oggy groaned as she nestled into the corner.

"I just had time to say goodbye to Lilka, are you not exaggerating?" Fronda pouted, stroking the crouched in his lap Jen.

"If you keep whining, both of you will get hit in the ear," Dea growled at them, very dissatisfied with this turn of events.

"I'm used to it, I can go to the end of the world, but maybe you can tell us one thing, where is Never?" Gerard demanded, carefully touching the bandage on his forehead.

"Do I look like the twenty-seventh volume of the Britannica Encyclopedia?!" Dea burst out. "He's gone, end of the story!"

"Where has he gone?" Fronda asked stupidly.

"Jesus Christ! Do I know that?! If I knew it, moron, I'd go straight to him!" At this point the RV skidded and the girl struggled to even out the ride. "Because of your whining, we will finally crash. Keep quiet and let me think!"

Gerard wanted to say something else, but changed his mind. It was better to be silent now, because Dea looked temporarily insane. It was hardly surprising, as the sudden appearance of the Order of Rast struck like a bolt from the blue. These people were excellent trackers, and it became clear that it was necessary to finally break with settled life, and even abandon contact between groups.

"We'll be on our own again," he thought resignedly. The fact that the life of the average vampire is a constant escape, he had known for a long time and even accepted it, but recent years made him a bit lazy, used to having his own corner. Besides, he saw less and less sense in all of this - to live in order to keep running away, he didn't really want to. How could Fronda stand it, having been a hunted animal for so many centuries?

34

He moved closer to him.

"Have you always been hunted?" He asked in a whisper.

"Yep. This is not the first group of fanatics in my life and probably not the last." Theo glanced at him and patted him lightly on the back. "It's not worth worrying about all of this that much."

"Maybe it's not worth it," his friend agreed with him. "But it gets very unpleasant, you'll admit it yourself. And where is Never? They got him?" No one has been able to answer this question so far. Dea had struggled to start banging her head on the steering wheel - she couldn't forgive herself having to leave Never at a time like this, though she admitted it was her only chance to save the rest.

She had met Never well enough to know that she was far from willing to sacrifice herself for others, and would certainly do anything to not only lead the Rasts out of the way, but to escape himself... but their efficiency was worrying her.

The ease with which they murdered the Gladiator was terrifying, and the form of the execution was chilling.

The RV trip lasted almost a week. They took turns at the wheel, but only stopped at gas stations, then looked around vigilantly, prepared to fight or flee. However, there was no chase after them. Never work effectively, his plan worked, but did he manage to survive on his own? They did not know and could not know. Their cells lay at the bottom of the Rhine, they were an excellent source of contact, and it was better to get rid of them and rely mainly on psycholocation. Dea didn't tell anyone where she was taking them, only giving directions as sleep seized her and she had to give way at the wheel. It was only on the last day of the trip that everything became clear.

At the foot of the Alps, Dea left the car in a paid garage, told everyone to put on warm shoes and jackets, and then she chased them into the mountains, in an area remote from the hiking trails, rather unfriendly and inaccessible.

It was terribly cold in the mountains, the higher it was, the colder it was, and despite warm clothes, everyone froze in a short time.

Especially Oggy, the more sensitive, was shaking so much that she couldn't even speak and plunged after her friends, drawing all her strength not to be left behind.

Nobody protested, because they had already guessed what hiding place she had found for them, and although these conjectures were a bit depressing, it could have been the best solution.

They finally got rid of all doubts when, reaching one of the jagged ridges, they saw Segovia.

He waited for them with an old-fashioned lantern in his hand, slim and delicate in his black tuxedo, a white bow tie at his neck. He seemed completely misplaced in this stark landscape.

"No one saw you?" he asked.

"Which is better: "yes" or "we hope so"?" Dea replied, rubbing her cold hands. He shrugged in response.

"Come on, you clydes." He led the way, lighting the road with a lantern. It led to a narrow, winding cave that formed a kind of rocky corridor that ended in a blind wall. Segovia pressed some seemingly random elements and the wall slid open to reveal a normally furnished library with a Persian rug on the floor, paintings on the walls blackened with age, and an old-fashioned fireplace on which a fire was burning.

"Come on in," he said. "This is my current headquarters."

The friends entered the library, and the wall slid slowly shut behind them. On the inside there was a carved paneling, giving the impression of uniformity. Segovia switched off the lantern and hung it on the hook that was stuck next to the bookshelf.

"Drop your jackets on the sofa," he said. "Would you like a drink?"

"Willingly," Fronda replied, releasing Jen from the carrier. "I'll have something stronger, please."

The chilled monkey cuddled up to him, while at the same time tracing his eyes with distrust over the unfamiliar surroundings.

Segovia pulled bottles of blood from a hidden refrigerator and set a decanter of cognac and glasses on the table. He pointed to the electric kettle and hot-drinker, which she eagerly used.

"Upstairs is the snobbish hostel 'Devil's Castle'." He said, settling himself comfortably in a large armchair by the fireplace. "I'm his permanent resident, hence my outfit.

I preferred you to come on the other side, not along the public route, just in case. I liked this place, I feel comfortable here, and I would not like to leave here just because you were not elementary careful."

"All right, don't grumble," Dea growled, drinking a second glass of blood greedily. "Your son is left alone in the fight against this sect of madmen, and you only worry about your ass."

"This bastard is grown up, let him take care of himself," Segovia replied indifferently. "The world is cruel, there is no place for the lame in it."

"However, you decided to help us."

"Only for you. I have a weakness for you. You can stay here for now, just don't expose my hiding place. As I said, I am attached to it."

Fronda added two scoops of cognac to his drink and stirred. He had a terrible desire to drink undiluted alcohol, but wisely refrained from taking this step. This was not the time to risk losing control of yourself.

"We'll do our best," he said. "But we do not vouch for those bastards who chase us. Hell, I said from the beginning that black and white are irreconcilable."

"They're not black, rather brown," Dea rubbed her left ear thoughtfully. "And they're led by a white girl. I think, Theo, there are people of all colors in their ranks. And that this is not the best time to flaunt your racism. Underestimating the enemy, considered a creature of inferior and lower quality, and caused the Nazis to lose in the end. The color of the skin has nothing to do with it."

Usually she ignored Fronda's genuinely racist statements, but this time they sounded extremely stupid to her. Even for someone who still had roots in the Middle Ages.

"Maybe there aren't, but it's hard to say they're the same as us, and it's not just a matter of coloration, or even what they look like from the face," he insisted. "It's enough to look at what is happening in Africa, which would probably have starved for the most part, if so much good from Europe and America had not been pushed there..."

"Shut up at last, Fronda!" Gerard shouted angrily. "You found a bad moment for ideological training! What do we care about Africa's problems now, we have our own!"

Segovia laughed with a hint of irony and spite. Everyone who knew him knew that such views were not alien to him, on the contrary - he was their stony follower. He did not even accept his own son, as he was also the son of a Hindu woman. The primacy of the white race was indisputable to him. While he ultimately recognized the right to the life and development of the "inferior" races, he ruthlessly condemned mixed relationships and hunted with special fervor those who were descended from such relationships.

The fact that he himself, in the approach of insanity, "dealt" with an Indian beauty, and worse, had a child with her, was a constant shame for him. Initially, he planned to kill the boy, but even he was unable to do so. After all, it was his son, he had his blood in him, his genes, and he was extraordinary. However, he did not want to know him and for a very long time he had no idea what he looked like.

"I like you, French," he said. "You seem to have a clear view on certain points. However, for now, it is actually better to put them aside and take care of those who threaten all of our clan. They are ruthless murderers, the more dangerous because they operate from a religious position. The hardest with such ones."

"Yes, the Brotherhood of St. Obadiah... a cult just like that. I wonder how many innocent people they took out before they improved their bearing system."

"According to them, these are inevitable costs of humanity. Anyway, now they kill people by mistake or when they suspect them of helping vampires. Like any sect, they have blinders on their eyes and a gudgeon in their heads."

He took a sip from his glass. When he sat there, lit by the fire from the fireplace, he did not look like a typical vampire image at all. Slender, not too tall, fair-haired, with a gentle smile and a delicate, aristocratic beauty emphasized by a black tuxedo, he resembled a descendant of an old family, sharing in the best companies.

"Are there many of them?" Asked Oggy, who, unlike the rest, drank her hand-made grog - cognac, boiling water, chili and sugar - and only now had it warmed up enough to regain the urge to talk.

"It's hard to say," he replied. "There is a lot of talk about it. In any case, as far as I was able to understand from the data available to me, the operational unit is only a small fraction of the entire grouping. It is not known where they have their headquarters, how many of them live there, what are the rules of recruitment... actually, nothing is known. I have some suspicions that someone is behind it, the real leader of the entire movement, and that, contrary to appearances, it is not Akheela. She is only an armed commander.

"And to think that Never has them on his neck right now and can't count on any help," sighed Gerard.

"He can do it. His mind is after me, not the idiot who gave birth to him. You will see, he will show up here, and we will not know when."

"He doesn't know where we are."

"He'll find out. You will see."

Meanwhile, Never tried not to think about his friends. He hoped that Dea had managed to take them somewhere relatively safe, since he himself, risking his own life, dragged away the group hunting them, but he could not even think with them. He now had to take care of himself first and, if possible, to work out the targeting system used by the Order. If they fail to meet him, all members of the clan scattered around the world will be in danger. The Van Helsing Institute and the other Hunters' groups had no tracking devices, they only used environmental intelligence and their own intuition, and how much damage they could do... If the Order had developed some sort of "radar", it was not a mere inconvenience, but a real disaster.

He couldn't lead the Rasts out of the way yet. He, who had always dealt with it, was now almost defenseless. Well, maybe not entirely defenseless - by using the old trick of flanking the opponent, he managed to eliminate two of the assassins chasing him. Still, they were hot on his heels, so he decided to use a method he knew from India - to climb to the roof of the nearest unfinished building and wait for his pursuers to pass this place. To his disappointment, however, instead of going far, they turned indecisively, unable to understand why the hunting object had suddenly disappeared into thin air.

He couldn't wait forever. Every minute increased the risk that they would somehow track him down on that roof, and that could have ended badly. Looking around, he found that the only place he could come down to the ground without being noticed was a steep wall where there was nothing to grapple with. He could only jump.

"High, bloody hell," he thought, and bit his lips. But he didn't have much choice, so he took a sharp breath and jumped.

He was prepared for an unpleasant, painful shock to the rocky ground, but to his surprise, he fell quite gently, as if it had drained.

It was so unexpected that he stood there for a moment, amazed, and wondered what had happened.

"What the hell is going on? After all, vampires don't fly, I know for sure," he thought. "There was no such accident. I should hit the ground. What happened?"

Only after a while did he come to the conclusion that there was no time or place for such considerations. He had to get away and fast. He took over what had happened and started running in the opposite direction of the chase. This part of Białołęka[4] was only half-inhabited - most of the houses were under construction, and they were scattered quite far apart. Lots of open space, which was an unfavorable circumstance. He ran from house to house, hiding as much as he could, but falling from behind one of the buildings, to his amazement, he saw a girl in leopard print, her head trimmed to the skin, right in front of him.

---

[4] A peripheral district of Warsaw.

He recognized the Rast leader at once and jumped at her before she could point her blaster at him. Since they did not allow themselves to be led out of the way, there was no time to lose.

"Here he is!" Akheela shouted before he could silence her.

"Third," he thought. "How many more are there?"

Certainly there were too many of them, and they must indeed have at their disposal something that rendered his efforts in vain, for they were going forward for granted, he had not been able to confuse them. Now he was also barely a dozen meters ahead of them, despite all his efforts. He ran through the bushes, dodging and trying to confuse the trail, but with less and less hope.

The bushes finally ended and he rushed between the fenced-in houses.

He looked around nervously and ran across the dark road, where the construction site was uninhabited at this time.

Too late he heard the whir of a motorbike, the slap of the bonnet of the big sedan tossed him aside. He sprang to his feet, but too slowly because they were getting close. The last thing he saw was a fireball rushing toward him.

*****

"How do you feel?" the older woman asked carefully, leaning over him.

Never opened his eyes and tried to focus his eyes somehow. There were still black and red spots in his field of vision, although it was getting better. He managed to figure out where he was - it looked like a bunker or a sewer. Walls of raw brick, clearly showing signs of erosion, darkness, a musty smell in the air. Some rags by the walls and a few lumps playing cards by a gas lamp. An ordinary hideout, but to the injured vampire, it seemed an oasis of safety.

"Better," he replied, shifting his gaze to the woman.

He didn't even know if she was old or middle-aged. She hadn't seen a bath in a long time, her hair was stiff with dirt, as were the rags that covered her. She had lice, he could see them clearly. She was certainly drinking a lot but her gaze was good, gentle.

"Lolo brought you here," she said. "You managed to hide from these bullies, but they beat you up well. You should see a doctor."

"Oh, there's no need to bother doctors," Never muttered, touching his tanned hair with his hand. "I was very lucky."

"Sure. What kind of people are they to go to a man with a flamethrower..."

The Indian sat up, barely controlling the curvature of his mouth and a groan of pain. He couldn't believe how he had survived, why he hadn't been killed. From what he remembered, he didn't stand a chance.

"How did it happen that...?" he asked and paused. He didn't know how to formulate the question.

"The police chased after them. Someone called. They didn't notice you," said one of the lumps. "They weren't even looking for, because that's a benefit of them."

"They thought you were a gypsy or one of us, motherfuckers," added the other. "And we aren't human for them."

"And you saved me..."

"It's Lolo. He said that he saw something like a huge animal at the construction site and went to see what it was. He was drunk, so he must be seeing things, because he didn't find any animal, only you. At first he thought, you are dead, but when it turned out that you were breathing, he brought you here."

"I'm very grateful to you guys, I really do," Never said, looking over what was left of his clothes. "But how do I get out of here now?"

"Mania, give this Gypsy something from our depot!"

"I'm not a gypsy, I come from India."

"If you say so, man... We don't care. For those also, as you can see, it makes no difference."

These homeless derailed people seemed to think that he was being hunted by racists, and it was better not to correct them. Besides, they weren't that far from the truth. After all, the actions of all Hunters could be summed up like this.

It turned out that the homeless people nesting in this forgotten basement had their own storehouse of clothes received from the Polish Red Cross or simply found somewhere in the garbage.

What the woman had brought was wrinkled and smelled of mice, but at least it fit all. Never's own clothes were unusable. It was almost completely burned, though luckily the wallet was saved. He looked at it with no little surprise - the good leather was durable, although it was well charred, the contents were not damaged either. Neither of the lumps seemed to have looked in it.

"I'm very grateful to you," he said when he managed to get dressed after several tries, despite the painful burns all over his body. "I owe you my life. I don't have much to repay because it's not the end of my troubles, but take it."

He took all the money out of his wallet. He didn't need them right now, and he knew that when he did, he could always steal them somewhere. He had no special resistance against it.

"Er," the first lump grunted, staring at the pile of bills. "A lot of this."

"Drink for my health." Never stuck money in the astonished woman's hand and twisted his lips in a forced smile. "Now I have to take care of myself. Better that no one knows that I was here, because they might hurt you too."

He left the basement, making efforts so that no one would notice him. But his pursuers seemed nowhere to be found.

The neighborhood was quiet, lit only by the moon and dim lights in the windows of several houses.

A favorable circumstance, given that Never was currently unable to fight.

He knew that his burned body would not regain full fitness for a long time, and yet he had to pull himself together. He had a very difficult task to complete, but most of all he had to send out a warning to everyone he could connect with.

To do this, he should return from Białołęka to the center of Warsaw, which might not have been too easy.

He had to find a means of transport, as well as some "afterburner", otherwise his body would refuse to obey him. Now, as his adrenaline levels dropped, he felt worse and worse, and he knew this was just a prelude to what lay ahead.

After a long search, he finally found a house, the owners of which left, trusting in the alarm system. He immobilized the plant and walked inside without turning on any light he did not need. First of all, he "borrowed" himself a set of clothes from the master of the house, he was relieved to throw off the rags he had received from the lumps and locked himself in the bathroom. Only now could he judge the extent of his injuries. His hair was tanned almost to the skin, and fresh burns were visible on his arms, torso, and back, revealing living tissue in some places. It was not good, and he knew it would not be good for some time.

He washed as carefully as he could, bandaged the wounds and plasters found in the home medicine chest, shaved off the rest of his hair. They would grow back quickly anyway, and the bare skull looked better than it was covered with irregular shreds of various lengths. Then he changed into clean clothes. Finally he searched the house and found, to his delight, a computer with internet access and a landline telephone. Fortunately, he didn't need a notebook. With his photographic memory at his disposal, he perfectly remembered all emergency numbers and could easily warn the clan members.

He left the temporary shelter only in the morning, having cleaned up as much as possible the traces of his stay.

He only took stolen clothes and a box of sugar cubes with him. Despite the gravity of the situation, he had to smile at the face of the owners when they saw what was missing. They will surely go dumb wondering what kind of weird thief has haunted them.

Now he had to think about how to get to Soro in Denmark - it was the most recent address he knew for Octavia di Mauro and his crew.

Fortunately for him, the lack of hair changed his appearance beyond recognition, although he felt that it could not solve all the problems. The Order had something more accurate than vampire tracking photos. Unable to think of anything better, he simply went to the airport, as soon as he found the secret safe with more false papers and took the money out of the account. He wondered what would happen if his "fresh" passport was questioned at the airport, but luckily it didn't happen. Only the cashier from whom he bought the ticket looked out of his window a little surprised.

"What is going on?" he asked him bluntly.

"Nothing," the man replied, clearly puzzled. "I thought you had a dog with you... I must have imagined something."

He did not look around, but there was nothing suspicious about him.

"It's out of exhaustion," assured the cashier. "You should rest."

He took his ticket and went to the check-in chamber.

The trip to Denmark was uneventful, although it was a torture for Never. The burns bothered him terribly.

The worst thing was the constant desire that made the pupils of his eyes glow red like a demon's.

Before the trip, he went hunting and drank as much blood as he could, yet he wasn't sure he would be able to stay calm. Immediately after reaching the destination, he hunted again, and only, fortified with another portion of life-giving liquid, began to look for Octavio. it was not that simple. For the sake of their safety, the vampires only gave each other approximate addresses, so that he had to use all his psycholocation skills to finally catch the trail that led him to the hideout, which was a new base of scientists from Spain.

He was a little surprised that the inconspicuous buildings were arranged quite carelessly and it did not seem that there was any laboratory here. Anyway, everything became clear immediately.

"Glad you still found us here," said Octavio. "We're moving again soon. Is the situation as bad as you said in the email?"

"It's terrible," Never said emphatically. "I've no idea where the Rast Order came from, but it is effective and very conservative. So much so that the Rasts killed the Vanhelsingers because they were using vampires like Gusto."

"Poor Gusto," muttered Octavio glumly. "He did them a service. What about Nuntia?"

"As far as I know, Nuntia does not exist anymore. Also a few other, smaller groups. Where are mine.. I don't even know. I told them to run away and they probably did, but I have no contact with them."

Never sat down on a round stool feeling suddenly dizzy.

"That's it, show me how they set you up." Octavio forcibly stripped off his shirt and whistled. "Oh boy! How did you even get here like this?"

"I was sucking on sugar," Never admitted.

"All the time? Congratulations then."

Pure sugar acts on vampires like amphetamines on humans, but leads to rapid burnout of the body and, in addition, causes severe withdrawal syndrome. He was not aware of it, but if he hadn't risked it, he probably wouldn't have made it to Denmark.

"Lie down," Octavio ordered. "You need care, and longer than you think."

"I know. I'm a doctor."

The red-haired Spaniard called his sister and Dr. Kralova to cleanse the wounds of necrotic tissue, and then apply appropriate dressings. Lying on the clean sheets, Never closed his eyes with relief. Now he could finally rest, knowing that the Octavia group would take care of everything. He could allow himself to get sick of what had happened to him.

Without artificial support, the body collapsed quickly and for many days Never was unconscious despite the bolster injections and intravenous nutrition. In fact, he was worse than unconscious - possessed by nightmarish dreams, he could not move or make a voice, and all he felt was a terrible headache and burning thirst. Happily, the day of the solstice has finally come and the patient has fallen into a restful, restorative sleep. The healing treatments ordered by Dr. Kralowa finally had the desired effect.

One morning Never regained consciousness, and although he was still extremely weak and his burns hurt, the fever consuming his body had subsided and he was able to think normally.

Most of all, he noticed that the move Octavio had talked about had already been completed.

He was lying in a nice, clean room, and through the semicircular window you could see the sea crashing against the rocks and seagulls flying high. Their long scream echoed outside, mingling with the sound of the waves.

Overcoming weakness, Never sat down. First of all, he examined his hands. The burn marks were covered with a pink, wrinkled tissue that seemed to be too loose for the areas undamaged by the fire, and there was a cannula stuck to the vein on the top of his left hand. He touched his head. His hair was already growing back, not as fast as usual, but still - it was about three centimeters long. He looked at the nails - well, these were far too long, he would have to trim them. He wanted to get up to look in the mirror, but couldn't stay on his feet.

On the second attempt, he knocked over his chair, and the noise caused a laboratory assistant from Dr. Kralova's department, temporarily renamed a nurse, into the room.

"What's that supposed to mean?!" She boomed. "Please go to bed now! Did you fall on your head to do such things?!"

"But I..." Never tried to protest, but it was to no avail.

The lab technician called Dr. Tamara Siemionovna, and together the two women forced him to return to the bedding.

"You're stupid, man, you just wanted to buckle?" Tamara grumbled, watching Never's scars diligently to see if they had cracked with the effort. "Do you know how few vampires recover from burn disease? In case of burns of twenty percent, you actually have to put a line on it, and for you it was almost thirty-five! Instead of being thankful to all gods for being alive and for our protection, you are already going crazy."

"But I'm grateful. Didn't I lie long enough?"

"What does it have to do with it? You can't get up yet. You are very weak. If you want to talk to Octavio, I'll call him, but you're lying there and won't budge, okay?"

"Okay..."

He didn't have to admit that the Russian woman was right. He felt terrible. He knew that he had literally escaped a close call, and though his active nature rebelled against lying in bed, he gave up on any further attempts to get up. Anyway, he felt dizzy, as if he were on a heavily rocking ship and had no strength for anything.

Octavio showed up after about ten minutes, clearly straight from the lab, still in a reagent-stained lab coat, and brought with him a strong smell of formaldehyde.

"I'm glad you're already conscious," he said, sitting down next to the bed. "We were afraid for you because it was very bad. It hurt a lot?'

"Just so you know. Like hell."

"That's good. Means the nerves are not damaged. It's a strange thing, though: your wounds should be deeper and more dangerous, not to mention the fact that in fact you should burn like a pile of straw, because it was napalm. We did a biopsy, the laboratory confirmed the presence of substances in the tissues used in the manufacture of this filth. You were incredibly lucky."

"I know. But I've grown a new skin, it shouldn't hurt anymore, and I'm still in pain."

"Oh. This is phantom pain. You owe your new skin to our experimental ointment, but nerve irritation is not that easy. With a vampire, it can take up to a year for the brain to finally tell itself that it's okay."

"Nice perspective."

"Not the only one," Octavio took a cigarette from his pocket and lit it. "We tried to find out how the scanner used to detect vampires works.

Dr. Mandez from the anthropology department has analyzed all the data available to us and seems to have found the answer. Well, our bodies are quite cool. Normal temperature for a vampire is around 30 degrees Celsius. Therefore, a thermal imaging sensor with the appropriate resolution is enough to catch a vampire from the crowd. However, such sensors are quite large and bulky, so I think they are only used for an approximate location, and an isotope detector, for example, calibrated to carbon C14, is taken for the chase itself. Every living tissue contains it, but in our case its content is very high. You understand, don't you? The only problem is that these detectors do not officially exist, but that's a minor problem: someone might have built them for the Order."

"So we have no way to defend ourselves."

"I don't know? First, we can try to confuse the spectrometer. Second, do you know what it might look like?"

"Don't bother, Octavio."

"It's big. However, there is a workaround for this. Every Order member likely has a sensor with a transmitter that works much like a normal cell phone. The signal is transmitted to the mobile unit where it is analyzed and the result is sent back to the sensor where the result is displayed. The whole operation now takes a few seconds in the age of microprocessors and telecommunications satellites."

Never closed his eyes for a moment. He had to digest what he heard.

"All right," he said after a moment. "So what do we have to do?"

"First of all, destroy this theoretical data processing center. It can't be far from the main pursuit party.

But you understand, it won't be easy. First you have to locate the headquarters, then pull Rasts as far away from it as possible, and then, normally, in a simpleton: smash it."

"I'm going to need a task force," said the Indian, sitting down on the bed.

Octavio held him firmly.

"Not right away, brother. You have to recover, and our scout has to find the Rasts."

"If only they didn't find him. This fight can cost us dearly."

These fears were well-founded, but he saw no alternative but to trust "Agent #1", whom he did not even know.

"How about the fake blood tests?" he asked after a moment.

Octavio waved his hand reluctantly.

"Ah, it's a pity to talk. Nothing of that. During the last experiments, I struggled to lie down for two weeks. During our research, after all, we discovered a very strong probiotic and made some money on the patent, always something."

The Octavia Group made a living off of this - selling drug and technology patents. They sometimes amused the thought that humans had no idea that some of the inventions that accompany them were actually due to a team of vampires with a scientific flair. The fact that all the glory falls on some man, who often did not even lend a hand to the creation of the final product, did not bother them - they did not crave fame that would be very dangerous for them, they were satisfied with tangible profit.

For all his impatience, Never had to stay in bed for two more days. Every hour the nurse changed the gel packs on his skin, and each time he felt a tingling and tickling sensation, as if something was seeping under the stratum corneum.

The recipe of the gel was a pharmacy doctor Mendoza's secret, and the only thing that could save the life of a badly burned vampire. The ingredients contained in it stimulated the reconstruction of the skin, had an analgesic effect and prevented the development of deadly tissue degeneration. He couldn't even feel the action of the mysterious ingredients inside his skin, and it was a pleasant feeling, but it did bring back nightmarish memories.

He still couldn't understand how he had survived. It was completely illogical and improbable, it seemed a miracle, though Never's cynical mind denied the possibility. He believed in miracles, but he did not believe that any God would waste his miraculous power on him. In any case, he experienced what seemed impossible and should be happy. And yet he approached it with distrust and suspiciously examined in his memories all the remembered circumstances of this incident.

"If it weren't for Eusebio Mendoza's specificity, you wouldn't have survived," Tamara Semyonovna said the day he was finally allowed to stand up, examining Never's scars.

"I don't know how you managed to get to Denmark after all this, because you should die of common sense from the shock. So far, no one in your state has survived."

"I'm an extraordinary individual."

"Yes. Though not a compliment, why," Tamara was sour and sarcastic as always. "Okay, you can get dressed. You don't have to lie down anymore, but take care. You are a convalescent."

"Ok, ok. I won't caress about myself like a countess."

Never carefully pulled on his new shirt and jeans, wincing a little as the new skin was still oversensitive and it felt as though it would be easy to peel off.

He was relieved to leave this room. Although the makeshift solitary room was nice and had a nice view from the window, it made him feel bad, and he wanted to visit Octavio and his group's new headquarters.

The institute now occupied a historic palace that housed the Andersen Museum. The museum occupied several rooms in the main part, while both side wings were rented to a fictional company Dunklung, dealing with the conservation of art objects of museum value. There were two specialists in this field on the Octavio team, and although they did something completely different on a daily basis, they sometimes took something to renovate to support the cover.

According to the documents, most of the rented rooms were used as antiques warehouses, some turned into living quarters, and it was even possible to obtain a permit to run the laboratory. It officially analyzed paint and canvas samples in order to synthesize materials suitable for the preservation of old canvases and tapestries. Unofficially, scientists continued their research there, interrupted by the ongoing campaign. It was impressive that every time a considerable team was forced to move by unfavorable circumstances, they managed to take with them most of the valuable equipment and reagents, as well as the entire archive. It is true that now it has become easier, because thanks to the development of computer technology it was possible to store a huge amount of data on a small disk that was easy to hide with you.

"Do you have any idea how we struggled to transfer our entire archive to storage media? It was an unbelievable job," said Octavio Never as he showed him around the facility.

"I think so. Well, now you have at least some facilitation... Octavio, this is really very interesting, but I'm interested in something else. Did that scout of yours say something?"

Di Mauro sighed and leaned against the sill of a tall window, half covered by a brick wall.

"He contacted me," he replied. "Our guesses were correct, the Rasts have a mobile data processing center that accompanies their operational group. Currently, their main branch, together with the headquarters, penetrates the forests of the Black Forest, perhaps they also have a backup headquarters there. If we want to catch them, we have to do some trouble there."

"We?"

"Yes, we. It's been a long time since I took part in similar operations, but once I was a soldier of Mark Antony. My name was Octavian Placidus then, and Mercedes was called Aecya."

"You really are old fart. Never mind, will you be able to lead the diversion? I'll get Rasts away from the switchboard, and you and your platoon will blow it up."

"It sounds nice, but in practice it means that you have left yourself the worst part of the task. You can die."

Never shrugged. He could have died, it is true, but it was nothing new to him... from childhood, he was accompanied by the fact that he could die at any moment, blue and red like a jaguar's eyes. He cut it then, he can do it now.

It is hard to expect that scientists, even vampires, would be soldiers at the same time, but the team of several dozen of Octavio di Mauro's men included five with military training and one ex-policeman.

According to Never's calculations, such a squad should be enough to carry out his plan, and it would have to do. The trouble with the undead is that they are mostly defensive, except for the mentally ill, who are eliminated very quickly.

Contrary to the typical portrait, known from books and movies, the undead do not seek confrontation with humans and prefer to run away rather than defend themselves. This time, however, the clash was inevitable, if they wanted to at least level the playing field.

"The switchboard they have is incredibly expensive. They certainly don't have a spare one, and even if they do, we'll find it too," Never explained at the briefing. "A much better method is destroying their facilities than killing their soldiers. It is better to refrain from killing, because it is a dangerous thing."

"Certainly, especially for the corpse," muttered the lab technician in the biochemistry department, Oleg Tarnov.

"For us too, because it directs the spotlight at us. We must avoid this. That is why we use tasers and paralyzing gas as weapons, and I recommend that you use them in moderation."

"And if they don't have this moderation?" Trelavny from the engineering department asked skeptically.

"They certainly won't," said Alex Spicery from the same section.

"I'm explaining that, we cannot give them a taste of their own medicine, because we will get so deeply involved that God also will not help," Never said patiently. "This isn't a vendetta or any jihad, here you have to think about the future. By refraining from killing, we keep our enemies' weapons out of hand, for we are depriving them of the most powerful source of hatred. We are also reducing the number of those who fight with us, because those who have taken their loved ones from them do not join them. And they are the most dangerous.

His interim squad seemed unconvinced, but no one protested. Octavio had instructed them before that they were destined to be dusted - if they managed to survive it would be a favorable circumstance, but they shouldn't count on it too much.

They agreed to die for the sake of the majority, though of course they hoped it wouldn't be that bad. Despite Never's clear position, they were also ready to defend their lives in any way possible.

"I have some experimental devices for you," said Octavio, who was not part of the squad but had attended the briefing nonetheless. "These are electronic emitters that will disturb the bearing of any sensor, regardless of its specification. Thanks to them, you will be able to approach the Rasts unnoticed, if, of course, you do not make unnecessary noise."

"Something constructive at last, because until now you and your department could only spread your hands," Sienna Laung from the medical section said sourly. "I hope there will be someone to tell if it works."

Never looked at the bracelet given to him - it looked like a metal ID for diabetics, but it seemed to be slightly warm from the inside. He fastened it on his left wrist, then turned to his squad:

"I haven't said this before, but you are to obey me absolutely, at least during the action itself. Then... well, what will happen next, you will see. In any case, I'm in charge, and even if I give you the strangest order, you are to carry it out. OK?"

He looked at the six vampires of both sexes and cursed silently. Had it not been for the forced situation, he thought, he would never have taken such a crowd on a dangerous foray - but he had no choice. He had to take what was there and thank his gods that he had anyone to go into battle with.

*****

Skiing by the light of torches, masked balls, evening banquets, film screenings... yes, "Devil's Castle" really knew what to offer to rich, sophisticated tourists.

Segovia, who owned the majority of the shares, made sure that the offer was in good taste and worth the horrendous fees. He also never looked for victims from among his guests, preferring to undertake long expeditions for this purpose.

"I didn't know you turned into a consummate businessman," Dea said as he told everyone about his snobbish little hotel and its income.

"I've always been able to earn," he replied. "I like a lavish life, and I don't like stealing. It's so plebeian."

"We steal a lot," muttered Gerard.

"Somehow it does not surprise me. What else could this Indian bastard have taught you?"

"This Indian bastard is your son," Dea reminded him coldly.

Segovia shrugged his shoulders contemptuously. He never hid what he thought about his offspring, and saw no reason to change anything here. Anyway, Never gave him a taste of his own medicine and never said a single good word about him.

"Segovia, tell me one thing," Fronda said from his chair. "I understand that "Devil's Castle" brings you a lot of income and so on, but why did you choose this particular place? There are so many other, friendlier ones."

"Maybe I just like the ones that are unfriendly? Besides, not only you like solving dark secrets, me too, but for me it's more of a hobby."

"How can you choose such a hobby? If we didn't have to, we wouldn't even touch most of our affairs. Then you have nightmares and a life of constant fear."

The fair-haired vampire laughed at these words and put his glass on the table.

"I told you, it depends on what motives you are working for," he said. "I'm not doing it for the money, so fear doesn't bother me."

"Okay, but what is it that you're investigating?" Oggy asked curiously, as she had just finished licking the tartar with egg bowl with her dog's tongue.

Segovia's eyes lit up. Slowly he got up and walked over to the wall, which was a camouflaged exit to the system of natural tunnels that had led them here.

"I can show you," he said. "But you gotta wear something warm. It's very cold there."

Intrigued friends dressed quickly. Since they lived in these secret rooms, they learned something new every day, but it sounded different and indeed interesting. It was true that it was so cold outside that it did not encourage them to walk, but they did not walk outside for too long. Soon Segovia ushered them into one of the rock corridors - it was cold there too, but at least there was no wind. The lantern illuminated the stone walls that formed a narrow vault over their heads, and the corridors branching off in different directions. Segovia walked without hesitation, it was obvious that he already knew the way well and was confident in his steps. Finally, one of the corridors ended with a huge grotto where their guide stopped.

"Now, be quiet and listen." He said

There was a silence, an eerie, unbelievable silence, in which after a while they heard something like a distant whisper in an unknown language. As they listened to the whisper, it grew louder and clearer, though they still didn't understand the words. They were definitely not words in any human language.

"Who are you? Can you speak our way?" Fronda asked before anyone could stop him. "What are your intentions?"

The whisper stopped, as if someone were listening to his words, then rang out again, but there was no indication that it could be an attempt to answer or initiate dialogue.

"Come over here and put your hands on the stones," their guide said softly, pointing to one of the sides of the grotto.

The surprise was even greater than with the whispers. Somewhere deep in the rock, they felt a pulsating rhythm, as if the slow beating of an enormous heart.

"These mountains live," Segovia said after a moment. "What we hear are thoughts of something we do not know and understand. People are needlessly self-righteous, not knowing how little they really know about the world in which they live. Man is not his first or the most developed rational inhabitant, only that he does not want to know about it. He avoids riddles like this, eagerly telling himself that such a thing does not exist. It's even fun, you know? Grown up, serious people, instead of examining the unusual, retreat cowardly, explaining everything with hallucinations or something like that. Like a small child who hides his head under a pillow and "there is no John". I'm going to find out something, and I think I'm close. I'm absolutely sure that on Earth you can still find representatives of long-extinct races, whose capabilities and intentions we know nothing about."

"Oh yes, we even had contact with such people. Only we called them "ghosts"," Gerard shook himself nervously. This place terrified him no less than the Haunted House.

"The apparitions are different. And what I'm talking about has nothing to do with supernatural phenomena. This is just something we do not understand because it is at odds with the image of the world that we are used to, which, my dear kids, is completely false."

He smiled his usual dry smile, which indicated that he considered his interlocutors under-educated or underdeveloped.

"And that's why you're sitting here?" On Dea, as usual, none of anyone's haughtiness made an impression. "I always suspected you were unevenly under the dome. Better read the short story "A Tale of a Man Who Went Over the Top" and let it go."

"Relax, I'll be fine."

Segovia's unwavering confidence did not really convince Dea and Gerard, but Fronda and Oggy accepted his words unopposed. They both did not care how this strange man would handle - they did not like him despite the fact that he had helped them, and they did not care whether he could handle it or not. They dreamed of giving up his company as soon as possible, but none of the newspapers they read every day in the Devil's Castle café had any advertisement informing one of the coding systems that the danger was over.

In this situation, they had to wait, deprived of the possibility of contacting their leader. It cannot be said that they were bored, but nonetheless they felt a bit like in a prison in this place. The lack of a message from Never left them awake all day long, and at night, when they were normally active, they were tired and depressed. They wholeheartedly wanted to be with him now, wherever he was, and yet they didn't even know if he was still alive.

*****

The scout was waiting at the train station and Never was surprised to see him. The slightly stout, bald, unshaven man in the policeman's uniform looked like anything but not a vampire. It immediately turned out that he is not at all.

"I'm an ordinary human," he explained freely. "I work for Interpol and Octavio uses it when he needs me. He pays royally."

"And... you don't mind who he is?" Never asked carefully.

"No," the cop replied, and smiled. "My wife lives thanks to him and his otherness. Doctors could not help her."

"So she... And you not?"

"No. Not because I don't want to. It just didn't work."

Never thought Octavio was careless after all, but he didn't say anything else. After all, he also used the help of people when it was impossible to achieve his goal otherwise, and although he tried hard not to discover his identity, sometimes they did find out the truth.

"Where are those you were supposed to track?" he asked.

"In the mountains," said the policeman, taking a hand-drawn map from his notebook. "Officially, they are at camping, but I managed to photograph the truck next to which they are supposed to camp. It is definitely not a caravan.

Taken with a telephoto lens, the picture showed a large, gray, armored truck without a logo and dark-skinned people in leopard print sitting on the grass. It was easy to recognize them as Rasts.

"New Hunters," Trelavny muttered, taking the photo in her hand. "Shame and disgrace, it looks like they come from my tribe."

"I don't understand one thing, why the Order of Obadiah?" Oleg scratched his head as he studied the photo over Trelavna's shoulder. "Who was Saint Obadiah? I have not heard of such man."

He did not frown reluctantly.

He wanted to explain to Oleg that if someone wanted to use people for a particular cause, the easiest way would be to create a cult and take control of their minds, but decided to postpone theorizing until a more convenient moment. He took the picture from Oleg and looked at it carefully. Akheeli was not to be seen among the assembled Rasts, and he looked to him to be all men.

"What are they waiting for?" he muttered.

"They are following a group of highlanders they suspect of vampirism," the cop replied. "I even think they rightly suspect them. If you want to do something, in my opinion you should hurry up, because these highlanders are peaceful natures. They form an artistic commune and I don't think they can defend themselves."

He took out a second map where he marked the location of the tiny village where the Rasts wanted them to live. Never remembered with some difficulty that he had heard about this village before, which did not even have a name - it was inhabited by freaks, endowed with artistic abilities. Their sculptures and paintings were sold for good prices in galleries.

"You're right," he said. "We're getting together. Where is the nearest car rental?"

"I will show you."

Soon the detachment drove straight to the village in a rented old-type Ford.

The car was converted by the owner of the rental company - it had a four-wheel drive and reinforced suspension, so you could risk driving it over mountain bumps. Once near the village, they immediately understood why the Rasts had not attacked it right away. Just a few hundred meters from her, a film crew was set up, shooting outdoors for a series, and it was probably only this fortunate circumstance that saved the nearby commune of artists from a terrible fate.

Artists may or may not be vampires. They must have behaved suspiciously to outside observers, but that was not the case. The Rasts would hardly have any regard for their outstanding talent, but they preferred not to risk the attack in the presence of so many camera-armed witnesses. They decided to wait, and this gave Never's squad time to act, but that time was running out as, as they drove past the filmmakers' camp, they noticed that they were gathering to leave.

They had to take a detour to avoid catching the Rasts's eye, which was difficult as night had fallen and the mountain trail was not illuminated by any lanterns. For safety reasons, the car's lights were turned off and they were guided only by the moonlight, which even for a vampire's eyes becomes tiring over time, especially when the road requires constant attention from the driver. Ignoring the warning signs "Private property, no entry", they drove to the village and stood just outside its borders. Two men with torches and armed with old-style shotguns came out to meet them.

"You can't drive in here, it's private property," said one of them. "Didn't you see the plates?"

"We saw it perfectly," Never replied, getting out of the Ford. "Briefly, brothers: we and you are of one blood."

The highlander looked at his friend and after a moment hesitating he repeated the password in Sanskrit.

"We came to warn you. There is a group of Hunters nearby for who your miserable shotguns will be worth as much as sticks," Never said approvingly.

"Hunters here?"

"Here. The warning was in all the major newspapers, don't you know the codes or what?"

"We don't read newspapers here, we want to be calm... Are you not lying sometimes?"

The men exchanged glances, then one of them approached Never and shone a torch on his face. For a moment he studied his pupils carefully.

"He's not lying," he decided after a moment. "Summon everyone to the common room."

His companion nodded and disappeared into the gloom between the domed huts. As Never noted, their peculiar structure was very functional - wide, overhanging eaves of the roofs protected against the sun during the day. The windows, covered with a special foil on the inside, did not reveal at night that the light was burning inside, and that the inhabitants were working or having fun.

"I'm Krabat," the highlander shook hands with Never, then with the rest of the squad. "Honza and I have a watch tonight. We felt something was going on here, but we had no idea it was that serious. Come to the common room, you need to talk to everyone and decide what to do."

"As soon as possible, because when the others attack, it will be too late for consultations."

Honza very quickly brought all the villagers to the common room - twelve men and five women. They all wore paint or clay stained aprons and looked very unhappy that they had been taken away from their work. They glared at the strangers with distrustful looks, but Never's first words made them listen to him attentively. When he was done, they whispered to each other, and then a gypsy-looking dark-haired man asked matter-of-factly:

"So what do you advise?"

"Get out of here now and hide somewhere," Never replied. "We will stay and deal with these fanatics."

"Can you do it?"

"It's our job. We'll be fine, but on the condition that you don't get tangled around."

Apparently, his words convinced the artists, as they immediately changed from working clothes to something more "formal" and, just in case, took their more valuable things. Soon none of them remained in the village, except Krabat. As the leader, he felt it would be his duty to support the strangers in the fight for the villagers.

"I was a professional soldier once," he replied to Never's protests. "I can fight, and I should do it, not just pass all the work on the passersby. After all, this is my and my friends' home."

"As you like, but do not get away with anything on your own," Never warned him, and proceeded to distribute tasks among the members of his squad.

His plan, though seemingly insane, was only dangerous to him, because he was supposed to distract the main group of Rasts from the switchboard and persuade them, because they chased him until the rest of them destroyed the moving center of the bearing. To this end, he decided not to wait, but to attack the Hunters now, allowing his squad to take control of the situation. He thought that probably not all of them would survive this action, but he did not say it aloud - as a commander he had to take care of the morale of his temporary subordinates.

Half an hour later they started the action. The plan was simple - lure the main group away from their mobile control room, then plant explosives under it and fire them remotely.

The Rasts chasing Never did not seem to associate the blast with their headquarters at first, as they hadn't even slowed down as they tracked the vampire stalking through the trees. They didn't need data processing now to track him down, he was very close. It was enough to follow the senses stimulated by the mysterious substance not to lose him.

This was what he had been counting on when he attacked them alone, drawing the attention of the main force. In this way, he pulled them away from the gray, armored truck, next to which they had set up their camp. It was their mobile switchboard - a real monster on wheels, filled with complicated apparatus and operated by a few people trained in this direction. He had no hope that his "task force" would at least try to get the technicians out of the truck before he dropped it off, but he couldn't think about it yet. He was followed by more than ten - he couldn't pinpoint how many - determined to do anything, armed with flamethrowers and machetes. There were still five armed men left by the truck, and Octavio's colleagues had to deal with them.

Running like a chased cat, he finally found himself in a more open space. It was a kind of wide valley, covered with dense, stunted vegetation. In the geometric center of the area was an oval-shaped basin about two meters long and a meter wide, resembling a sand-like basin. It was struck by Nevera that here in the heart of Black Forest, no birds could be heard, that there weren't even insects above that shallow valley, nothing. He paused uncertainly.

There was a heavy silence all around, and, even stranger, the plants growing on the edge of the basin were leaning away from her, as if trying to escape.

He stepped closer and stopped again. He knew he should go on, but he stood still, oblivious to the Rasts pursuing him.

Something held him in place, some indescribable horror emanating from that sandy shoal in a sea of deep green plants that felt equally dreaded and tried to keep as far away as possible from what must have been there... but what was that?

He felt that the answer to this question could not be found in any human language.

He stared at the smooth golden sand, slowly realizing that its surface was rising and falling very slowly, as if the place was breathing... that the Rasts were right there, that they were about to surround it and aim their blasters at it. For some reason, the thought was indifferent to him now. Only when he heard them behind him did he turn, slowly and heavily. They surrounded him in a semicircle, taking their blasters off their shoulders. He stood. He just stared.

However, this time the flames shooting from the barrels did not reach him, they faded in the air as if they were hitting an invisible wall. Out of the corner of his eye, Never noticed that the vegetation around him was suddenly graying, as if a ghostly wave were walking on it - yes, that was the most accurate comparison, for the sudden fading widened, crept unstoppably like a spilling thick liquid. He felt a penetrating cold, as if a sticky fog had enveloped him, and at the same time his strength was completely drained. He couldn't even move.

After a while a wave of gray reached the Rasts, neither of which made a sound, but a terrible change took place in their appearance - their skin turned a pale-dead color, began to wrinkle violently and shrink. The bodies dried up in the eyes, turned brown, cracked, curling like leaves under the influence of the harsh sun, fell off bones in pieces, and finally the skeletons, even unsupported by the appearance of life, crumbled with a crunch, like mummies from thousands of years ago.

He didn't look at all of this while waiting for his turn, which... didn't come. The ghastly wave retreated slowly back to its lair, the plants regaining their saturated hues, though they still trembled as if they were aware of what had happened.

The bitter cold that chilled the Indian to the bone was slowly subsiding. Comprehending what had happened, he turned, overcoming the willpower of the stiffness in his muscles. He looked down at the sandy rag, which was slowly changing its color from gray to golden natural sand. After a while it began to rise again and fall in a pulsating rhythm as if nothing had happened.

Barely daring to breathe, Never lowered his gaze and saw the thick darkness hugging his legs.

Under the influence of his astonished gaze, she floated a bit to the side and blurred, disappeared, although Never knew that he only stopped seeing her, because he is still with him.

Feeling a sudden weakness, he sat down on one of the few boulders that adorned this unusual place. For a moment he was bothered about how he knew her, then he remembered - he had seen her once when they were solving the Meredith Johnson case.

Yes, that was what the former pastor "clung to" and must have torn away from him when they forcibly took him into the world of Vandis. Apparently, they found Never afterwards and now he was "haunted". He had to accept the facts: now he had a Companion, and you had to get used to his presence. Interestingly, he didn't sense any threat from it. Powerful, undoubtedly, it was very powerful, but it was not his enemy, even if it was evil in human understanding. He already knew that it had saved him from dying in the flames, it had given him the strength to reach Denmark, and probably also supported him somehow during his treatment. And now it had saved him from something that had killed the Rasts.

"I don't know what you are," he said aloud, standing up. "I don't know what you want from me.

That girl who was with Johnson said we would regret what we did, maybe she meant you. But I'm not going to be afraid of you. Let it be as you like, but I will live the same life as before. I've seen too much and lived too much for you to scare me."

He felt a little uncomfortable at the thought of ghostly company, but decided that if he accepted the Shadow, he shouldn't care about that silent Companion, as he chose to call him. Although he did not know his intentions, he did not know his motives, he decided to assume that whatever they were, he would be able to handle it.

It took a while for him to reach the point where his squad had destroyed the Order's headquarters.

The smell was still drifting over the entire hall, the grass was covered with a black hoof and charred remains. He found his branch several dozen meters away. Nobody suffered too much in the fight against the control unit, although it was obvious that they had a problem - they clearly did not know what to do with the captured Rasts. Four white men and one dark woman sat tied under the trees and were silent as if they had bitten off their tongues. They seemed to be in some kind of trance.

"Are they high?" he asked.

"Could be," replied Oleg Tarnov. "We've secured some of their powder, we'll examine it. How did you manage? Where are those who chased you?"

"They're dead," Never replied shortly. "Don't look at me like that, I didn't kill them. I'll tell you later. We have to deal with those here now."

Sienna Laung looked into her first aid bag and took out a syringe and a large ampoule of some liquid.

"I'll let them sleep," she suggested. "They'll take a nap and we'll disappear. This is probably the best solution."

He nodded his head approvingly. He wanted to leave the Black Forest as soon as possible and find his friends.

"Wait," he remembered after a moment. "If this was their operational unit, where is Akheela?"

"She wasn't here," said Alex Spicery with a shrug. "If we want to look for it, maybe we will volunteer to look for a needle in a bottle of hay?"

"Very funny. You better watch out, we only won one battle. We don't know where their training camp is, we don't know who their leader really is or how many people they have.

We only dealt with one pesky squad. We may suppose that it was an armed arm of the cult that they were the best of their people, but that still means that we did not tear off the hydra's head, at most the tail. We've bitten that organization, it's true. However, nothing more."

"They're asleep," Sienna reported.

"Then take the restraints off them and we're going out of here. Be careful not to unfasten your bracelets. We will have to tell Octavio that they have worked perfectly well, let him start mass production."

"Better to kill them," Oleg said grimly.

"You're probably right, but we won't," he snapped. "Once we start, we won't be able to stop."

"Leave them to us," Krabat suggested. "We hand them over to the police on charges of assault. I'm betting they're here illegally so we'll get them over with."

"Excellent," Never said. "You can also tell yours to go home. Luckily, these idiots didn't set your village on fire, so they have something to come back to."

He thought wearily that once again everyone would expect him and his friends to finally settle the Order.

For a long time in the vampire milieu, they were regarded as somewhat of the clan's permanent security guards, which brought some material benefits, but at the same time was a great burden. Although, on the other hand, what was to be done?

As Lambdon Tygier once remarked with a sneer, most vampires are not powerful demons known from movies, but intimidated losers who, over time, cease to cope with life's problems at all.

There was a certain irony to that. The immortal blood kept the tissues from degenerating, but it could not protect the crumbling psyche, which seldom adapted to change as well as it did in Octavio or Fronda. For di Mauro, this ability was probably due to his high intelligence, and on the contrary, to the fact that he was not intelligent enough to care too much about anything. He only glided on the surface of the events, not penetrating what was deeper and thus kept his sanity.

*****

Analysis of the mysterious powder found in the damaged switchboard showed that it was not strictly speaking a drug, but was a no less dangerous chemical.

It was a blend of plant alkaloids known to biologists, including tetrodotoxin and Datura extract, but Octavio said, to test their integrated effect, they would have to do human experiments.

The individual ingredients were used in trace amounts, so that the end result must have been their interaction - and this has not yet been tested in the laboratory. So, biologists have developed a probable profile of the compound's action on the human brain. It turned out that it paralyzes the self-preservation instinct and eliminates all manifestations of empathy, and also increases susceptibility to suggestions. The latter property, as Irka Kralova stated, could be used precisely to defend against the Rasts.

"Do you have consciousness manipulation specialists here?" Never asked distrustfully.

"The anthropology department does," Octavio replied. "They may not be specialists, but they deal with the behaviorism of mankind, so they are no strangers to such matters."

He didn't grimace a little, but he held back the unpleasant comment that struck his lips.

After the action in the Black Forest, he felt so bad that he decided to take advantage of the hospitality of Octavio and his group for a while. After several days of strengthening treatment, he got out of bed like a newborn, although, as the beautiful Russian assured him, he should still be ill for quite a long time. First of all, he went to the city and began sending an appropriately worded advertisement to a dozen newspapers.

Luckily the Rasts either didn't have "steps" in the banks, or did not think of a similar action, as their friends' accounts were safe. It is true that they were usually empty, because everyone preferred to carry money with them (there weren't that many of them anyway), but it was better to have access to it. Right now, only Never and Dea had something on their accounts, and he was now using his meager resources to pay for the listing.

Returning from the bank, he deviated a bit from the road and went to the fjord. There was no one there, for the bitterly cold wind was blowing and the sea was threatening with a storm, as usual at this time of the year. Never stopped on a high cliff. There was a pebble beach at the bottom and the tide was lashing against it. Overhead, gulls screamed, hunting the little creatures, but apart from them there was no living spirit around. He looked around again, then took a deep breath and jumped. It was very reckless. He could break his arms and legs, he knew it well, but the urge to see how things were going was stronger than the voice of reason.

Last time, he had been too nervous to pay attention to details, nor did he know what was happening - now he was watching.

Something surrounded his body like concentrated air, and held it so that it fell gently, in slow motion, until his feet touched the beach. It didn't even feel like something was holding him - rather like his body had suddenly lost weight.

It might even be enjoyable if he didn't realize where the power that carried him was coming from.

"Stranger and stranger," he muttered to himself. He walked down the beach and after a while he turned, trying to enter the restless sea that crawled almost to his feet. He saw the rising tide and walked towards it, determined to fully investigate what was happening to him. The wave rushed straight at him, and after a while, as if it had hit something invisible, it splashed right in front of him into billions of ice-cold splashes that soaked him to his skin but knocked him down and did not take him out to sea, as it should have happened. It was all clear.

"So you're still there," he said loudly. "All right, then be here. We will see how it will work for us."

He still felt a little insecure, but the feeling of the strange slowly faded away. After all, he had dealt with so many extraordinary things that he had gotten used to the bizarre, as it were. He couldn't understand why Meredith Johnson thought she was "damned" because of his symbiosis with it - because it was certainly a symbiosis, though he didn't quite know what it was.

The Ghostly Companion knew how to be of help, as it turned out, but did not protect against every inconvenience. By the time Never reached the Andersen Museum, he was chilled to the core. Shaking his teeth chattering, he stripped off his wet clothes, dried it heavily with a hairy towel, and crawled under the covers. Work was booming all over the wing, and no one paid any attention to his return, so he didn't have to explain to anyone. After warming up a bit, he thought that he would sleep for a while, and when he opened his eyes, it was already dusk outside the window.

He felt refreshed and strong. He dressed, shaved, combed his rapidly growing hair and left the room. After finding Octavio, he thanked him for his help and announced that he was already on his way.

Good luck, said the Spaniard. Here are bracelets for your crew and some new gadgets. You can tell them cell phones are safe for now, they can use them. Rasts do not have the technology and power to eavesdrop or triangulate their cell tracking.

"Still don't know who's in charge?" Never asked.

Octavio shook his ginger head.

"We still don't know much. We must be careful. In any case, once you get yours together, try to track down the organizer who trained these freaks.

We'll transfer as much as possible to your accounts so you don't have to bother with the money, but you take care of it."

Never shrugged his shoulders slightly. He had expected it, but honestly wished it hadn't been said.

"We're the only hope again, right?" He said. "Why doesn't someone else try this job?"

"You know why. Only you somehow manage it, and you are a great commander. You haven't lost a single person from the branch we entrusted to you, and we counted on the fact that a good half would not come back."

"Well, we can try, but I don't promise miracles."

He left the museum around midnight after saying goodbye to the entire team. With the money he had received, he bought an old, but functional car and hit the road. The burn scars had ceased to bother him. Strengthened with fresh blood, the body worked at top speed, and the presence of the Companion, though it should have depressed him, gave him confidence. He had no doubts that his friends would read the announcement he had written for them and that they would go to their designated meeting point, which means that they would be together again in a few days. And then... is it so important what will happen next?

He smiled grimly. Well, then, he will have to explain some things to his friends, and this may not be easy, especially since he himself was not so sure what this unexpected alliance meant for him. How to check it, if it does not say something and does not communicate telepathically, which would be logical in this situation?

"Friends?" He asked aloud.

He looked down at his clenched hands on the steering wheel and saw a black shadow crawling over one of them.

He wrapped himself around Never's hand for a moment, as if he were trying to shake it, and disappeared.

Never smiled as he crank up and turned to the international road, whistling "A hard day's night". He felt great.

Part 2

The Curse of Millhaven

I was named devil's filth

and the curse of the town

But it was Millhaven who brought this bad luck upon me

Quite pretty green eyes I have

And my loose fair hair

And pretty lips when I smile

Fall to your knees everyone!

I know the best path to the Lord!

Tra la la tra la la la...

You do not know the day nor the hour - only God knows it!

By Roman Kołakowski based on poem by Nick Cave

Investigation officer Laszlo Kun was beginning to be concerned when the lock on the door clicked. A man with swarthy skin and black hair tied up at the back entered the room. The springy movements made it clear that he had to be fast and agile. Almond eyes, an unbelievable shade of gold tinfoil, rested on the policeman who shuddered nervously.

"So, do you know who killed?" He asked.

The other shrugged.

"Oh, I know who killed," he replied. "But I have no idea why he did it. Hello everyone."

"Hello, Never," two men greeted, an elegant lady and a frail girl in an unfashionable dress waiting with Laszlo for his return. He knew their names, but they told him no more about each other. And he didn't ask.

With a sigh, the newcomer threw himself on the old-fashioned armchair in front of the TV set and closed his disturbing eyes.

"This murder doesn't really make any sense," he said. "No logical motive."

For a week or so, Laszlo had had the help of this man and his no less peculiar friends. Their friend recommended them, warning them at the same time:

"Don't ask anything and don't try to learn anything about them, and you'll be fine."

Such a condition seemed unusual, but Laszlo accepted it, for he had no choice. He was in danger of relegating, his account was empty, and this case was of prestigious importance. He had to, he just had to solve it, no matter how bizarre the private detectives he hired with his mortgage money.

"Give me the materials," he said. "I'll find the motive myself, as long as I have the evidence."

The man named Never threw a leather briefcase on the table.

"There you have everything I got. It would be enough for two life sentences, not just one."

Laszlo opened the briefcase and began leafing through its contents.

"Peter Wang was right, you are very effective. I also know from him that you are looking for the founder of the RAST organization. I could help you, I have access to materials that you won't get in the normal way."

"How much for this?" The lady in the black suit asked sharply. Her name was Dea, she had red hair and a belligerent gaze. All of Laszlo's experience told him that it was better not to get in her way.

"It's not about the money. This time... exchange of favors. I wonder..." Laszlo paused for a moment and walked slowly around the room.

He was thinking hard about something. Finally he sat down on the sofa and asked:

"Is it true that you are specialists in paranormal affairs?"

Never laughed, revealing two rows of sharp white teeth that gave the impression that there were twice as many as there should be.

"Peter can't keep his mouth shut, huh? Specialists are an exaggeration, but we had several such cases. Not all of them could be logically explained. What is it all about?"

Under his careful, penetrating gaze, the investigator felt uncomfortable. For many years he had been in possession of a secret with which he could do nothing.

He realized that once he started talking about what he knew, he would be finished, and worse, no one would believe him, and he was not a suicide type or comic book hero.

He wanted to be able to live normally and work normally, and the label of a lunatic was the last thing he needed. Still, he was tormented by what he had to hide, and this mysterious man and his no less strange colleagues might have been just the ones who would prove to be the right one to look at.

"You will probably find that my head is not in order," he began, stuttering slightly. "But I swear to you by my mother that what I will say is true. Not far from here is Millhaven, a fairly large town, located off the beaten track, between the swamps. Seemingly, not much is going on there, it is not a so-called dying city, on the contrary, it is prospering even well. However, it has one specific feature: it is impossible to escape from this city if you were born and raised there. If someone leaves, he dies under strange circumstances. Maybe I should say: scary."

"I heard something... there was a song about that. Is it about this city?" The woody man with a sickly appearance and an elf's face frowned.

"About this one, about this. What I said isn't enough. There is something else. After dark, none of the indigenous people of Millhaven will leave their doorstep, and they will not turn off the lights until dawn. Those who disregarded this general phobia were sometimes found torn apart... and sometimes not found at all, only scraps of bloody clothing, remnants of hair, a torn purse... you see for yourself."

"My word, the same thing again," muttered Gerard. Jen jumped on his shoulder and began tugging at his hair affectionately. He stroked the monkey automatically.

"Well, what do you expect from us?" Never asked, showing no emotion.

Laszlo coughed embarrassedly.

"It would be perfect if you could explain why this is happening, but if you fail, why not try to get a woman named Emma Simms out of there."

"Cherchez la femme[5], cripes," snorted the tall, strikingly handsome dark-haired man they called Fronda. "She's from a local family, I understand?"

"Exactly. Will you do it?"

"We don't promise. We never give a guarantee. However, we will do our best, but you must know that our services are not, whatever the outcome, how to say..." Never began diplomatically.

"Do you have money?" Dea interrupted unceremoniously.

Laszlo nodded.

---

[5] Look for women (French), implied: she must be the cause of the problems.

"I have money from the loan. I will give you as much as I can, just please try to help Emma. For me it's very important."

"I expect that," the young lady looked slightly disgusted, but was clearly trying to hide it. "So, sir, address, advance payment and please wait for contact."

He pulled his wallet out of his pocket and pulled out a thick bundle of bills.

"I will not account for this," he said emphatically. "And if you do it successfully, I promise to help you find a Rast animator."

"If we don't, it's probably because something will eat us," Gerard said. "Rajah, do we really have to take matters where every now and then something is trying to skin us alive?"

"We have to, because somehow nobody wants to entrust us with the investigations consisting in looking for the missing kitten," Never answered him sharply. "Don't be surprised. Pack better, you too."

Gerard wanted to say something, but changed his mind and fell silent. He had known for a long time that going against Never was a lost nerve and nothing more, because you can't win against him.

The worst part was not even that he didn't know how to oppose him, but that he let himself be dominated without a fight. More than once he reproached himself for being too passive towards this Hindu demon, but he could do nothing about it. While at one time it was still possible to argue with Never, since he had an ally in the person of Dea, he stopped taking the opinion of the other three into account at all.

"There can only be one commander," he said when one day there was a fierce argument over this. "A ship with two captains on board will sink quickly. Whoever does not like it may leave, but whoever stays must accept that I'm in charge."

Fronda had pouted like a resentful child all day, but as the anger passed over him, he explained to Gerard and Oggy why he was staying with Never:

"I can't deny that he's just the best. And this in every way possible."

It was indeed difficult to argue with this. He was already a tough opponent for anyone who hunted him (or whom he hunted), but now that he had a mysterious Companion, no one could really face him. At first his friends felt a certain dread of the unnamed force fused into their leader's body, but soon the horror passed and they began to treat the whole thing "just".

For his part, Never's companion did not cause any trouble. He rarely manifested his presence and was hardly annoying, only sometimes you could see that the Indian cast a second shadow, or that his golden eyes flashed red and green.

"Is he taking something from you?" Dea asked skeptically when it was once known. It was inconsistent in her always sober head that such a symbiosis could be disinterested.

"He's taking," Never replied. "It probably cannot exist outside some material object, and the human body is an excellent home for it. And a tool for self-realization."

Gerard couldn't understand why his friend would agree to such a deal, but Never had his reasons. First of all, the Companion was better than titanium armor, since he could protect his host to some extent even from immediate danger and mask his trail enough to hide from his pursuers. It also stimulated the body in some way - after all, He could never have died of burns when blasted fire hit him, let alone burn like a dry branch. Of course, it was doubtful that such a symbiosis would prove dangerous in the long run, but the Indian vampire had no intention of worrying about it. For now, the whole thing suited him, and that was enough.

The last day in Los Angeles was remembered by friends as an event as grotesque as it was dangerous. Fronda, who successfully pretended to be a rich lost man, got an invitation for two to a banquet for the local high society and persuaded Dea to accompany him. The others, tired of the investigation that had just ended, went to bed shortly after ten o'clock, not letting themselves be tempted by the night movie on television.

At three in the morning they were awakened by noise and wailing complaints.

"What happened?" Gerard asked half-consciously, jumping up from the bed.

"What happened, what happened..." Dea pushed Fronda into the room, twisting with pain. "It just so happened that I'm not going to any party with that idiot anymore! Some friend of his was there..."

"Jackie the Liar." Fronda groaned, huddling on the carpet.

"Whatever. The moron had made a bet with him that he would eat a tablespoon of caviar and wash it down with champagne."

"And what?" Never asked, only now lifting his head from the pillow.

"He won thirty bucks."

"I'm dying, oh mother, it hurts..." Theo moaned, curling up on the carpet.

"Of course it hurts," Dea grunted mercilessly, taking off her elegant gown and putting on a crumpled apron out of the suitcase. "Good for you. Hold that donkey, I have to do gastric lavage for him. If it fails, it will have to be cut or the sympathetic nervous system will be paralyzed, and goodbye."

Looking through the contents of the suitcase, she took out a twenty-centimeter syringe and several catheters, from which she chose the thinnest.

"What is this?" screamed Fronda, forgetting his suffering and leaping up from the carpet.

Never and Gerard grabbed him, despite his cursing and brave resistance, twisted his arms behind his back, and Oggy brought a bowl and water. The operation was going to be difficult, as the vampire's esophagus is not only narrowed but also extremely innervated, so there could be problems even with inserting a catheter into the stomach. It was hard to dream about using an ordinary rubber tube, as in the case of a human.

Dea forcefully forced Fronda to open his mouth, numb his throat with lignocaine spray and, despite his resistance, tried to insert the catheter. The second time her efforts were successful, and around six in the morning Fronda, exhausted but with a washed out stomach, fell asleep on his bed. Only now could everyone rest.

"How could something like this come to his mind?" Oggy muttered as she tidied up the shambles the room had turned into.

"I'm curious what he will come up with next time. This isn't his first stupid prank. You can expect anything, even a drink of gasoline and a burning match." Dea put her tools away and went to shower.

She did not add, although she could, that she was also very curious about how Fronda coped in the past when there was no one to watch over him.

*****

It took them all night to get to town. "Near" turned out to be a relative and inaccurate concept, in addition, there was a mistake in the map received from the detective, and only by lucky coincidence they found the right path. They pulled into Millhaven just before dawn and stayed at a small motel next to a gas station, clean and well-kept. The sleepy receptionist grabbed the money given to her and gave them the keys, not interested in who they were or what they were bringing with them. Apparently that was the custom here.

Having checked in, Theo and Dea, who were "moths", went to bed, and Never, Gerard, and Oggy set out to explore the town that was waking from sleep. One thing they noticed at once - the city, like the motel, was very clean. You had the impression that either someone was constantly cleaning the streets, or that the inhabitants were not in the habit of littering.

"It looks very nice," Oggy said appreciatively. "Compared to many cities we've been to, it's like a museum here."

"Exactly. And I don't like it," Never looked around with a concerned expression in his eyes. "Notice something, there aren't any animals here. If you see one, tell me."

Confused, Oggy began to look for even the slightest manifestation of animal life in the streets, but she could see nothing. You couldn't hear birds or insects, no dog barked anywhere, no cats slipping by. The curious girl finally began to sniff eagerly, taking advantage of her canine predispositions

"And you know you're right," she said after a moment. "I bet there aren't even rats here, I can't smell them."

"Humans do look and act normal, though," said Gerard.

It was indeed so. Residents rushed to their classes, bought various products in stores, children, yawning from lack of sleep, went to school - everything looked completely normal, only the lack of animals was strange.

However, after a long look, they noticed a few dogs, small parlor specimens - two pugs, a Yorkie being carried by an elderly woman in her arm, and a pair of cat-sized mongrels. They never seemed to be unleashed. Even these animals were acting weird. They did not bark and were very careful about the legs of their guardians.

"I think if the three of us walk like this, we'll get people's attention more easily," said Gerard suddenly. "Let's split up and check everything on our own."

"Good thought," Never agreed. "We meet in the motel tonight and compare our findings. Just a side note: no hassle, okay?"

"Sure, sure."

Gerard's observation was accurate because when they split up, they really stopped drawing the attention of passers-by. One by one, they could penetrate all nooks and crannies without being too conspicuous to anyone. At least that's what they thought and they did. However, the effect was slightly different than expected. Although even the very sensitive Never could not notice he was being watched, all three of them had that stinging, unpleasant feeling that someone was watching them all the time and never taking his eyes off them.

This town was definitely strange, with a strange, unpleasant aura. Never, the most experienced man in this field, even discovered something that surprised and disturbed him: the aura was fairly homogeneous in structure, not made up of many human-dependent components, as is usually the case in crowded places. It was truly alarming, for it made an association with Stonehenge and what they discovered in the stone circle.

He did not fail to share this observation with his friends when they met at the motel.

"No, again?" Fronda groaned.

"I said it was an association, not an identification. It is not the same, but it feels similar."

"Maybe this city is located in an old Indian cemetery, like in "Spirit"?" Gerard clearly remembered the movie that seriously scared him.

"Eh," Ghost ", Dea waved her hand contemptuously. "The "Pet Sematary" was better, and it also talked about an Indian cemetery.

Oggy shook her head doubtfully.

95

"I had a little chat with the local "element"," she said. "Don't look at me like that. It's a good way and I didn't risk much.

I gave them a bottle and cigarettes, they rejoiced and even offered them to taste... There were never any Indians in this area. It is said that a group of pioneers established a settlement here for this very reason. They were quiet people, and they didn't want to deal with redskins who, you know, could be pretty decisive about scalping."

"And that's what the white visitors taught them," Never replied coolly. "They didn't make it up themselves. Anyway, never mind, that was a long time ago. Come on, what else did you find out from these scums?"

"Not much, actually. They complained a little about the swamps that they were poisoning the area. One said that probably a large pharmaceutical company, which has a factory relatively nearby, was getting rid of some waste in these swamps and attributed all the strange phenomena to it. But what are these phenomena, he did not really want to talk about."

The Indian narrowed his eyes. He, too, had heard of a company that had plants some distance from town - townspeople seemed to blame it for all their problems, though many of them had worked for it until recently. But no one said anything specific.

"And you, Cheetah?" He turned to Gerard. "What did you find out?"

"I figured out where Emma Simms lives," the actor replied with studied calm. "I went to the post office and they told me where to look for her."

"So where, Cheetah?" Dea looked at him appreciatively, which was very rare to her.

"For some time, the girl has been working in Hidden Cove, a mansion outside the city. Apparently, she was employed by the owner of half of this town."

"Hidden Cove?" Theo asked incredulously. He didn't like the name and didn't like small towns for a while. Admittedly, it was not that small again, and it was all the stranger.

"She worked at the clinic before, but this guy just requested her to work for him, and it looks like she had to obey for some reason," Gerard poured himself a drink and sipped it slowly, his eyes half-closed.

"Damn it, America," Never muttered, disgusted. "I guess the guy has half the locals in his pocket."

He hated this country and didn't feel like believing that he was here again. However, it was here that their trail of a new enemy had failed, and it was here that they lost him. They still did not know who commanded the Rasts and why he sent them on these deadly hunts. There was one such person, but they couldn't figure out who it was. If Laszlo knew that, it was necessary to do everything possible to get him to speak.

"The word 'residence' indicates that we are dealing with local notables," he said after a moment. "Before we try to talk to Emma Simms, we need to find out more. We don't need to argue with the 'untouchables' here."

"Do you believe in the curse?" Oggy asked.

He shrugged his shoulders slightly. Born and raised in India, he had seen and heard things, so the "curse", whatever it was, could not surprise him. Something was happening in this town, all his experience had told him so, and it was worth investigating.

"And you two?" He looked at Dea and Fronda. "Nothing to worry you?"

"The water in the taps is a little cloudy, otherwise not too bad," replied the girl, continuing to wear makeup in front of the mirror.

"Now you guys rest while Theo and I check out the nightlife in this hole."

"Be careful," he warned her for the sake of order. "From what Laszlo said, it's not safe."

"Let him scare Grandma with an umbrella," Dea corrected the contour of her eyebrows a bit and tucked the crayon into the cosmetic bag. "Fronda, are you ready?"

"For you, always," Theo replied with the courteous and seductive smile of a man who knows the strength of his charm well. However, Dea was not impressed by his tricks.

"So let's go," she said, getting up from the mirror. "In case of emergency we call the boss's cell phone, so do not turn it off. Good night."

Never want to say "Watch her," but gave up. He knew from experience that it was rather Dea who could watch over Fronda so that he did not do nonsense, after all, she had an eminently masculine character, which more than one guy had fool himself about and regretted long after.

The town looked frozen. There were no passersby anywhere, no prowler or police patrol - no one. Only car traffic appeared to be normal. Dea and Fronda stayed in the shadows, not wanting to be seen by anyone, but it was not easy as all the windows were brightly lit. It was really fascinating. Throughout the night, as they traveled through the silent streets and alleys, they did not see a single inhabited house where no light was on.

"Peculiar. It never happens, it is usually half and half, and at certain times almost 100% of people are asleep, so the lights should be off," Dea murmured as they both decided they had seen enough to confirm this phenomenon.

"It isn't said that they are awake. However, for some reason they are afraid to turn off the light.

From this the conclusion is that whatever haunts the inhabitants is afraid of the light," Fronda looked around and pointed to the unlit nook.

There was a decaying hovel that would be a great haven for local drunks and vagrants in any other city. Here, however, it was perfectly empty and silent.

"If our theory is correct and it only attacks in the dark, let's find out," he suggested.

"Why not?" Dea pulled out the miniature camera, turned on the infrared mode, and looked around, fixing it in place where the brick had fallen.

There was a lot of dust and debris in the abandoned building, broken pieces of some old furniture, rubbish, but nowhere could you smell the rat smell of such places.

Instead, there was a barely perceptible, pungent odor, unlike anything but incomparably hideous. As soon as Fronda became aware of its presence, he sniffed around the room like a hound, looking for the source, and finally returned to his companion.

"I have no idea what it smells like in here," he said. "It's not from some specific place, I don't know... From the air?"

"Do you know that smell?"

"I don't know? Probably not. It's a bit like what bedbugs emit, but it's worse. Only you can barely feel it. What could it be?"

"We'll see." With these words, Dea turned off her flashlight.

The Fronda followed her example. They both saw as well as cats in the dark, using flashlights out of human habit rather than real need.

But the darkness that covered the ruined house was anything but ordinary. They had seen such people before and knew that they did not bode well.

But they only went numb for good when, somewhere in the middle of the darkness, an amazing melody came, played neither on a toy xylophone, nor on the black keys of a regular piano. It was soft, almost childish - light tapping on invisible keys, like a single finger, without deep chords.

They formed a melody that was as evocative as terrifying, penetrating to the bone marrow. As it resounded, all surfaces - walls, floor, and broken furniture - began to be covered with some peculiar, phosphorescent white mold. It didn't look like it was rising - rather it was crawling up from the depths of the building, covering everything it reached. It moved slowly, blindly, but not mechanically, and that was the most macabre because it seemed to be some primitive, animal form.

As it was dangerously close, Fronda and Dea suddenly discovered with horror that they had lost control of their bodies. Whether it was because of the weird music or that faint odor, they didn't know, and at that moment they didn't care. They became helpless in the face of impending danger, unable to break the curse that bound them, or the charm, or anything that held them captive. Phosphoric mold was already flooding most of the room, covering everything she could reach when a thin screech sounded at the entrance to the ruin.

The strange substance suddenly became cohesive and rushed towards the sound in a long, resilient wave.

The invisible bond abruptly gave way, the ghastly music stopped, and they realized that it had never really been there. Released so unexpectedly turned to see Jen.

Taking advantage of someone's inattention, the monkey had to get out of the cage and followed the Fronda trail - to its undoing. Before they could even sigh, the white stain engulfed the animal like some giant amoeba. Dea yanked the stunned friend's arm.

"Run for your life!" She screamed.

They both ran out of the ruins and only stopped at the nearest street lamp. Their hearts pounded against their ribs in some absurdly rapid rhythm, their lungs burning as if they were inhaling poison gas.

"Jen..." Fronda groaned.

"We couldn't help her. She died so that we would survive," Dea interrupted him brusquely, not letting him feel sorry. There was no time for that.

"What could it be?" Theo gasped for breath, his normally calm hands trembling.

"It could be anything," Dea replied, trying unsuccessfully to conceal that she was at least as scared as he was. "I haven't seen anything like that and heard of anything like that. In any case, it's afraid of the light, we know for sure."

"It ate Jen!"

"Not only her. It consumed everything that was alive and stupid enough to enter the dark. That explains something I didn't understand before."

"What?" He looked at her with confused eyes.

"In this city, almost every corner smells like gasoline. I bet every inhabitant has a gasoline generator and plenty of fuel in case the power plant collapses."

"What a horrible place! Do you think we've seen enough or are we still looking for something?"

"No, the investigation is over for today. Whatever it is, it is deadly and very powerful. We return to the hotel, we need to consult what to do next."

They set off, sticking to the most lit places. They understood well now the fears of the people of Millhaven, who would not be able to leave this place, trapped by a mysterious curse, something no outsider even believed existed.

"You know, Dea..." Fronda began after a while. "I already remember what the name of this city reminded me of. It's not just a song. Once I read about a series of murders in Millhaven... guilty was a fifteen-year-old girl, Loretta White, well-liked, calm, pious... She was considered insane and probably was, but was it not because of this?"

"Perhaps," Dea said dryly. "We don't know how this thing affects people. We don't even know if they can see it."

"How's that?"

"Just like that. I'm not one hundred and fifty percent sure, but I don't think they can see. Don't forget that our eyes are different, more sensitive. This stuff was barely visible even to us, people probably don't know what is attacking them. I think they don't even know for sure, or they'd go crazy for it."

Theo shuddered, but on reflection agreed with his friend. He hadn't paid any attention to it before, but the phosphorescent "mold" could indeed lie outside the spectrum of colors perceived by the eyes of an ordinary person. The mesmerizing influence probably did its job as well.

A nasty surprise awaited them at the motel. Their friends were gone, which also explained why Jen managed to escape from the carrier she usually slept in.

If anyone had stayed with her, she would have cuddled up to him and not looking for Fronda. Theo picked up the empty baby carrier and stared at it for a long moment until his eyes watered. He became very attached to the little tamarin and could not come to terms with the fact that he had lost her.

Meanwhile, Dea discovered a piece of paper lying on the table with a short note: "We went for a scout. Wait until we answer." And she cursed.

"Fronda, stop cry with it!" She demanded angrily. "It's not the time to feel sorry for the monkey when people die. Grab the phone and try to warn Never, I'll call Gerard."

She shrugged impatiently, seeing that Theo wasn't listening to her words at all, and took her phone out of her pocket. Unfortunately, all three numbers were silent, and Dea remembered angrily that Never had always ordered the cameras to be turned off in such situations, so that they would not expose the scouts at the least appropriate moment. So there was no communication, although it would be most useful now.

"What we do?" asked Fronda, having controlled himself and realized the situation.

"Nothing. We sit and wait. We don't know where they went anyway. Nothing will help them if we also lose ourselves. We sit and hope they don't get into more trouble than necessary."

Theo hesitated, but on reflection decided Dea was right. And there was so little they could do without knowing where their friends had gone, especially since their psycho-localization could prove unreliable under these circumstances, and it was better not to rely on it. So they have to wait.

Meanwhile, the rest of the team was already outside the city. The decision to leave the motel was not spontaneous - it was dictated by accidental information about the "haunted factory".

They heard it in the cafeteria where they went down to buy some drink. Oggy, pitying as usual, put a bottle of cheap gin on a washed-up tramp who was counting up some last pennies in the corner. The derelict kissed her hands in gratitude, and Gerard and Never's displeasure subsided when they discovered that the drunk man was a mine of information.

"This factory has been closed for ten years. Everyone is avoiding it" he said, glad to find an audience. "Apparently, strange things used to happen there. People were killed, torn to shreds by machines, or pinned down by stacks of goods, and some went in and didn't go out at all! Never heard from again! That's why the factory closed. After all, no one wanted to work there."

"Have they seen something, maybe heard?" Never asked.

"Not at all! They did not see or hear anything! Considering that in this god-damned city, a poltergeist or an ordinary ghost are the most ordinary things in the world, it is truly extraordinary, because nothing happened in the factory, and only people were dying."

"Indeed, like nothing." Gerard muttered sarcastically. He suddenly remembered the short story from Ghost Stories, specifically a passage about the tenants of the haunted house:

"It was the terrible fear that overwhelmed them upon entering a completely empty room, the only one where absolutely nothing happened, that prompted them to move out, not the strange phenomena which they explained with wild imaginationspon."

"You know, people in this goddamn town were used to weird things, but that was too much," the tramp went on.

"The factory owner has been accused of breaking sanitary regulations and would have been put on trial if he hadn't died too, during the inspection of the equipment, when he tried to prove that everything was fine.

He was electrocuted by an unprotected wire. It was about a month ago. From now on, the factory is closed and nobody wants to have anything to do with it.

"Don't you know if there's still something going on there?" Never asked, adding gin to him.

"Sometimes a light comes on there. Alone, I give you my word! And if something more, no one knows, because no locals would come there and the passersby, even when they get there, probably won't leave anymore.

Never narrowed his eyes. He had quite radical ideas about apparitions and ghosts, and did not believe they could cause short circuits in mechanical devices. In his opinion, technology was beyond the reach of supernatural forces and constituted a separate world that could not mix with the supernatural in any way, just like oil with water.

The old drinker chuckled.

"You look like a be on the lookout cat now, boy," he said. Even though he had drunk almost the entire bottle, the effect of the alcohol was unseen on him.

Indian smiled and ordered another one.

"You are angels," the tramp solemnly declared.

Friends left him alone with the gin and left.

"What do you think?" Oggy asked.

"I think we have to check the factory," Never replied. "Best now."

"Why?"

"Not to waste time. After all, we don't want to stay here. Let's find out what's scary there, and when Fronda and Dea return, we will be able to brainstorm."

"If we still have brains," muttered Gerard skeptically.

"Don't be ridiculous, you lived to see today, and you will still do. I don't know what's going on here, but I'm pretty sure no ghosts or ghouls are messing around here. I've not heard of a ghost terrorizing an entire city before."

"Or maybe there are several of them?"

"No. Ghosts, apparitions, they are all single phenomena. Whatever they are, they are not "flocks". Get your things, let's go. Note: we turn off the cells, they are too noisy."

The "things" were cameras and miniature sample containers. Never insisted on taking them wherever he could, then tested them with reagents and wrote down the results in his notebook. What he was doing, no one knew, but no one asked either. It was known that he had his own ideas, his own aspirations, and that had to be respected.

Armed with this simple equipment, they drove to nearby buildings and parked in some relatively safe place. The factory buildings were divided into two sections - in one, as they guessed, production had taken place in the past, and in the other there was a warehouse. Once medicines, or rather parapharmaceuticals, were produced here, now it really looked like the place was completely abandoned. A high barbed wire fence, stretched over a solid, though rusty frame, was closed by a gate with two large padlocks.

"I wonder if the fence is charged with electricity..." Gerard wondered, looking for the warning signs.

"I suggest not to check," Never reached into the glove box under the steering wheel and pulled out a bundle with lockpicks from there.

He knew how to operate them, although he was far from Fronda's craftsmanship, and these padlocks did not look particularly complicated.

The problem turned out to be something else. Nobody opened them for a long time and the hoop sticks and sockets were heavily rusty. Never have to hit each of the padlocks with a large stone to break the layer of rust, and it was only after this operation that he managed to pry the locks open with a pick.

The leaves of the gate, freed from the chains, could hardly be tilted enough to allow them to slip inside. If anyone has been in here since it was closed, it wasn't through this gate anyway.

"Okay, then we're in," for some reason Gerard lowered his voice to a whisper. "What's next?"

Never looked around. There was clearly no one on the property, but the vampire's keen senses gripped something, for lack of a better word, might have been called "sensation of presence." Under its influence, the Companion awoke and extended its phantom tentacles on the back of its host's hand.

"There's something here, isn't there?" Oggy asked, shivering slightly.

"It looks like it," Never agreed. "Laszlo was not exaggerating, and if, than not to much. Cheetah, go to the warehouses and penetrate them. It shouldn't take you long, they are relatively small. Me and Oggy take care of the factory."

The actor nodded without enthusiasm. He didn't feel any mysterious presence, but the whole complex made a depressing impression on him.

Not for the first time, he wondered if it wouldn't be possible to live without terrible places, monstrous creatures, and supernatural phenomena at every turn.

It was what he dreamed about the most - an ordinary, quiet life, work from eight a.m. to four p.m., then returning home, dinner with his family, TV, newspaper...

Unfortunately, he had no chance, and if he tried to live like that, he would be detected and eliminated very quickly. Hunters were still scouring the world for vampires, and you had to be very skillful and clever to hide from their scouts.

The warehouses were still full of boxes of outdated drugs. Nobody picked them up when they were produced, nobody came here to get them, so there were piles of boxes, bottles, blisters with factory names, which meant nothing to Gerard. There was a smell of dust and chemicals everywhere, and there was an unbearable silence. He walked on, shining his flashlight, the light of which picked up piles of boxes from the darkness, he peered into every corner, but there was nothing to be seen.

Only deep in the warehouses did he discover something not entirely normal - an open basement hatch. He hesitated for a moment. He wasn't sure if he should go underground on his own, but then he remembered the mockery of Fronda and Dea, who thought he was almost a loser and half-jokingly called him a coward. True, he was not as "plucky" as they were, but he could not be called a coward! This has to be proved. With this in mind, he started down the narrow stairs to the underground depot.

Seemingly, there was nothing suspicious going on there - just an ordinary cellar, some broken boxes lying around the corners and nothing else.

However, Gerard quickly discovered that it was not just one room, but rather a complex. It seemed strange that it had not been used in some way while the factory was still in operation, and probably not, because the underground rooms looked completely unused. Nothing happened in them either. The flashlight illuminated the same concrete walls, chipped here and there, stained with damp patches, silent and uninteresting.

Convincing that there was nothing to look for in the underground, a bit disappointed, he decided to go back upstairs, but as soon as he turned around, the flashlight fell from his suddenly numb hands.

The path he followed was now blocked by a human skeleton that he knew damned well hadn't been there before. He stood erect, staring directly at Gerard through his empty eye sockets. The bones of the skeleton were not white, rather brownish, rough, covered with dried lumps. The actor was gasping for breath, staring at it with wide eyes, when suddenly the skeleton twitched and started toward him in an unsteady, duck-like gait.

"Stay away from me!" Gerard shouted hysterically.

He backed away, never taking his eyes off the slowly moving skeleton, until he felt the wall behind his back. He felt as if he were going to go mad with terror. Though he had seen a lot and heard a lot more, something was beyond his comprehension. With nowhere to go, he pressed his back to the wall and slumped over it, still screaming. He screamed for as long as he finally got a hoarse voice and fell silent, huddled against the brick wall, terrified to the bone.

The skeleton bent over him. At the bottom of the black eye sockets faint flames flickered like some ghastly pupils with which he seemed to be looking at his victim, or maybe that was just what Gerard thought.

He yelped despairingly as the white bones of his fingers touched his chest. He expected the creature to tear his heart out, like Mictenacutli from a horror movie he had recently read... but nothing bad happened. The skeleton was simply reaching for his notebook. The actor watched with the utmost amazement, still unable to contain his frenzied heartbeat, as his tormentor clumsily grips the pen and writes something on a piece of paper torn from his notebook.

"Don't... hurt... me, you calm..." he deciphered the almost illegible scribbles with difficulty as the skeleton held the paper under his nose. In a sudden flash he realized that without the vocal organs or the lungs, the creature could not speak. Writing, as you can see, was extremely difficult for him, but at least he could do that somehow.

"Who are you?" he asked, still trembling. The terror didn't go away that easily.

The skeleton struggled to run the pen over the paper.

"Rescue," Gerard read after a moment. "I don't understand. Rescue? Whose? For whom?"

The ghastly, bony hand traced the strange words "Bare ghara" and "Mairjaldi se bhigha ma mgati hum". After that, the barely readable "Casa Grande". Finally, the skeleton dropped the pen from his fingers and fell with a crunch of dried bones, suddenly losing all semblance of life and falling apart like a bundle of wood.

It was only after a long moment that Gerard summoned his courage and stood up. He picked up the scattered pages, then, clinging to the wall, hesitantly left the room. Once outside, he dared to take a deeper breath and wipe the sweat from his brow. It didn't do much, because he was sweating in this escape from the walking skeleton, so that his shirt and hair were wet, as if someone had poured a bucket of water over him.

"No, it's beyond my depth," he muttered. "And I thought vampires didn't need to be afraid of anything anymore."

He pulled a cell phone from his pants pocket and pressed a speed dial key.

"Where the hell are you guys?" he asked grimly when Never answered the call. "I almost died here, and you are playing somewhere."

"You almost died? What are you getting into again?" the Indian worried.

"I was checking this warehouse and I came across something amazing... Hurry up, I'll tell you. Didn't you hear my scream?"

"No. It's weird..." Never's voice was genuine surprise. "Is there anyone?"

"Not really, empty. Apparently, they closed this place earlier than they say about it, because for a month you wouldn't get so dusty here."

"Okay, we'll be right there. We also have some news, or rather a handful of observations."

It was a euphemism for what they discovered. Penetrating the factory, Never and Oggy found four dead bodies in different states of decay - all crushed, as if something heavy had rolled over them. However, they did not come across any trace of what could be responsible for this tragedy. There was no sign of a struggle anywhere, as if death had taken these people by surprise.

"It's not that far from the warehouse. Why didn't you hear me?" After meeting the walking skeleton, Gerard did not pay any attention to the revelations about the corpse. He was too much of what he had witnessed.

Never shrugged, and Oggy shook her head helplessly. Her hearing was phenomenal, and so far she couldn't understand why it hadn't alerted her.

"The warehouse is probably soundproofed," she guessed after a while, "I don't know why one in a pharmaceutical factory, but maybe it was just necessary for something."

"I don't even want to know for what," growled Gerard.

"That's not easy, for now we won't find out anything about it," Never looked at the camera he was holding in his hand, "we have some photos. Let's go back to the motel, this needs to be discussed."

These events made the friends return to the motel only in the morning. At the sight of them, Fronda exploded with a stream of resentment and excuses, in which indignation was mixed with enormous relief. Dea listened to him and Never arguing about priorities, responsibility, and freedom of action for a while, then interrupted them with a sharp command to shut their mouths.

"Now, it's better," she said as silence fell. "Now let's compare what we found out."

"I'll never forgive him for leaving the cage open." Fronda growled.

"I said I'm sorry, what else can I do?" Never stood up. "Hit the floor with his forehead or make a sacrifice of barley pies?"

"Silence!" Dea shouted. "What happened, happened, we won't take it back. If you have to argue, do it later. Now talk about what you discovered and we'll tell you what we came up with."

She shaded the windows because the sky was starting to turn gray and the meeting was going to be long.

After two hours of intense conversation, the friends came to the conclusion that despite appearances, the matter is not unequivocally paranormal. Yes, some premises, such as the skeleton that terrified Gerard so much, indicated the influence of psychic forces, but when Fronda and Dea described what had happened to them, Never immediately ruled out the supernatural origin of the strange substance.

"Let's not go crazy," he said firmly. "Ghosts, ghouls, and the like don't eat rats or monkeys. This is absurd."

"So what was that?"

"How do I know? I didn't see it, and you took only few samples."

"We were too busy running away."

"Okay, I'm not making excuses to you. I understand you freaked out because that was your only natural response to such a threat. However, we need to check what it was. It would also be useful to find out what moved that skeleton in the basement. Or rather who."

"Are you sure there is a specific person behind this?" Gerard asked, trembling involuntarily.

He still couldn't think emotionally about what had happened to him.

"Specific and very material," Never assured him. "It was a typical manifestation of psychokinesis. I've seen something like this before... in fact, about 75% of haunted houses aren't haunted at all, only one of the residents has psychokinetic abilities that manifest without him being aware of."

"But nobody lives there!" the actor was close to exploding.

"Doesn't matter. Sometimes such a person is strong enough to animate objects from a distance, a big distance."

"So who are we looking for?" Oggy asked, unknowingly growling.

Never looked at the page on which he summarized the information he had obtained.

"We are looking for a person cut off from the environment, perhaps a deaf-blind person, or perhaps with closure syndrome or severe autism," he said after a moment.

"It's not a baby. It can write and knows the world, but for some reason it has no contact with the environment.

Therefore, cutting off is an acquired matter, not an innate matter. Moreover, it knows Hindi. These words mean "Great house" and "I beg you quickly." This someone needs help."

"And what attacked us?" Fronda was clearly not convinced, although he did not protest.

"It's a different story. Completely different. You see little in the video, but enough to understand it. I have a theory, but I will have to check it. Everyone sleeps for now. If we are to be fully operational, we must be well rested, full and content."

Fronda muttered rebelliously that there was no question of satisfaction in this situation, but obediently went to bed. It was quite impressive as for one night.

Never didn't want to sleep despite his own declarations. He waited until his friends' breath said they were all four asleep, then stood up and quietly set up his chemistry kit. He managed to collect a dozen samples today and decided to check their nature as much as he could. Octavio Di Mauro had provided him in his time with a whole lot of strips soaked in reagents and comparative tables of results. In this way, he could obtain a lot of data allowing to exclude or confirm any suspicions. He dissolved the test sample in distilled water and examined it, writing the readings on a piece of paper, and then compared the read data with the tables.

"What's times that even an honest, ancient vampire cannot do without a scientific background," he would say when asked about the legitimacy of all this work.

Usually, he failed to detect anything that was significantly abnormal, but today was different.

All samples were heavily contaminated regardless of where they were taken.

The pollutants were mainly chemical in nature - reading the substance profile with the help of tables, Never thought that it was mainly benzodiazepine, ephedrine and barbital acid derivatives. Ethanol was also present in a few samples. On the other hand, in the dust, taken from the surface in the old ruin, where Fronda and Dea operated, there was additionally present ammonia and hydrogen sulfide. This not only explained the strange odor, but also supported Never's theory as to the nature of the strange phenomenon.

"It's alive," he muttered thoughtfully. "Whatever it is, it lives and hunts to live."

He watched the infrared film from Dea's camera again. It was not clear, but you could see a moving mass, like a moving sheet, covering everything it reached.

Upon reflection, he separated this matter from what was happening in the factory. A strange creature would have eaten the uninvited guests to the last bite, yet the shattered bodies were intact.

"Yes. These are two, maybe even three different things," he decided finally. From the collected messages emerged a gloomy, slightly surreal image which he did not like very much. Glumly, he folded his miniature laboratory together, cleared the table, and rang a knife at the tin cup.

"What's going on?" Fronda asked, lifting his head from the pillow.

"Are you crazy? Let people sleep," Dea yawned, coming out from behind the screen where she slept with Oggy.

"You've had enough sleep," Never said firmly. "And I found out something we need to discuss. Gerard, am I supposed to honk at you?!"

Theo shook his friend, who sprang to his feet semiconscious and senselessly shielded his head with both hands. Fronda laughed.

"Come on? I had a bad dream," Gerard excused himself as he regained his clarity and realized he was in a safe motel with his friends.

"Sit down both of you," Never ordered. "You girls, too. And listen to me carefully.

The parapharmaceuticals factory we saw has been operating in this area for quite a long time.

Everything indicates that the people managing it acted without any scruples, they simply poured chemical waste into the surrounding swamps, which was much cheaper than the removal and disposal, because only a bribe for employees.

Chemicals seeped through the soil, permeating everything. At some point they caused a mutation in some protozoa, which, under the influence of the mutagen, began to produce a kind of mobile thallus that could disperse in case of danger and hide everywhere. When necessary, individual individuals combine into a movable "thallus" seen by Fronda and Dea, which forages, releasing digestive acids and absorbing dissolved organic components.

"Gosh, nice," Oggy muttered in disgust. "Like a giant starfish... or something like that."

"Yes. Starfish, sea snail, similar foraging. For some reason, this thing is photosensitive and it runs away from the weakest rays, so you know how to protect yourself from it. From secondary premises, it can also be concluded that the creature's foraging territory is limited to Millhaven, as it is as dependent on the chemical mix present in the air and water as the people inhabiting the area.

"Can you beat it somehow?" Fronda asked.

"I don't know, and it's none of our business," Never replied. "We're not here to deal with people's problems."

"Wait a minute. What you said doesn't seem to chase people out of town, it doesn't have a brain," Dea remarked soberly.

"A very fair point." Never nodded his head approvingly. "I didn't understand that either, until I examined the profile of the chemicals in the samples. Those who try to move elsewhere are not killed by any mysterious force, only a severe abstinence syndrome. Without even knowing it, they are constantly under the influence of substances that make them addictive."

"That's creepy."

"Okay, what about this skeleton? In your opinion, I had hallucinations?" Gerard interrupted.

"No, not at all. That's a completely different question, and I shall venture a guess that it is related to the cause that brought us here. As you can see, Mr. Skeleton wrote on a piece of paper "Casa Grande". In Spanish it means residence... Previously, he also used Hindi to mean the same. There is only one in the area, and it belongs to that mysterious millionaire who recently hired Miss Emma. The question is, in what capacity did he hire her. Secretary?"

"No," Oggy shook her head vigorously. "Emma is a nurse."

"So as I thought. The psychokineticist who used the skeleton to convey a message to Gerard lives in this mansion and is sick in a way that cuts him off from the outside world. Emma looks after him as a nurse. We need to get to Hidden Cove and talk to this girl. And leave this terrible place as soon as possible."

"See, even you have had enough," muttered Gerard.

It wasn't just a tease, but rather a statement of fact. Never protested, even his golden gaze said that he was tired of strange phenomena and mysteries that he had to solve together with his friends. Perhaps he was already suffering from the poisoning of the ubiquitous chemicals in this town - vampires were tougher than humans, but not indestructible, and they had to feel the effects of inhaling chemicals in the end. For this reason, it was better to hurry, although in the light of the previous arrangements, the safe removal of Emma Simms may have turned out to be impossible.

"So what are we doing?" Oggy asked softly.

"We wait until dark and then we move," Never answered her. "By the way, are you okay, little one?"

Oggy shook her shaggy hair.

"Not really," she confessed. "My head hurts and I'm so... as if I snapped a glass."

"Exactly. You're already poisoned. We are less susceptible, but the atmosphere here is also not good for us. We need to hurry up. So go to work - shower, shave, get a haircut and whatever else you want. I will settle the bill just in case, so that we do not leave debts behind.

It was Never's rule of thumb. Wherever they were, he paid all the bills, often adding a generous tip (depending on local customs) so that he could be sure they would not leave any undesirable traces. Experience has taught him that hoteliers, eateries, bartenders and rental owners rarely remember customers who paid on time and cleaned up after themselves. And that was the point: not to be remembered.

As dusk had fallen, the friends vacated their rented room and went on their way.

However, before they reached the mansion something unforeseen and trivial at the same time stopped them - they had a flat tire. It was necessary to pull aside and start changing the wheel in conditions when all around the darkness had already thickened into darkness, deadly in this town. Never turned on the headlights and rear lights, and strictly forbidden to move away from the car, unnecessarily, because no one wanted to.

The men went to work briskly, and the girls voluntarily took on the role of sentinels and looked around diligently for any sign of any threat. The place seemed perfect for some kind of ambush - a side, little frequented branch of the road, forests and swamps all around - but nothing happened, everything was silent. There was even no wind. It was only thanks to this eerie, unnatural silence that Oggy caught the slight reverberation of the sliding branches with her ear.

She nudged Dea to the side and pointed slightly in the direction. Someone's eyes flashed there for a split second - you had to have the super-resolution vampire eyesight to see that.

Dea gave a slight whistle. The men abandoned the changing wheel and turned so quickly that they could see a shape slipping silently behind the bushes.

"Fronda, to the left! Dea, watch the car!" Never shouted, throwing himself into the bushes.

Theo, trained in such things as hardly anyone, has come full circle, and Oggy and Gerard have cut off the fugitive's way into the swamp. Together, they finally scared the runaway into the open space, and only then could they see it.

It was young, maybe even very young, and thin and looking a little clumsy because of his disproportionately long limbs.

It had quite dark hair, a narrow face with frightened eyes, and skin so pale it almost glowed in the dark.

Seeing that he was surrounded, he gave up on his escape, threw himself to the ground and clenched his curved fingers in the grass.

"Please do it quickly," he yelled.

"What are we supposed to do?" Gerard was surprised.

"He's thinking that we want to kill him," Never explained brightly. "No, get up, man, we're not Vampire Hunters... rather the opposite. We just want to talk about what's going on here."

The boy looked up and shook his hair off his forehead. He was scared and did not look too scary, though the established facts contradicted this impression.

"Youuu, don't you want to kill me?" he asked, his voice trembling.

"No. If we wanted you would be dead by now. Get up and let's get out of here. This swamp has a depressing effect on me, in fact this grove too."

Never have the rare ability to modulate his voice in such a way that it influenced people in a way that was not compelling, but compelled to listen.

No wonder he was able to calm the slightly scared boy. He got up and followed Never with his head down. Fronda, Gerard, and growling anxiously Oggy walked behind, shining their torches.

"Come on, what's your name and what's up," Never said as they reached the circle of car headlights.

Under the halogen light, you could see the young boy's tousled hair was dark gray, and his eyes were hazel, almost black in that eerily pale face. The poor man looked so miserable that Dea could not help but hardly remark:

"And who did you drag along here? It dies of fear."

"We see, don't we? We're not blind." Theo turned off his flashlight to save battery power and leaned against the hood of the car.

"Talk. Who are you and why did you follow us?" Never asked severely.

"My name is Dean Terence. I didn't follow you, I was just curious what you are doing..." the boy tried to explain himself. He was still shaking so much that his teeth were chattering. In the spotlight, his clothes were stiff with dirt, as was his hair.

"Okay, what are you doing here, all alone, and this... in the dark?" Never continued. "We know the people of Millhaven avoid dark places, and we even know why."

"I know too."

"You know and you're not afraid?"

Dean looked around, his eyes round with something like fear mixed with a feeling of deep shame.

"You don't understand yet?" he whispered. "I'm worse than THAT."

Dea looked at him closely.

"I don't think so," she said dryly. "You are a rather young lame who could use a good bath, a hairdresser and a change of clothes."

The boy gave her a tortured look. He was clearly hesitating between wanting to run away immediately and confessing everything.

His craving for the latter option seemed to prevail. But suddenly he shuddered more violently than before and cried out in pain.

"What's up?" Dea worried.

The young man didn't even hear her. In desperation, he threw himself to the ground, as if he were begging for something.

"Oh no, again..." he wailed loudly, "Leave me alone, leave me... No!"

Dean's clothes began to crack, his skin puffed out strangely as if something was pushing it up from the inside. Suddenly, multiple, thin, bristled legs shot out from both sides of the boy, his face lengthened and flattened, losing human features. Huge jaws grew up on either side of the mouth, eyes turned to the top of the head. There was a nasty insect stench in the air.

An inexpressibly hideous shape that had been Dean a moment ago and now resembled a whitish spider leapt on Never, who was standing closest but as agile as a cat, the Indian managed to dodge. The monster hissed and fled through the trees with a speed that amazed everyone, though you might expect it from a creature with four pairs of legs.

"What was it?" Oggy shook, tucking her head defensively against Fronda's arm. He embraced her instinctively.

"Xenomorph," Never replied calmly. "I never thought I'd see one. They are extremely rare. Almost extinct."

"Yes?! So why this freak is alive at its best?!" Dea attacked him, shaken more than ever. "Instead of enjoying, better say if this thing is also hunting the people of the city!"

"Rather unlikely. I mean, he will definitely eat someone from time to time, but he is not the one who gets those who leave here. He has nothing to do with the mysterious deaths outside the township."

"And where did he come from? fell from the moon or what?"

"More like he came out of the ground. I don't know exactly, but it seems that xenomorphs are formed by combining a normal mammal with some kind of symbiote...

As far as I know, a parasitic organism is not intelligent, it reacts purely instinctively, but for understandable reasons those who chose the human body, not an animal, as their "seat". Once associated with the host, it cannot be removed by the usual methods, it forms a whole with it."

"I see. It's like you and your Companion," Gerard nodded. He seemed to be the least shocked, as if escaping the animate skeleton had exhausted his ability to give in to fear, and even his ability to wonder at anything.

"Gosh," Theo grunted. This was beyond his comprehension.

"Could it have anything to do with our discovery?" asked Dea, whose medical mind was trying to find some explanation for what her eyes could see and her mind could not accept.

"Maybe, of course he can. Xenomorphs have typically been reported near active volcanoes, so their chemical mutation is possible. As parasites, however, they are basically no different from the migrating larvae complex and, it seems to me, you can get rid of them in the same way," Never replied calmly.

"Intravenous pesticides?"

"Of course. Poison the yard dog and then surgically remove it."

"And it is impossible without poisoning? Since there is only one symbiote..."

"No. The symbiote sticks to vital organs, and if it is alive, surgery means death to the host. Dea, Oggy, a combat assignment for you. You will follow Dean and try to convince him to go to therapy. The three of us are going to Hidden Cove as planned, only to finish the wheel change."

"Okay," Dea agreed. "But be warned, if you turn off your cell phones, I'll bite you. Contact should be all the time."

"It will," Never promised her solemnly.

Oggy looked sour but said nothing. She would have preferred to stay with Fronda, but she realized that in this situation such whims would be childish. She was given a serious task and it had to be fulfilled.

The friends of the three completed the wheel change and continued on their way. Soon they also saw their destination - a huge, gloomy house.

Hidden Cove was on the far side of the town - a huge mansion, surrounded by a large piece of neglected land and well fenced off on all sides. Soldered to the gate were several small standard warning signs and one larger that read "Sir Cornelius Higgins, esq." The security guards were nowhere to be seen, but Oggy's keen eyes spotted some of the typical security cameras. Whoever Sir Cornelius was, he surely did not wish for unannounced visits. The great house seemed uninhabited.

There was no light in any of the front windows, and the fenced-in area seemed completely empty.

Only a slight movement of the cameras indicated that the monitoring was working, so probably someone inside was following what was happening outside.

It took a lot of dexterity to get past these cameras, but the three friends were already well trained in such stunts and soon managed not only to get into the area no longer monitored, but into the building itself. It turned out to be surprisingly easy as the door was not locked and gave way as soon as Never pressed the handle.

It was dark inside, though not thick enough for vampire eyes. Thanks to their ability to see in the dark, they did not have to turn on their flashlights to see that they were situated in a hall typical of this type of house - wide, branched into several branches.

You might think that the residence is uninhabited were it not for the faint smell of some dishes and a delicate hint of perfume in the air. Never smelled something more and lifted a finger in warning.

He pointed to one of the corridors. Trying to walk noiselessly, they moved in that direction. The hallway led into a large drawing room, empty, dimly lit, and upholstered in black linen. In the center, on a dais, was an open coffin. They all felt what had alerted Never now - the smell of death. There was a dead man in the coffin. Certainly dead.

They hesitated on the threshold. They hadn't even heard a murmur behind them, only dispersed when the bullet intended for Never whistled in the air. Had it not been for the vigilance of the Companion, it would have smashed his head, but the ghostly symbiote jerked its host violently to the side, causing the bullet to pass right past his left temple. But it whistled so close that his skin stung.

Gerard, who had instinctively jumped closest to the shooter, threw himself to the floor, cutting his legs. Fronda came to his aid. The two of them managed to overwhelm the attacker and tear off his hunting rifle before another person appeared in the mourning lounge, a young woman in whom they had immediately guessed Emma Simms. She turned on the light and, seeing the intruders, was so terrified that she forgot to scream.

"Hola, don't pass out here," Never said, grabbing her arm. "You're not in any danger. We are here on the recommendation of Laszlo Kuna."

"Emma, do you know these people?!" cried the shooter, trying unsuccessfully to free himself from the strong hands of Fronda and Gerard.

"I don't know, Mr. Higgins, but I know who they are talking about," the girl replied. She was still shivering, but she was already starting to calm down.

"Laszlo sent you to get me?" she asked hopefully. "He promised he would."

"About that later," Never turned to Higgins, held on the floor. "Forgive us for so unceremoniously burst into your house. We have no bad intentions. We are neither robbers nor murderers. We are conducting an informal investigation into strange phenomena happening in this city. Let him go, boys."

"He was shooting at us!" Gerard protested.

"What you think? Three bulls would climb into his hut without asking, what was he supposed to do? But now we will talk as rational people."

Sir Cornelius Higgins rose and tugged his rumpled clothes.

"What do you want?" he asked aggressively.

"As I mentioned, we are investigating and one of the leads led us to this house."

"What's the investigation?"

"Forgive me, but we are the ones asking the questions," Fronda interrupted, catching Never's menacing gaze and justifying excusingly. "Come on? I've always wanted to say this."

"Don't be a fool! This is a serious matter. Well," here Never turned to Sir Higgins again. "First of all, who is this man in the catafalque?"

He walked over to the coffin and looked at the dead man. He could have been no more than twenty years old and looked wasted by some serious illness.

"He's my son," replied the host gloomily, and turned his back to the intruders. It was obvious that he wasn't going to say anything more.

Emma turned out to be more open.

"He died last night," she said. "The professor tried to find a cure for his ailments, but failed."

"If only I had been bolder..." Higgins blurted out. He fell silent as he realized that he had said more than he wanted.

"You have my deepest sympathies," said Gerard. "What was wrong with him?"

"Cystic fibrosis."

"Well, I don't understand why you feel guilty," Never said to Sir Higgins. "There is no cure for this disease."

The professor shrugged his thin shoulders angrily. Now that everyone had cooled down a bit, they could see clearly that this was a man who had undoubtedly been through a lot. He was slightly stooped, bony, chalky pale, with an ascetic face and tight lips. His clothes, while undoubtedly of good quality and brand, looked as if he did not care for them at all. The whole house made a similar impression.

"Does man they say own half of Millhaven have no cash to hire some servants?" Never muttered, looking at the dusty, cobwebbed walls.

"Who's coming here? There is no such stupid one. Nobody from the town will want to serve me, and the newcomers quickly learn that it is better to run from here," growled Sir Higgins. "Emma is an exception. She looked after my boy like a natural sister and practically did not leave the residence, although sometimes... it is strange here."

131

Never looked at him with cold sympathy.

"It's weird everywhere here," he said.

Emma shook her head.

"You don't know what's going on here," she whispered. "I saw something monstrous myself. It cannot even be described."

"Some kind of monster, miss? Or maybe a ghost?"

"Don't be kidding," growled Sir Higgins angrily. "Emma really deserves a lot of respect for persevering here, because it scared all the servants out of here. Only the caretaker remains, who is so old that he is blind, hard of hearing and doesn't care... I suspect that the monster is responsible for my nephew's disappearance. It probably devoured him."

The friends exchanged knowing looks. They all thought the same thing and asked almost simultaneously:

"What was your nephew's name?"

"Dean Terence, what's the matter with you?"

"Of course," Theo muttered.

"That explains why he sticks to this area," added Gerard.

"What?"

Never took the professor's arm and explained as carefully as possible what had happened to his nephew. Sir Higgins could not believe what he was hearing at first, but since the Indian had an exceptional gift of persuasion, the host soon stopped doubting his words and began to inquire frantically about the prospects of healing the boy.

"First, let's see if the girls found him," Never answered him, and turned on his cell phone.

At his signal Dea pick up.

"Do you have him?"

"We got lost him somewhere in those bloody smelly swamps. What do you actually want? He knows them like his own pocket and we are here for the first time!"

There was a clear bit of bitterness in the girl's voice, mixed with resentment. How did this puppy dare to escape just like that? After all, she wanted to help him! What an ungrateful... Dea hated when someone rejected her help or any other manifestation of "kindness of heart."

"Oh, come on," Never said. "Look, girls: we're in Hidden Cove. We'll get a little bit more here, so why not join us? Do you have enough battery in your flashlights?"

"Yeah, don't worry about that. They shine like halogen lights, nothing will come close to us. We are going to you."

Never turned off his cell phone and looked at Sir Higgins. It is unbelievable how a ray of hope can illuminate a person from within - the old professor was ten years younger and his eyes brightened like lanterns when he heard about the possibility of healing his nephew.

"Professor," the Indian began. "You must know something. Whatever you want to do, you must do it here, because leaving the city, so far, means death for the inhabitants of this area. Of course, the cause is not any curse..."

"I know. Rather, the cause is direct action."

"Why direct?" Theo looked at the professor in amazement. "Are you saying that somebody is murdering these people?"

"There are those who must murder in order to live."

"You mean serial killers? Do you have any here?"

"You could say that."

Never slightly drew his silky eyebrows. Something about the professor's words and tone disturbed him, but he couldn't somehow pinpoint what exactly. After a moment's thought, he put that anxiety down to his strained nerves and began explaining how to help Dean.

"And he will survive?" asked Sir Higgins doubtfully after the Indian had finished.

"It's, as I said, possible. It's enough to poison the symbiote and then surgically remove it. Please don't be afraid of decisive action, xenomorphs have nothing supernatural about them."

He wanted to say something else, but stopped as his eyes fell on Gerard. The former fan of French cinema looked as if he had just seen something inexpressibly terrifying, something beyond comprehension. His skin was pale and gray, his green eyes turned the color of jade, his cheekbones and jawbones were more pronounced, like on a skull. He staggered on his feet and would have fallen if Fronda not caught him by the arms. "What's wrong, Cheetah?" he exclaimed.

"Someone's here," whispered Gerard. "I have already felt this presence... It's very strong, stronger than anything in our blood that we have dealt with so far."

"Who's stronger?" Never asked.

The actor turned his burning gaze to him with his suddenly pale eyes.

"I can smell our blood," he gasped with difficulty. "He is here..."

His words went off and the bullet whistled right next to Never's ear, making him hurt. Sir Higgins, about whom all three had forgotten for a moment, gripped his rifle again.

"You tricked me! You are vampires!" the professor shouted, drawing himself up for the next shot.

A deathly pale Emma squeezed into a corner, covering her head with her arms crossed. It seems she understand nothing, but explaining it to her was better off until later.

Friends scattered, hiding behind what who could. Even their very resistant bodies could be permanently damaged if the bullet hit the heart, spine or head, and the professor's rifle was for a special type of cartridge. Never did not immediately recognize them by the sound of the shot - they were bullets, the cover of which, after hitting the target, split into several sharp claws. If it hit the heart, it literally ripped it to shreds like paper.

Sir Higgins seemed not only familiar with this weapon, but also proficient in the technique of fighting against several opponents. Despite all their efforts, they could not get him from behind, and all three finally felt like cats intimidated by a mouse: one elderly gentleman kept them in check, and they only managed to avoid direct hits. The absurdity of this situation did not diminish the horror of their situation, especially as they left their guns in the car out of distraction. Finally, the situation was saved by Fronda, who managed to crouch behind a small bookcase.

Safe behind this concealment, he unfolded his inseparable slingshot and, instead of a pebble, he inserted a small glass button to the paper. He had barely dealt with it when Dea appeared in the corridor, followed by Oggy, who at the sound of the shots immediately took the form of a dog.

"Girls, get down!" Theo shouted.

He jumped into the center of the lounge and spun the slingshot in a flash. The glass bullet stunned the professor just as he was already taking his bow tie thrower.

"Have you lost the reason?" Never said angrily, getting up from behind the catafalque. "You've completely exposed yourself. He could have killed you."

"I had to. Otherwise, I would probably miss it, but he could hurt our girls." Theo looked at Emma huddling in the corner. "Miss, please do not be so afraid, we will do nothing to you, my word of honor."

"Whay the hell are you so sweet to her?" Dea huffed furiously. "Get up, stupid! And you guys, what kind of shooting was that? You can't be left alone for a while, only problems with these guys..."

She went to the catafalque.

"And the corpse, as I can see, you have already passed..."

"No foolishness, this is not our job," Never began, and broke off, looking at Gerard. "And why are you so pale again? What do you feel?"

"On the ground!" the actor shouted.

They all dropped to the floor instinctively, thanks to which the blade, whirling at a height of about a meter, only cut through the air and stuck, vibrating, in the wall. A figure flashed in the corridor. Gerard jumped up from the floor, jumped, and grabbed her just as she bounced her feet off the wall, doing a somersault and landed on the floor beside the unconscious professor. Fronda whistled in admiration, even Never looked surprised. Their young friend had never shown such advanced skills before.

However, congratulations had to wait, for the time being they both rushed to his aid, as the captured attacker struggled furiously and the actor would not have kept her alone for more than a few seconds.

"Who is this?" Dea asked, watching the scuffle with interest. "It looks like our Gepcio knew who to take in the jasyr. Not bad."

The mysterious aggressor turned out to be a young, slim girl, dressed in black pants and a black tunic blouse, about 16-17 years old.

Checked in by three men, she was huddled on the floor, her head bowed, veiled with long, fair hair."

"Relax, you'll be fine," Never said, picking up the peculiar device she dropped off on the floor. "Is that the thrower of those spinning discs? Interesting construction."

"Who are you?" Theo asked gently as he crouched down next to the girl.

She looked up and pushed her hair out of her face. She had large, slightly slanted eyes, almost as green as Gerard's, and her soulful face was reminiscent of the Madonnas of Raphael. She was indeed pretty.

"They gave me Loretta when I was baptized, but I prefer the name Lottie," she said softly.

Pressed into the corner, Emma Simms gave a shrill scream and once again covered her head with a defensive gesture.

Lottie smiled gently at the sight of her horror.

"I don't understand." Dea, intrigued, trailed her eyes from one to the other.

"She's... she's a murderer! Twenty years ago she was locked up in a psychiatric ward for three murders that were discovered, though it is not known how many really were... It's Loretta White!"

Never made a disdainful face. He didn't seem to be somehow moved by what he heard, probably because he had known more than one serial killer in his long life. However, Lottie's case seemed different. Looking into her eyes, he felt fascination and fear, which did not happen to him every day.

"What are you doing here, child?" he asked gently. "Why did you break in here with such an exotic weapon?"

"You really don't know?" The girl raised her eyebrows slightly. "Then what are you here for?"

She closed her eyelids and lightly touched the tips of her fingers to her temples. Gerard screamed weakly and clutched his head. He gasped for a moment with his half-open mouth, then croaked in a hoarse voice quite unlike his usual gentle tenor:

"In the basement... In the basement..."

Lottie opened her eyes and looked at him, really surprised this time.

"You have such a strong medium and you don't know anything?"

"What's in the basement?!" Dea shouted angrily. She didn't feel like solving rebuses, and she didn't understand anything about the scene.

"Well, we don't know," Never explained. "Hey Emma, is there a way down to some dungeons?"

"What do you expect to find there, you crazy Indian idol?"

"I don't know. I guess that's the answer. So where is this descent?"

Emma was too scared to be able to respond efficiently. She just groaned and pressed herself into the corner, as if she wanted to merge with the wall and thus disappear from the eyes of the intruders who were terrifying her. Never professionally bound the still unconscious Higgins and ordered Oggy to watch over both of them. Oggy barked in agreement and sat up, her silky ears upright. It was evident that she did not intend to return to human form for the time being.

Loretta White seems to have gained confidence in her new acquaintances, as she secured and hid her thrower in a small haversack, slung over her shoulder, and followed them in search of the cellar mentioned by the actor.

Soon they found a descent, but to use it, they had to force through three pairs of solid doors, equipped with complicated locks, which even Fronda had big problems with. After opening the last ones, they saw a real surprise.

Lab. Computers. State-of-the-art equipment for millions of dollars. In the center - something like a laboratory table, and a young, naked man tied to it. An emaciated body, marked with traces of either medical procedures or torture. Stitched eyelids. A leather band around the mouth, fixed so that he cannot take it off.

Lottie rushed to him immediately. Her nimble fingers quickly found the clasp of the leather gag, while Fronda and Never unfastened their fastening straps.

The prisoner's mouth was also sewn shut, the headband was only meant to be an additional security measure. Dea leaned over the table with the look of a professional.

"They're just stitches," she said. "Just cut it. Boys, it's Segovia!"

"No kidding," Never straightened abruptly.

Now he too recognized Neville, his cursed, half-demented father, and felt a shiver of terror. How did it happen that Segovia ended up here, how is it possible that he would not be able to defend himself against a single, well-aged scientist who had imprisoned him in such terrible conditions?

Dea looked around the lab and found the entire medical kit to her satisfaction. With a tiny ophthalmic lancet, she slit open the sutures and removed them with tweezers.

Segovia was unresponsive to her treatments, he was unconscious, or rather in some kind of catalepsy.

Dea and Never studied him intently, Theo got to one of the computers and downloaded files to a flash drive, and Gerard slowly backed out of the door so as not to alarm anyone.

Once inside the door, he sped up and almost ran upstairs, into the living room, where Oggy was still keeping an eye on Emma and the now conscious professor. He knelt down and cut his bonds.

"Get out of here both of you," he ordered. "Hide with an acquaintance or friend. Quick. They're busy getting Segovia up for now, but then they'll remember you and your wretched fate. They will never forgive you for what you did to this guy."

"I tried to isolate the healing factor. I did it for my son," growled Sir Higgins, rubbing his numb wrists. "I had pity on such a monster...?"

"I'm not asking for explanations," the actor interrupted sharply. "Take the girl and disappear as soon as I change my mind. I'm not joking. You can't protect yourself from angry vampires, and I warn you that half of them are immune to sunlight and the day won't save you. They won't leave a single drop of blood in your veins."

The professor nodded after a moment and started, dragging Emma with him. It looked like he would be reasonable. Gerard hoped so. He watched the people away, and was relieved when the knock of the door told him they had left the residence.

Oggy barked in surprise. He looked at her and smiled slightly.

"It's the right thing to do," he said. "They would tear those two, and Lottie would certainly do.

I didn't want to have them on my conscience. Never probably won't want to strangle me for such willfulness, but I can deal with him."

Suddenly he felt how tired he was. He sat down against the wall with his back against it. He stroked the wolf's neck and kissed the silky head between the triangular ears.

"You're lovely, you know?"

Oggy whimpered and licked his face to show that she understood and approved of his actions. Gerard embraced her, and he himself did not know when he had suddenly fallen into a restless nap.

A sharp tug on his arm woke him. The furious Never stood over him, and the evil flashes in his golden eyes did not mean any good.

"What have you done, you idiot?" he hissed.

Oggy snarled, baring her fangs, but the Indian paid no attention to her.

"Leave it," Theo interrupted unexpectedly.

He was standing behind Never, holding a semiconscious Segovia in his arms, and didn't seem to be at all surprised by what had happened.

"Leave it," he repeated. "He did very well. Revenge wouldn't fix anything, but rather it could hurt. Your father and Lottie have to leave as soon as possible anyway, and Emma, as we agreed, couldn't be taken away. We better get out of here."

Never wrestled with himself for a moment, then turned on his heel. He led the way, followed by Fronda, followed by Dea and Loretta. Gerard got up and joined his friends with Oggy.

It was dawn, it was necessary to find shelter quickly, because they did not want to return to the motel. It wouldn't be safe. Fortunately, even though they had two people more, they somehow got into the car.

"Where to now?" Gerard asked as he took the wheel on Never's brief order.

"At the second fork to the right," Loretta said. "And straight. I'll tell you when it is time to stop."

She helped Fronda arrange Segovia so that his head rested on her knees. Neville allowed his body to be manipulated with the passivity of the doll. It looked like drug addiction or poisoning with ubiquitous chemical fumes, but Never said it was more of a trance.

Gerard obeyed the instruction without a word. Glancing every now and then in the rearview mirror, he wondered in passing how Segovia could get along with this girl. Vampires usually shunned this type of person. Mental illnesses aroused a superstitious fear in them, especially that in the event of attacking someone who was ill, they could temporarily affect them. Segovia, on the other hand, was considered insane himself, and long ago. All vampires avoided and got out of his way, for he hated the company of beings of his kind, even those he (occasionally) made himself.

He made an exception so far only for Dea, who lived with him some time after recording in his headquarters at that time. So why the acquaintance with this juvenile serial killer? And why did he record her, since, first, she was not fully mature, and, second, her past completely discredited her? After all, certain rules were followed even by those like him, and this one was adamant and exceptions were not tolerated.

Fronda must have been thinking the same thing, as he suddenly asked:

"Lottie, did you really commit all the crimes for which you were convicted?"

"Theo..." Never growled warningly.

Loretta brushed her hair back from her face and replied calmly:

"Majority. But if you want to plead guilty better in bulk, right?"

"What actually pushed you to such atrocities? You were barely a child then."

"I'm not the only one who got crazy in this town. After all, the other murders also had their perpetrators. This place was cursed by God before I was born."

"Nonsense," Never said firmly. "You were poisoned by chemical waste from the factory. I bet they were sneaked into that little river of yours without being cleaned. Because they poured hectoliters of filth in the swamps, we know from rumors. Cheetah, take a turn."

"Why are you snooping around here?" Loretta asked after a moment. "Were you looking for him?"

"No. And you? You did a poor job, my lady, Segovia has been in captivity for a long time, and you just today went to free him?"

"I couldn't find him. Only you guided me to the trail. If I had known what was going on, the professor would be dead today."

No one had any doubts about one thing. There was something about this slender girl that was truly scary.

On the sidelines, small, low buildings appeared - a gas station, looking like a miniature museum.

The fuel dispensers had been polished to a shine and probably were even functional, even though no one had worked there for a long time.

They couldn't sense human presence, there were no pets or used disposable cups anywhere. No sound disturbed the silence.

"It's here," said Loretta.

The place seemed unusual for a vampire's hideout, but, as they soon found out, it provided ample protection from the sun.

Fronda carried Segovia to the corrugated pavilion and placed him on the bed indicated by the girl.

"He needs gallons of blood," he said with concern. "Nev, do we have anything more?"

Never returned to the car and after a while he brought two half-liter containers.

"That's all left. It will have to be enough for him. We don't even have more to ourselves for now. I think we'll have to rob the local hospital."

"Not good," Dea sighed.

She was already very hungry, and she could feel that the others too. This is a dangerous condition for a vampire. The essentially natural feeling was somewhat suspicious now, it had come too early. After all, they all ate not so long ago, they used up all their supplies, only those two pints were left.

"It would be worth the hunt," Fronda said quite openly, while Never carefully poured the life-giving liquid into Segovia's mouth.

Neville swallowed with obvious difficulty without opening his eyes, his gaunt, scarred body trembling. Despite the apparent focus only on what he was doing, the Indian heard very well what was going on around him.

"Don't you dare!" he growled sharply. "Categorical hunting ban in this area, understood? Whoever tries will deal with me."

"Have pity, we're all starving," groaned Gerard. "What about Oggy? She needs meat!"

"There are dog biscuits in the trunk, she must have enough. And you guys get a grip. One would think that you have not seen a good fasting on your eyes. You will endure."

"But why starve?" Loretta asked matter-of-factly. "It's a inhabited neighborhood."

"I know. But the people here are too contaminated to take any chances. Better not to touch their blood. I don't want to scare you, baby, but if you hunt the people of Millhaven, by drinking their blood you absorb what poisons them."

The girl did not seem to be concerned about it. Now that they could get a better look at her, everyone saw more and more clearly in her eyes, features and movements, what could best be described with the words "out of this world."

146

"Do as you like," she said. "I go hunting as soon as it gets dark. I've been living like this for twenty years, I can do a little more."

"I'm not keeping you. Life is what you make it, do what you want. We must rest, otherwise we will fall."

*****

Friends slept most of the day. When they woke up, Loretta was no longer with them, probably as she had promised she had gone hunting in town, while outside, two huge Latinos were messing with the fuel pumps. There was a huge truck with Mexican numbers beside it. Only now did it become clear why the girl and her master kept them in such good condition - it was an excellent trap for passersby.

Silently as shadows, the friends circled the drivers and attacked at the sign Never had given. It was a long time since they felt such relief when the life-giving fluid filled their mouths. The leader did not allow his friends to relish the blood of young men for too long, healthy, hot, with a taste of nicotine and alcohol.

"Now put them in the cab," the leader finally commanded. "Fronda, pour some fuel into the tank, let it be full funnel anyway, they deserve something. Cheetah, you'll drive them a few miles, then park them off the highway, and come back."

"Sure," the actor muttered eagerly, wiping his mouth on his sleeve. "It will be done."

Theo and Never helped him shove the two huge bodies into the cab of the truck, and the slim Gerard somehow managed to squeeze into the third there. He carefully started the motor and started down the side road to the highway. He did not know the area, but his sharpened hearing with time easily caught the characteristic noise of many cars, which unfailingly heralded the way of express traffic. There are many legends about the sensitive senses of vampires, and not all of them are true, and the fact is that their eyesight and hearing are slowly sharpening in them. This can be very helpful, but it also keeps very old vampires away from cities and avoiding not only the sun but any brighter light.

He parked the truck on the side of the road, checked that both drivers were breathing, and jumped out of the cab. Holding the shadows, he returned to the path and walked quietly, hardly hiding anymore, back to the station. It didn't take him as long as he thought it would fade away. Without realizing it himself, he acquired a certain condition and strength greater than he had as a human being. Now that he was additionally charged with fresh blood, his legs carried him swiftly and firmly, as if he were flying over the ground.

He quickly reached the gas station and, entering the warehouse, saw that Segovia was no longer lying, and was sitting on the bed, propped up against rolled blankets. He still looked like a ghost, but he was already awake. Never had managed to find his spare clothes, and now that his bony body was not visible, he did not make such a pathetic impression as before. The marks of stitches brutally placed on his lips and eyelids were already fading into narrow scars. In two or three days there will be no trace of them.

"Hello, amant," he greeted. "I was just asking where they left you."

His voice was barely audible, raspy and choppy.

"They didn't. How are you?"

"Say "like a zombie" and you'll be close. This time, I seriously thought it was over. What about that hell professor, you got him and his doll?"

"No. We are not judges, let alone executioners," Never said flatly seeing that Gerard did not know what to answer. "As far as I am concerned, I even thought that you should be left in their hands, for you would be useful as a test animal at least once in your life. But the others disagreed."

Hearing this ingenious lie, Theo could barely suppress a laugh and even Gerard smiled. He would never admit that he cared about his father's fate, although this father never cared about him and was an extremely unpleasant guy.

"You can think what you want," Segovia said calmly. "But be careful: Lottie will finish them off first, and then you, since you spared their lives."

"And you?" Theo raised his eyebrows slightly.

"She considers me her property. Why was she trying to free me?"

"I don't know?! Perhaps in gratitude," Dea suggested dryly.

"What are you talking about...? I can see you don't even have a clue who you're dealing with."

"We hear she's some juvenile murderer from a lunatic asylum," Fronda said, stroking Oggy who was holding her head under his arm. "You had to take her..."

Segovia shook his head.

"You don't understand. Lottie is a real monster. She had never drank tinned blood in her life. She hunts because she likes it, not that she has to. She drinks not only blood, but also spinal cerebral fluid. I know what you're gonna say, I should kill her, but I can't. She is, in a way, my daughter."

"Did you go crazy to record a seventeen-year-old? Do you know how you risked?" Never asked. "You both should be dead, as a matter of fact. Plus, you probably knew she was a psychopath. How could you be so stupid, you, my so-called father?"

Segovia licked his dry lips.

"You don't understand. It was not my initiative," he explained. "When I found myself in a psychiatrist for extremely dangerous criminals, at first I did not pay attention to her at all..."

"What were you doing there?" Dea interrupted him, frowning.

"I was playing journalist. I printed under a pseudonym... never mind. The head doctor introduced me to some patients, including Lottie, whom he was especially proud of. He claimed that he had healed her already and therefore allowed us to talk relatively freely. I don't know how she figured out who I was, but she showed no sign of herself. She is very clever."

"We noticed. What happened next?"

"The next night, when I went out hunting, I was stunned by a blow to the head and woke up in an underground bunker. Lottie murdered a nurse, a doctor and two watchmen, escaped the hospital and, one could say, took me prisoner. Professionally. I was nailed to the ground with long stakes so that I could only dream of freeing myself."

"Ouch. It must have hurt," muttered Gerard sympathetically.

"Just so you know. Lottie came by every night, sat down and looked at me. She said nothing, listened to my insults and pleas with equal indifference, until I was seriously afraid of her.

I don't know where and how she spent her days, but as for me, she had her own plan and carried it out consistently. She waited until I began to cry out of hunger and beg for blood. Then she gave me hers.

Do you have any idea how I drank? Then she suddenly stuck a medical scalpel into my artery and took what she wanted herself without asking me for my opinion."

Theo opened his mouth.

"Wow. I have never heard of an event like this."

"I was scared to death, especially when she started to change. She didn't go through the lethargy phase and... it was a macabre sight."

"I definitely believe you," Never muttered.

"Why so macabre?" Gerard asked, looking at him questioningly.

"Because the lethargy phase is necessary," he explained to him, "whoever does not go through it behaves like a madman and also undergoes uncontrolled, often nasty physical transformations. It doesn't take long, the changes are going backwards, but at first the sight is indeed ghastly. Go on, Segovia."

"I was almost mad, pinned to the ground and defenseless. She set me free later, when she was gaining strength and I felt completely weak for a change. She brought victims for me until I healed my body. I tried to escape her twice, but each time she found me, marking the way with dead bodies, and brought me back. She can exert psychological pressure so strong that I can't resist her."

Never narrowed his eyes with indescribable pity.

"What do you say, Dea?" he asked the doctor

"It looks like the Stockholm Syndrome to me," the girl replied indifferently. "Although, I think that at his age he should know how to deal with such a brat... What are we doing?"

"First of all, we need to find the professor and Emma. And we have to do this before Lottie finds them. Then we'll see. Father, how did Professor Higgins get you?"

"Oh, I don't know that," Segovia spoke with increasing difficulty. "It seems to me that it was a coincidence, but I will not bet on it. I have a memory gap. I also don't know how long he abused me in this lab. I lost track of time."

Dea nodded her chin slightly.

"You used the skeleton to scare Gerard?"

Not scare. It was the last thing I thought about at the time. For lack of any other possibilities, I searched the area mentally. Suddenly I found your friend.

I used my telekinetic capabilities because it was my only chance. I wanted to let Lottie know, not him, but... I don't think she has a psycho-localization sense and doesn't pick up telepaths. She needs to see someone to be able to act on them. This is her weakness, unfortunately too small to be used against her.

It made sense, and even Never have to agree to it.

"Nobody is perfect. But why the skeleton? Why was he writing? Why did you use Hindi?"

"A skeleton, because I had to direct something, and only he was fit for it. He had to write because getting articulated sound when something didn't have a larynx is impossible, so how was he supposed to get the message across?

And Hindi... you know, I was too tormented and at the moment my languages were mixed up. I have spent a lot of time in India, Hindi is like my second native..."

"You could have died from this. Like from what Loretta did to you."

Segovia looked at him glumly.

"Don't kill her," he asked softly. "She's so young..."

"She's deadly. Now I understand what did not suit me. Sure, she's the one who murders some people who want to move out of here. For revenge, for fun, because who knows why? I was convinced that the cause of their deaths was abstinence syndrome, but it only kills some. The weaker ones. It only makes others so that they cannot defend themselves."

Segovia denied vehemently

"Most of them fall prey to the xenomorph. He is hiding in the local swamps. Even we don't get in his way."

Never smiled with contemptuous superiority.

"Don't talk. Xenomorph doesn't need much. He could kill one, two, and the rest? Sweet Lotka just likes to kill, she loves her life as a nocturnal predator. She moves so fast that it is hard to see. And she drinks all the fluids out of the body until it disintegrates. Does that tell you something?"

"What are you talking about?" Gerard asked.

Never even didn't look at him.

"She's not an ordinary vampire, she's a Tengu!"

Segovia turned his head as if he couldn't bear his son's burning gaze.

"Suppose, but what do you care? You don't live here, and she won't leave these swamps."

"What is tengu?" the actor screamed, who didn't understand again.

"Tengu is a Japanese term," Fronda explained to him. "They are so rare, even greater than xenomorphs, and we have no idea what causes someone to become one.

The PAS factor is definitely not at stake. Tengu have a number of skills that make them excellent predators. If Loretta is one of them, we are no match for her."

Never snorted angrily.

"Cheetah and Oggy stay to watch this idiot," he ordered. "He's not allowed to get out of here, okay? You have my permission to shoot both his knees if necessary."

"O... OK..." Gerard muttered.

He felt faint at the thought of doing something similar, but he didn't protest.

It was better to keep an eye on Segovia than to participate in a hunt for a fair-haired sylph, more murderous than any vampire he knew. He also knew that the boss wanted to take him with him. His skills, far beyond mere psycholocation, would be very useful in finding Loretta, but no one doubted that this time the job would be too hard for him to handle.

Leaving the back room, Never stopped at the station's office. He took the knife out of the case attached to his left calf and, maneuvering with a well-sharpened blade, cut his long hair as short as possible.

Fronda and Dea exchanged glances. The Indian rarely cut his hair, because it had a will of its own - it grew back with indecent speed, and when it was short, it could not be modeled into any particular hairstyle. They only arranged the way they wanted them to, and you had the ghostly impression that they were "alive". How he treated them now could only mean one thing: he was preparing for a truly difficult journey.

"You think it's gonna be very nasty?" Theo asked, trying to sound sloppy and casually checking to see if he had all his combat gadgets with him.

"You can bet on that your's medallion."

"It's a gorget."

"Doesn't matter. We're dealing with a case not as rare as it seems. You know, it's convenient for us to pose as innocent victims... but the truth is, the Hunters call us mankind's misfortune for a reason. People like Loretta White come across every now and then..."

He went out to the car and opened the little hatch under the steering wheel. From there he pulled out a flat metal box that looked like a large cigarette case.

"I was hoping I would never have to use it," he muttered, twirling them between his fingers.

"What's that?"

"Death, knight. The only absolutely sure way to get a vampire, other than to be dismembered and burned, which we may not have time to do."

He opened the box. Narrow compartments held one next to the other thin syringes with insulin needles. The contents of the syringes sparkled with all the colors of the rainbow, like a stain of gasoline on water.

"And precisely?" Dea asked, looking over Never's shoulder.

"I have no idea. Production secret. All I know is that it contains silver nitrite, among other things. It works fast and ruthlessly. Get in, it's a waste of time. By the time we get there, it will be completely dark."

Never traveled the road to the town so quickly that he would have been stopped by any, even the most liberal police. Along the way, he tried to catch Loretta's thoughts with his own psycholocation sense, but it was in vain.

Also Theo couldn't somehow accomplish this play. Dea didn't even try. As she explained, she prefers not to connect with such a mind in any way, because she cares too much about her own mind. It was not the first time that it was noticeable that the doctor acts in a very pragmatic manner and never takes risks without a real need.

Driving into town, Never slowed down and tried to search for Emma Simms' thoughts. It was not without some difficulty that he recalled the pattern of this girl's aura.

He had contact with her for a short time, but managed to consolidate the most important psycholocation aspects. He was sure that she was still in the professor's company, and it was him that a vampire obsessed with revenge would seek. She treated Segovia as her property, who knows, maybe she was really emotionally involved with him? Because they were lovers, there was no doubt. What a couple...

A fresh structural trace ran irregularly here and there, which indicated a chase, but eventually it became clear that it led to a small biology museum on the other side of town. Never hit the gas again, hoping that Segovia hadn't misled him and that Lottie did not really know how to use psycholocation. Because if she can... oh, it could be completely bad.

"Get out and silence," he ordered, stopping the cart. "The professor and Emma are on the premises of this facility. I don't know if Loretta is there, but rather we have to reckon with it."

The security guard's booth was open and empty. Behind her, they discovered the bodies of the two guards, in a dark corner, slowly growing in phosphorescent mold. The seats occupied shrank and collapsed while the rest looked normal. The disfigured bodies lay in embryonic positions, their faces still visible, only empty. Of course, that didn't mean they didn't know what had killed them. After death, the muscles lose their tension and all descriptions such as "The insane terror was still visible on the face of the deceased" should be put into fairy tales. Examination of the cadavers might explain, but they did not dare to touch them to see how they died.

They moved deeper into the buildings, following the ever clearer trail that the three of them could already sense: the scent of fear and blood hung in the air, and straining their ears, they could hear not too far, muffled sobs.

Never's companion showed sudden concern, suddenly appearing in the form of a thick shadow that wrapped around his host like a hooded cloak. He very rarely did it before the action, usually manifested his presence only seconds before the deadly event, only in crisis situations he appeared earlier, as now. Dea and Fronda exchanged knowing looks. Keeping the mysterious symbiote told them clearly that the journey would be difficult.

Professor Higgins and Emma were hiding in a small store next to the Natural History Room. They were both battered and terrified that when they saw their three friends, their first instinct was to run blindly. Their friends caught up with them in the Hall of Great Discoveries.

"Relax, we're here to help!" Never cried, grabbing the girl by the half and at the same time cutting the professor's legs. "Do not try to run away, because we will lose, we only have a chance together."

"She's here somewhere! How do we know if she sent you? She is the same as you!" Emma screamed hysterically.

It was evident that she was in a state of shock and that nothing would reach her now. Sir Higgins looked more alert, but his eyes shone with unparalleled terror, and his hands, stained with reagents, trembled like a malaria attack.

"She's here somewhere," he said. "She found us easily. We ran all over town, knocked on so many doors, and nobody wanted to hide us."

"Long live small towns," muttered Fronda sarcastically.

"What is there to be surprised, everyone is afraid," Never rebuked him with a sharp look and shook Emma. "Take it easy, both of you. We're taking you out of here. They can handle the withdrawal syndrome in any hospital, as long as we get there."

Before he could say the last word, there was a sweet girlish laugh in the room, and a velocity-blurry shape flashed past the Indian. Emma screamed, and, breaking free from his hands, ran forward, knocking over furniture and display cases.

"Dea, follow her! Fronda, help me!" Never shouted. He held one of the syringes in his clenched hand and looked around carefully, ready to jump.

"Be careful, she's damn fast. I've never seen anything like it in my life," Theo warned.

He, too, tensed all his muscles and attention to catch the girl who was moving with absurd speed, but he knew it might not be enough. He felt one of the pills sewn into the cuff of his shirt and, putting it in his mouth, chewed on the plastic lining. The burning liquid was absorbed almost immediately, sharpening his senses to the limit.

Fronda spat out the casing, took a deep breath, and looked around. The effect of the chemical concentrate, which was an invention of Gusto Vanderbelt, perfected by Octavia di Mauro, allowed him to predict where his opponent would be, literally a second before that. If it were not so poisonous, it could be used more often, but even taking a single dose was a huge risk.

"Left!" he shouted, throwing himself in the spotted direction.

Lottie slipped out of his hands literally in the last fraction of a second, and only thanks to the action of the preparation he managed to avoid stabbing a knife in the neck.

"Attention, Nev!" he screamed out loud, knowing that he wouldn't have time to cut the girl's way.

Sir Higgins stumbled back to the wall, by chance rather than reflexes, to avoid death rushing at him.

The attacker immediately changed the direction of the attack. Never twisted in place and slammed the back of his hand with the face gliding at him at a rapid pace.

Sharp teeth ripped his hand open, a high-pitched squeal almost strained his auditory system, but he managed to lift the syringe and stab it with the needle. A blow to his hand knocked him off balance and knocked him down, a strong grip twisted the hand sharply.

Fronda leapt at Loretta like a charging tiger, threw her against the wall and, scared to death, stopped above his lying friend. He knew there was no antidote to the poison in these syringes. Never lay on his back, clutching a syringe in his bleeding hand. He was stunned, but luckily nothing more. Slowly he raised his hand to reveal a bent, disarmed needle to Fronda.

"If it weren't for my Companion, I would be dead by now," he said softly. "Let's hurry."

Theo helped him to get up and they both looked around. Professor Higgins lay nearby, twisted in some unnatural position. Closer inspection revealed that his neck had been broken with a single, well-aimed blow. There was no sign of Lottie, and the two, without exchanging a word, rushed towards the direction from which they could pick up Dea's psycholocation. However, to their amazement, it turned out to be wrong. Their opponent was much more dangerous than they had previously thought - she might not know how to use psycholocation, but she was able to create a false echo of someone else's presence.

Only the second lead turned out to be the right one, and it led to the back of the museum, where their friend lay on a small patio, and nearby - Emma Simms, over whom the slender figure of Loretta was bending over.

At footsteps, the girl lifted her chalk-white face and blood-dripping mouth from her motionless body. She looked like an actress in a cheesy horror movie.

They stared at each other's eyes for a moment. Then the girl straightened, without saying anything, fixed her green eyes on her friends and spread her hands.

Behind her, a phosphoric cloth appeared, slowly creeping up. She was getting closer and closer and suddenly split apart, bypassing Loretta in two streams and reuniting behind her. She was crawling clearly towards Emma Simms' body and towards the two men.

"She can control it," whispered Fronda.

Never unhooked the flashlight from his belt with trembling fingers and directed a beam of strong light at the "mold". Theo did the same, wondering he hadn't figured it out before.

The phosphorescent white retreated lazily and froze. Loretta let out a long scream until her friends' ears hurt. A profuse, blood-stained foam covered her mouth.

The lenses in the flashlights broke and their light dimmed. The phosphorescent mass lunged forward again, accelerating. And then something hissed in the air.

The friends turned, clutching their guns in sweaty hands. Behind them was the old tramp, the same one they had served at the bar. Now he didn't look like a drunk lump at all. In both hands he held what appeared to be a launcher with gleaming metallic arrows attached to it. The pure silver detectors woke up and beeped warningly.

The movement of a finger on the trigger and another dart, released from its bearing, whistled through the air.

Loretta made a short, sharp feint, almost avoiding the hit. Her pale, bloody hair lifted up like a strong gust of wind, the girl spun and suddenly jumped somewhere so fast that even Fronda's chemical-enhanced senses barely noticed the direction of the movement.

"Leave her alone," Never ordered, leaning over Dean.

Contrary to his fears, the girl was fine, she only fainted from a blow to the head. She had a large bruise on her right temple, but she was breathing.

He felt a gigantic relief and at the same time remembered who had saved them. Startled, he looked at the tramp standing motionless. He withstood his gaze without blinking an eye.

"Get out of here as soon as possible," he said. "Forget about this place, and I will forget about you too."

Then he vanished as if engulfed in darkness. Apparently, he was not afraid of what was hunting while avoiding the light, because he was a hunter himself, and perhaps much more dangerous than they had known before.

Never picked up the doctor from the ground while Fronda examined Emma's body.

"There is nothing we can do to help here," he said glumly. "We have failed."

"We should hurry up. I fear for Gerard and Oggy," Never replied without commenting on the humiliating conclusion.

"This guy... Who do you think he is?"

"Lone Hunter, who else? We should be glad he didn't try his launcher on us. Probably he's hunting mutants like Dean. There are probably more of them here."

As soon as they could, they reached the car and placed Dea, still unconscious, in it. It was dark again on the patio, and the phosphorescent thallus could crawl out of its hiding place unhindered. Until morning, nothing will be left of the bodies of the murdered.

If, when driving to the city, Never was driving like a speeder, now he probably broke all possible records in this respect. Fronda sat huddled in the back seat, shaken by nausea, completely useless now. It was not for nothing that Octavio warned them against reckless use of "accelerators", as he called these substances. Used carelessly, they could kill, and if taken according to the recipe, they could save a life in combat - but they brought many unpleasant sensations.

Opel only braked at the station. Theo got out, swaying as if drunk and immediately doubled over. He vomited blood. Never left him and ran into the warehouse with the safety pistol in his hand. Even if he couldn't kill a vampire with it, he could at least overpower him.

"As I thought," he muttered, pausing in the doorway.

Gerard was sitting on the floor, holding his bloody head with both hands, and beside him Oggy was kneeling in human form, wrapped in some kind of cloth, washing the deep wound on the actor's forehead and crown with a piece of wet cloth.

"Segovia buffaloed us," she said when she saw Never. "He got away. Sorry, we didn't take proper care of him."

"We didn't show off either," the Indian came over and examined Gerard's head. "It needs to be sewn together, but for now let's get out of here. Let's run as far as possible while we still can."

He helped the actor get up. Oggy trailed behind them, holding the dirty sheet to keep from falling down.

Having seated Gerard in the car, Never handed the girl a dress and slippers, and while she was getting dressed, he started to rejuvenate Dea.

After a few minutes, he managed to get her eyes open, so he left her and walked over to the huddled Fronda.

"Are you feeling better?" he asked brusquely. "If so, wipe your mouth and get in. We have to get out of here as soon as possible."

"And Loretta and Segovia?" Theo groaned, getting to his feet unsteadily.

"We won't find them if she doesn't want to. She grew up here, she knows every nook and cranny here and knows every tuft of moss in the swamps. And if she wants to find us, I honestly wouldn't pay a penny for our skin. We leave this case."

"Are you coward?"

"If that's what you say, then yes, I'm coward and I'm not going to pretend to be a hero for free. Better to be a living dog than a dead lion. Get in at last."

Fronda, completely devoid of his usual knightly quixotic, silently obeyed this order.

He sat in the back seat, and so did Oggy, who was already dressed. Squeezed between the two, Dea was slowly recovering, though she was still stunned. The punch she received should have shattered her skull and she was lucky that Loretta took care of Emma Simms without checking if the first opponent was dead or not.

"We didn't make it?" she asked finally, her voice weak.

"It make it, because we're alive," Never replied brusquely. "However, we screwed up the task, and I will have to inform Laszlo about it. He certainly won't be happy."

"What are you gonna tell him?"

"Truth. Emma Simms is dead and the town isn't cursed, it's poisoned. I will not mention this couple from hell. It does not make sense."

For some reason he now remembered Dean, the unfortunate Dean no one would help anymore.

For the rest of his days, he will wander the swamps, attacking lonely travelers, until someone with the stronger nerves simply shoots him.

Someone like that Hunter pretending to be a lump. There was a bitter irony to it. They knew how to help a symbiote-possessed boy, but could not.

"You don't always win, like in the movies," he finished quietly.

"And Segovia?" Dea moaned, adjusting the cold compress on her head.

"We can't help him either. It is doubtful whether he wants it. He's completely possessed by his Lottie," he speeded up.

"He's found his little private hell," Theo muttered. He still looked nauseous and pressed into the corner, as if he wanted to hide between the seat and the car's wall.

Opel passed a shabby signpost reading "Millhaven - 10 Miles". No one chased them, the city remained behind them, and with it its dark secret.

"So we won't get word of the Rast leader," Gerard said after a long moment.

He was sick too, but not excessively, he could stand it. Each of them absorbed some dose of poisoned air and poisoned water, but fortunately their bodies could handle it.

Never shook his head slightly and opened the window, letting in a stream of night air and something they had almost forgotten, the buzzing of night insects and the distant hoot of owls...

"Not this time. However, this doesn't mean never."

"So we are not giving up on this case."

"No. We will track them. Till death. Ours or theirs."

Part 3

Nemesis

Motto:

Obadiah Obadiah

Jah Jah sent us here to catch vampire

We have the chalice to lite up Jah fire

When I am nigh catch them vampire

I am nigh I go set them on fire ...

Sinead O'Connor

I don't think anyone has ever seen a vampire, a fellow of the priests of the goddess Kali, famous for his composure and coolness, be so furious. It was not the first time that Fronda had upset him, but never to such an extent as that night. Even Gerard, who had remained on the sidelines of their conflicts, now huddled into the corner and tried to remain invisible.

They were in a house off the beaten track. It was not so much a villa for rent, but a pre-war house, which they had taken over due to old age, without asking anyone's opinion. Eventually they had to stay somewhere, and they became afraid of hotels. They could not afford any good, and in the lesser ones they had been mugged twice recently and survived with difficulty. The Rasts acted decisively and efficiently, even reaching where the Van Helsing Institute had failed.

"This is because the Vanhelsingers work by scientific methods and the Rasts use only instincts," Dea explained. If you don't twist this hydra's head right up, we're all loosing."

Dea separated from the team and returned to Poland, to a detective agency led by Stasiek Zakrzewski. As she said herself, she would rather follow unfaithful wives for a lot of money than risk death for the sake of mankind. This was, of course, an exaggeration, as "humanity" was usually the last thing their little team had in mind. Usually they just tried to survive and earn some money at the same time. The doctor decided she was fed up with living on the edge and they didn't even hold it against her. Poland was still considered a relatively safe country, where you could live peacefully without fear of a sudden visit by the Hunters. As long as basic precautions were not neglected, of course. On his way to the country, Theo accompanied his friend, who insisted that she shouldn't go alone after all. Nobody suspected anything. After all, his overprotection towards the fair sex, bordering on ordinary sexism, was nothing new. However, what he did next...

"How can you be such a moron!" Never thundered at the whole house. "And at your age! Over six hundred years and you haven't learned anything! The older the dumber! If I seriously believed in any of the gods of my nation, or any other, I would pray day and night to him that he would give you brain! Although it is doubtful whether even all the gods could advise you on your stupidity and stubbornness... And what are you smiling so much, moron?!"

"Because you look so funny when you get angry," Fronda answered innocently, resting his chin on his curled fist, as was his custom.

"Himmellherrgott!" In moments of greatest desperation, Rajah usually cursed in German, although no one knew why. "Do you really understand nothing? Are you such an idiot?!"

Gerard, in the corner, shrugged. He had had enough of this brawl.

"How long will you ask about it? You are getting boring. The answer is basically clear. Yes, he is such an idiot. And what is the result of this?"

Never looked at him furiously and suddenly, as if someone had unexpectedly cut his knees, he sat helplessly on a dilapidated bed against the wall.

"What am I going to do with you now?" he groaned desperately.

His upset was all too justified. Fronda did not come back from Poland alone. He had brought with him the person least expected and least desired in their little company - the blind girl he called Lily Ann. This alone would not be so worst and probably could have been sorted out somehow if not for an additional problem.

"How could you preserve someone who will never be able to take care of himself and will always be dependent on others?"

The Indian asked this question without any hope of getting any meaningful answer. Theo struggled to suppress a laugh. He did not want to irritate the commander of their small unit even more, but he was clearly enjoying the whole situation.

Gerard smirked at Never's expression. He, too, appreciated the humorous tone of the scene, regardless of the embarrassing case that caused it.

"He read dumb books. One of them says that vampire blood heals everything, including blindness. And he tried. Because why not?"

Never looked at him, then at Fronda, who shook his head.

"It's not like that," he explained, "I read the book, yes. Maybe not the smartest one, but it's well written. Only I didn't believe it, of course, not a single word. Maybe I'm stupid, but not that much. The author has never met any of us. But she has such a fantasy that everyone would have it."

"So why...?"

"Maybe I'll say something," Lily interrupted unexpectedly.

She was sitting on the sofa in the corner, Oggy in her wolf form snuggled against her legs.

She immediately stuck to her new friend, which was probably influenced by the fact that recently she spent more and more time "in dog's skin".

The change was slow, and they didn't quickly notice that something was wrong. And once they figured it out, they had no choice but to accept the fact that their proven friend is more and more willing to accompany them in the form of a shaggy tetrapod.

It meant they had to get used to a lot of new things. Also, as a shepherd dog, she felt an irresistible urge to look after someone for whom her help would certainly be useful. It was especially visible now.

"Okay," Rajah agreed with resignation, "speak, Lily Ann."

The fair-haired Polish woman folded her hands on her lap. Her calmness might have seemed strange to someone who had only become a vampire twenty-four hours before and had broken with her former life, leaving everything she knew behind. But Lily was just like that. Cool, calm, unfazed. It was hard to guess what fascinated Fronda so much that he broke the most sacred principle of his brethren for her. She was not even particularly beautiful, although she undeniably had something in herself. It resembled a Byzantine icon - very slim, with a classic neckline, aristocratic hands, a slightly too long face, small lips and large, oblong eyes, captivating with an unusual play of colors, from dark gray to azure. Perhaps it was they, although they were blind, that charmed Theo so much that he could not resist them?

"First of all, nothing happened that I myself did not want," she began. "I understand your objections, but I can assure you that I'm not a helpless being who needs to be led by a hand. I grew up in an institution for the blind, where I was prepared for life. I've been living alone since I was eighteen and I'm doing great. The more I can manage as one of you."

"You don't know what you're saying," Never muttered.

"I know. My senses are very acute. I know, for example, that we are now in a remote area, away from the communication routes, in an old house built partly of wood and partly of brick.

It is much neglected, even in ruins, and for sure no one has cleaned it for a long time. The only permanent residents are rats and cockroaches.

Little? I can determine the height of each of you, and if you were ordinary people, then also age and ailments that trouble you.

I know exactly how far away you are from me. I can tell what the passing man ate and when was the last time he washed.

What vehicle was he driving? When he changed clothes. Sometimes even what medications she takes. I know when he is afraid and when he is joyful. I can easily determine the quality of the food to buy. By touching the material, I can tell whether it is artificial or real, dyed or raw, new or old. I recognize the denominations of coins and banknotes so that no one deceives me when spending the change. I can easily determine the distance from the source of any sound. It is enough for me to snap my fingers while in a closed room or in a built-up area, and by the quality of the reflected echo I will know where the walls are. As a teenager, I competed in the Paralympics as a runner and had pretty good results. I can swim and skate, I can also deal with equestrianism. By treating me like a helpless person, you're embarrassing yourself."

Theo finally allowed himself a little chuckle. The leader paid no attention to this.

"I'm not questioning your abilities, but I don't think you understand. How dangerous our life is, especially now. And even for someone with no burdens. It's not just about sucking blood, pretending to be a great lord, and having fun forever."

"We don't have much fun, and in bad taste," muttered Gerard from his corner.

The girl smiled slightly, with subtle irony.

"And you are implying again, you think I'm an idiot, or your friend is a fraud. Meanwhile, Theo didn't hide anything from me.

I know perfectly well that you are being hunted and that you are dealing with paranormal phenomena. I'm not afraid of Hunters or ghouls. He also warned me, by the way, that you would be very dissatisfied, and I was not afraid of that either. It's not easy to scare me."

She put her hand on Oggy's head, and she narrowed her eyes in response and opened her mouth, tongue hanging all the way out. There was incomprehensible satisfaction with all her doggy form, as if she had only now found her place in life. Looking at her, Never suddenly lost the will to continue talking.

"Cheetah, do you have any cigarettes?" He turned to the actor. "Would you please? I have to smoke."

"Sure," Gerard rose from his seat, "let's go outside so as not to annoy our ladies. They both don't like smoke. I will also smoke, just for the company..."

Despite the passage of years and a radical change in his lifestyle, he still smoked a lot, and now he had no additional incentive to get rid of this habit.

"Because what? Because I will die," he used to say when someone persuaded him to quit cigarettes.

This did not really threaten him anymore, since vampires are not susceptible to typical human diseases, so he could indulge in his favorite addiction as much as he wanted. His friends allowed it, as long as he walked outside the house or car they were in.

As they left, Theo kissed Lily heartily and put his arm around her protectively.

"It'll be okay," he said reassuringly, "it will pass soon. As always."

"Why did you want to be a vampire so much?" Oggy asked curiously, cuddling up to the fair-haired Polish woman on the other side. "Do you want to live forever?"

Lily smiled at her.

"Eternity is unlikely to be an option," she replied, "Theo explained everything to me exactly. It's just, as if to say, I was tempted by the aesthetics of such a life."

"Aesthetics?"

"Yes. You know, I never liked my body and its natural functions. Vampires don't digest, excrete, or produce sperm, have no gas, runny nose, or other disgusting ailments that have disgusted me since my early childhood. The most beautiful, sexiest man with silk-smooth skin, brilliant intelligence and a wonderful voice is in fact a bag of mucus that deteriorates over time, various smelly liquids and dung. Once you get it, it's really hard to fall in love with anyone. He even hates himself. Now all this stuff is beyond me."

"Vanitas vanitatum," Fronda summed up her statement. She did not make a special impression on him, especially since he knew well this approach to the physicality of man from his own, ancient times.

"There's something to it," Oggy agreed, "let's wait for the boys to come back. Perhaps Rajah will calm down when he smoke. He doesn't usually do that, and maybe that's why he's so pissed off.

Never really used tobacco rarely, although sometimes when he was very nervous he used this form of de-stress, just like now. He took a cigarette from a packet offered to him by a friend, lit it, and leaned back against the wall of the house.

"I don't know what to do now," he confessed after a moment.

Gerard shrugged his slim shoulders.

"Nothing. What could you? The damage is done. Fronda brought this young lady to us and confronted us with a fait accompli.

As always, because it's his favorite way of doing things. It shouldn't surprise you, after all, you've known him longer than I have."

"That's true. And yet he continues to surprise me. It's kind of an art, don't you think?" Rajah flicked the ashes from his cigarette and stared at the moon. "Of course you know why he did this?"

The ex-actor considered.

"Fell in love?" he risked finally.

"That would be nothing new. He is still in love."

"He helped a lady in need, like a knight?"

"Probably that too. Don Quixote of La Moron, hellishness... But there is more to it. He wants an immortal companion, one for all eternity, and you know how difficult it is in our world. Relationships fall apart after being consolidated... Well, he had a "brilliant" idea that a blind woman would not run away from him. Creep!"

"That sounds logical," Gerard admitted, "but I don't know if he'll be perturbed. Lily looks to me like the one who can really handle it anytime. With or without Fronda. If she wants to leave, she will leave without looking back at anything, and he will do nothing. I know women like her, they are tougher than many men. What amazes me is Oggy's reaction. Usually she snarled at Fronda's mistresses, and now she is downright happy. It's hard to understand."

"And I think it's not that hard," Never puffed on the smoke and for a moment he played little rings as he watched them fade in the moonlight. "Oggy is a dog, not a wolf.

Alsatian sheepdog, also incorrectly called "German". These dogs have a coded need to care for the weaker in their blood, as they have been used to herd sheep for centuries.

So far, our little one has not had the opportunity to look after anyone, we rather had to protect her from the world. Or we thought we had to."

The actor took a second cigarette from the box, and lit it from the cigarette butt.

"Do you think?" he asked after a moment, "There may be something to it. You know, I never thought that the umbrella we spread over her would cause her any discomfort."

"As you can see, the emotional needs of werewolves may not be what we think. Now Oggy can discharge her instincts whether it is necessary or not."

"It looks like."

"Uhm. Besides, most dogs have a special attitude towards the blind, as if they sense their handicap."

"Because they can sense. Dogs are very smart. I used to have a dog myself, and a sheepdog as well," Gerard thought about the old days. "I don't think we understand the nature of werewolves. Oggy is someone on the border of worlds, her mind works in a way that is unavailable to us. Let's just let her be herself, even if that requires us to accept her sudden friendship with Lily."

The Indian looked at the sky as if he expected some advice from the stars blinking on it.

"I predict trouble as hell," he said after a moment, "it's not the first time that Fronda is capturing his girlfriend just because she asks him to do it. It always ends badly, because whenever a woman is involved, this goddamn idiot immediately starts thinking only on one thing.

In his case, there is no question of scrupulous checking for and against, or even the usual novitiate. He just can't say no to the lady and that's it.

For the first time, however, he broke a most holy rule. It is true that he also had an affair with a blind woman for the first time. Until now, even he had too much shame for a something like this. This Polish woman must have gotten under his skin pretty well."

"What is this novitiate?" Gerard asked. He hadn't heard of anything like this before in relation to their underworld, though he had spent so many years in it.

"Eh, that's something people tried to obey in the past. A candidate for a vampire had to be observed and assessed for some time by at least two of us before being preserved. In fact, it was rarely used too strictly...

Control was tightened at certain times in history, but you know, with people like us it's hard to talk about a consolidated society, so it usually ended with no one to watch over it. Because who and how? We are, as you probably noticed, rather something like a clan culture, some live here, some live there, and we have neither a common religion, nor even a spiritual homeland. And without that, it is difficult to talk about universal traditions."

The actor remembered his own beginnings and smiled sadly. In his case, the "novitiate" probably took place, it was finally observed before preservation, and for quite a long time. However, he himself had only a few minutes to make a decision, and it would be difficult to speak of a free choice when he was dying.

"But preservation can heal even fatal diseases," he noted.

Never shook his head.

"Only some. And not so much heals as freezes and activates the body's additional defenses. It doesn't always work, and it doesn't work for everything.

Neurological diseases do not give up at all. If you had fixed the epileptic, you wouldn't have cured it. You'd just be in a goddamn trouble because you'd be responsible for a vampire with epilepsy. The same is true for someone with a ruptured spinal cord or suffering from multiple sclerosis, for example. Can you imagine a vampire in a wheelchair? Nice picture, isn't it? As for mental illness, you already know. Therefore, we must be very careful."

"Well, now it's probably too late for caution."

"I know. That's why I was so carried away. Even if we assume that Fronda acted arbitrarily and on his own, everyone, as a team and as a clan, is now responsible for Lily until she stands on her own feet. And that may never happen, no matter what she imagines and what our chivalrous head believes. That's the truth."

"Tough case," muttered Gerard, and he probably never said anything truer.

They had no time now to look after the "jailbait", that is, the newly preserved human.

They returned to Paris at the desperate call of Francis Bell, the last of a Parisian clan once slaughtered by the Hunters.

After somehow surviving the Wild Hunt, he gathered a few survivors around him, and together they did their best to survive.

Unfortunately, they belonged to the most primeval variety of vampires known as "oysters."

Their psychophysical structure precluded any travel. Always attached to one city, one village, sometimes just one piece of land, they could not leave it, lest their cells began to fall apart.

Vampires generally do not like to travel at all, but in most cases they are not in any particular danger. "Oysters" were an age-old exception to the rule, paradoxically considered by many people to be representative of their species.

You never know who from preserved will become one, and it happened so rarely that the danger was underestimated. It seemed bitterly ironic that these handicapped "oysters" were a particularly difficult nut to crack for the Hunters.

They were virtually undetectable by their methods, although it should rather be the other way around.

There were usually a dozen such vampires of both sexes in Paris. Why exactly there?

No one could answer this question, but it was the City of Light that generated the greatest amount of "fossils" as they were sometimes referred to.

In others, the "oyster" happened only once in a century, in the French capital there were always up to twenty. As long as they were only threatened by vanhelsingers, they were very good at avoiding danger. But now the conditions have changed.

Bell claimed to know all about the Rasts and their leader, but did not want to speak on the phone. Whether they wanted to or not, they had to return to where they had once fled in panic and where many dangers lurked for them. While there were many who insisted that Transylvania was the spiritual homeland of all vampirism, in fact it was... Paris, at least in the modern world. No wonder that the Van Helsing Institute began its criminal activity there, and that this is how the Rasts, heirs of their ideas, found their central headquarters. But to know that this headquarters is in Paris is one thing. Find her is one thing and without getting killed is another.

Francis Bell was not going to fight for his group. Their tactic was defensive. They hid as best they could and avoid trouble as long as possible. They also usually isolated themselves from other undead, which had their justification. "Oysters" differed from ordinary people not only in their "diet" but also physically. They usually had very pale skin, bluish lips and always red eyelids, which gave them a characteristic, rather spooky appearance. However, it seemed that this time the activities of the Hunters terrified this tiny clan to death as they sought support. A decaying house in the suburbs as a meeting place was supposed to be a guarantee that it would be safe. If it could be at all. The Indian walked around the city before Fronda returned from Poland and came back upset. As he said, he had the impression that their pursuers were everywhere. It was due to the ubiquitous fashion for dreadlocks, so eagerly worn by Rasts.

"They may not come from Rastafarians, but they copy things from them. Even the hairstyle, clothes and terribly primitive decorations. This is a hint.

Not very precise, but still. We have to be careful," he said as he returned from this escapade. "Oggy, find everything on the internet about Rastafarians, Rastamans and others. So far I have not been interested in such cults, and maybe it's worth it."

The girl obediently turned on her inherent laptop, a new model, much smaller and lighter than what she had learned to surf the net and the basics of hacking. Never stood behind her and began to read over her shoulder as she flipped through the pages.

"It's not an ordinary cult," she said after a long moment, "rather a socio-philosophical movement. A little bit like hippies. They burn pot ritually. They are obsessed with healthy food and stuff like that, they like music and they have their own religious rites. They basically want good. That there would be no divisions, that there would be no evil."

"The starting point. We are evil. Such a Babylonian harlot," the Hindu pointed a slender finger at one of the verses.

"Except Rastafarians avoid violence," Oggy said. "It's a very peaceful religion. Whoever organized the Rasts into a fight used only the facade of the movement. He had a purpose in it."

The Rajah was silent for a long moment.

"Yes," he said finally. "Something that "enlightened and modern" people completely ignore. The power of faith. It's an extremely powerful glue, stronger than anything else. No matter what name is given to a deity in one of the human languages, it's important that its followers really believe. With all my strength and all my heart. Then nothing beats them."

Gerard entered the room, stretching and yawning. He liked to take a nap sometimes in the "middle of the activity," as he called it, whether it was day or night.

"Anyone talking about beliefs?" he asked.

"Yeah a little." Oggy stood up and took a piece of raw beef from the refrigerator. She devoured the meat greedily, then licked her fingers, announced that she was "going for a run" and, transforming into a dog, jumped out through the open window into the neglected garden around the house. The men barely paid any attention to it.

"And what enlightened conclusions have you reached?" Gerard asked ironically. He never concealed his atheism, although he had seen things that should really make him think.

"Virtually none," Never honestly admitted. "We are in a dead end."

"Then why do you turn to religion? Is it supposed to help?"

"We're not turning. We are trying to find out how the Rast leader is manipulating them. All indications are that he is using religion for this purpose.

The Obadiah brotherhood was a radical branch of rastafari, insignificant, and it seems that our persecutor has taken over them.

And he made them Rasts, who hunt vampires for the sake of humanity, not really caring about who will die along the way. Such a new cult. The problem is, they really believe what the bastard put in their heads. They don't think for themselves. The Vanhelsingers and those of Medlab at least used brains."

"It's not a big difference for us... They all had it in for us in the same way."

"Maybe so, but the others had something to do with it. They tried to "help". Remember what O'Grady said?

They wanted to restore our "human face" and had a certain self-preservation instinct. They did not risk themselves unnecessarily, so they could be intimidated.

The Rasts want to kill and only kill, no matter what the cost. Likewise, the vanhelsingers. It was possible to lead them out into the field for decades. Here, unfortunately, we have the matter put on the edge of the knife. Either we or they."

"Maybe Fronda can think of something," Gerard yawned again and went to the refrigerator for preserved blood. He has been gone for over two weeks.

Unfortunately, the awaited return of Theo did not help in any way, and even, for the aforementioned reason, made the situation impossible.

No quarrels could now change the fact that the friends had additional trouble, at the most inconvenient moment.

*****

Francis Bell showed up after ten days of waiting for his visit. Were it not for the fact that he had warned them about it earlier, they would not have waited so long, but had just looked for it themselves. As he himself said, he tried to circulate so as to confuse any potential tracker and, as he said, he hoped he succeeded. He wasn't sure of anything.

"The Rasts are either way smarter than the Vanhelsingers, or they have a damn good targeting system. One does not exclude the other. We must be on guard all the time. We stay in the group, because we have to put up guards, otherwise we would not sleep at all," he explained. "We have the impression that they know our every step and that they are everywhere. We'd run away to the end of the world, but you know we can't. You are our last hope."

"Didn't you try to contact Octavio di Mauro? He could send you some detectors or whatever."

Theo looked at Bell sympathetically. Even for an "oyster" he looked very bad, like someone constantly bullied and tormented to such an extent that he is constantly awake until he falls on his face from exhaustion. He certainly wasn't making it up or exaggerating.

"Octavio and his team are unavailable," Bell replied grimly. "We tried on all the phone numbers we got.

We posted coded advertisements in newspapers. We wrote to whomever we could. Not only he is silent. Also, those to whom we sent letters and messages did not respond. Only you..."

"Not good," Never muttered, and frowned.

"You think that all of them... already... this?" Gerard asked carefully, squinting at Lily. He didn't want to scare her, but perhaps he was unnecessarily worried about it.

She sat quietly, one hand resting on Oggy's head, which was crouched next to her in human form, and listened to the conversation as calmly as it was about the weather for tomorrow.

"Spit the words out! I rather think that they huddled like a mouse under a broomstick so as not to tempt the devil. Although, of course, some of them certainly caught up," he added, glowing even more.

"As Fronda says, vampires have been hunted for centuries, and they will continue to be hunted," said Oggy. "Unfortunately, there are always dead bodies in war. The only question is how many there are this time."

"Yes, that's the question," the leader of the group looked around. "And where did our knight go again?!"

"He said he had to meet someone and that he would be back before dawn."

"Not again..."

Lily, who had been silent until then, raised her eyebrows, arched in perfect arches.

"You are afraid of something?"

He looked at her. He had only known this girl for a few days, and he still couldn't get used to her. There was something in her that depressed him and that he didn't quite understand, as if she were from another world. In a way, she really was.

"The Fronda's friends are quite specific, so to speak," he explained reluctantly, "sometimes even dangerous. In the end, one of them will knock his head off and it will finally be silence."

"You always anticipate the worst. Or maybe he just took a trip to the cinema?"

Gerard suggested, "You know how he loves horror movies, especially those in which someone who is possessed by an evil spirit or infected with something suddenly gets crazy and goes through with ulcers."

"He himself is one big horror movie. And the age-old ulcer on my ass. Freak, too," Never thought about it. "Maybe he actually broke off to the cinema that would be his style. After all, you didn't make an appointment at a specific time, we thought you wouldn't show up until after midnight."

Bell sighed heavily.

"It's safer right after dusk. When it is still a little bright and crowds everywhere. You can do something, even hunt. You'll powder your mouth and they'll think you're gay at worst. It gets nasty after midnight as the lanterns dim, fewer passers-by, and the Hunters are active."

"Always been like that."

"I know. Except the Rasts are damn effective trackers. We have not had such on our necks yet. Vanhelsingers could clean their shoes."

There was silence after this statement.

Bell said finally, "Vanhelsingers were never quite as dangerous as they posed.

They tried to give the impression that they did not care about the human cost of their activities, but they were actually very careful and made sure that no outsiders were hurt. They did not want to attract the attention of the authorities so that they could conduct their research quietly. The Rasts don't care about science and care little about human life. What matters is the mission that Great Jah has given them. Or at least they believe that He commissioned it to them. Well, there is no conversation with fanatics."

"But fanatics must have a leader, they won't organize themselves," Oggy remarked soberly.

She wrapped her hands around the dress, trying to tuck the tail under it. She couldn't deal with it. For several weeks, even when she took the form of a human, the dog's tail remained and had to be hidden from human sight. To that end, she now wore slightly voluminous and longer dresses, and she tied the unruly organ with a sexshop lace garter to her thigh when she had to walk between people. It wasn't very convenient, but it worked.

"Yes of course. Until we track him down, the fight will be hopeless," Never agreed. "Francis, are you sure he's based in Paris?"

Bell nodded.

"Yes, we know that for sure."

"Well, I hope you are right. Because we already had several such signals and it always turned out that "sorry, wrong number"."

"Not this time. Believe me, he's here. He's based here. Only we don't know where or who."

"So where...?" Rajah did not seem convinced.

"For a while, these lunatics gathered in the Boulon Forest. Nadine attached a "bug" to one of them."

"Who's Nadine?"

"Regular visitor. One of us, but a shame to say the whore. She sells herself because she likes it. Seriously. She gets excited when someone pays for her services, and that's it."

"Deviations can be different," muttered Gerard.

He had managed to get used to the fact that the vampiresses he encountered were usually quite horny.

For some reason, the fixative acted on them as a prolonged aphrodisiac, or perhaps merely relieved their subconscious, repressed needs. There were those who liked it. It put him off, but luckily he had little to do with the female members of their species.

"There are," Bell agreed with him, "What someone likes. Nadine is what she is, we accept it and sometimes even use it, as we do now. Sometimes you have no choice."

"So she put a bug to one of the Rasts and what?" Never interrupted him impatiently.

"He found it quickly, unfortunately. But we overheard and recorded a few conversations. Then we analyzed them for hours. They show that although Rasts roam the world like stray cats looking for victims, they always return to Paris, as if they were receiving orders from here or had their main base here. Which, in my opinion, is one thing. Their leader must live here somewhere."

"Yes. It is quite possible," the Indian admitted after a moment's thought, "it sounds quite logical. In any case, it's enough for us to launch an investigation in this town. What do we have to lose anyway?"

"Heads," Gerard said maliciously.

He didn't want to say something sharp, but then the door slammed and Theo burst in. He wore new pants, trendy shoes, and a black shirt, all from Calvin Klein, plus he was neatly combed and smelled of good cologne. A new men's black leather bag was slung over his shoulder.

"Oh, are you here already?" he asked when he saw Bell.

"What "are you here already"?" Rajah bridled. "Rather, where have you been and what have you been doing so far? You tarted yourself up, damn it, like Mowgli at the Festival of the Woods... You robbed the model runway or what?"

"Exactly," Gerard agreed, "we're broke, and you show up here looking like James Bond on a date. You must have spent a few thousand bucks, apparently."

"Don't stick your nose into someone else's wallet, Cheetah," Theo advised, unhappily, "It's not your business, where I got the money. It was mine and I had the right to spend it as I wanted. By the way, you would get it too, if you hadn't insisted on giving all your money to that detective for the Millhaven action."

"This is really insolence! We didn't complete the task, so we couldn't stop it!"

"And since we almost died, does it no longer count? We deserved something for it, though anything. Anyway, never mind." Fronda kissed Lily on the forehead, ruffled Oggy's head, and looked at Bell. "Did you tell them everything?"

Francis nodded his head.

"That's good. And I set us up to meet someone who can help us track down the bastard's seat."

"With who?" Never asked distrustfully.

"Oh, it will be a surprise."

"You want trouble?!"

"You wouldn't believe it if I said anyway. This is an extraordinary persona," Fronda was not scared at all by the threat of his leader. "Francis, will you stay with us?"

"No way," Bell rose from his chair, "I already know your buddies, one better than the other."

"What buddies?" Lily asked.

"Hell's. He attracts demons like a magnet. Or at least what come across for demons. Like that scary woman who has flames instead of hair. Or the one you see only as darkness, and besides, not at all. Thank you for such contacts."

Theo laughed heartily and waved his hand.

"You were always chicken. Okay, go. We'll do it by ourselves, as always."

"I'll call you in a few days," Bell said for goodbye, and left, disappearing into the darkness.

"Has he seen Cyrotte?" Gerard looked at Fronda questioningly.

"Not only her. He believes he has seen demons from hell itself, hungry for blood and destruction. He is terribly superstitious, anything can scare him. And you will admit, Cheetah that our world is teeming with strangers out of nowhere. It is a grace of God that people don't usually see them."

"Interesting... My favorite writer wrote the same," Lily said thoughtfully, "I have some of his books in audio, on a Walkman. I even took them with me. Dagon, Cthulu, Yog Sottoth, Mi-Go..."

"Well, maybe it's not as bad as The Loner from Providence said," Theo chuckled. "But it's an indisputable fact that we are not alone on Earth. And there is a reason people fear the dark so much. Creatures coexisting, so to speak, hate light more than those of us who are "moths". That is why in the era of widespread lighting of cities and even villages, so little is heard about them. However, this does not mean that they are gone."

"You'd shut up, Fronda," Oggy muttered with an involuntary shiver. She didn't like horror movies. Unlike her best friend, she was afraid of them and preferred not even to be talked about in front of her. Then she had bad dreams.

"Stop saying nonsense," Never said, "Where do you want to take us?"

"To theater."

"You're kidding?!"

Theo laughed at the expression on his leader's face.

"No. I'm taking you to the Theater des Champs Elysee. Well, in a way."

"I will kill you!"

Fronda's tendency to joke at the least appropriate moment was, to say the least, annoying, which he himself did not understand. His Indian friend should get used to it, but while he had time for it, somehow he still couldn't. The former knight's infantility irritated him more than he could put it, but he was unable to deal with it. Theo was what he was and he wasn't going to change.

"Just take it easy, take it as entertainment," he said cheerfully. "Theater is a beautiful place anyway."

"The most beautiful," whispered Gerard, so softly only Oggy could hear him. Despite the passing of decades, he still missed the stage and the applause of the audience - something he was deprived of forever.

"I have no idea what we're supposed to be doing there," Never growled, but he obediently followed Fronda. Always been like that. Though he had shouted at him he is idiot, nominally he was the leader of their team, in the end he recognized the authority of Fronda. And it always came out in the end that he listened to him despite all his doubts.

"I have twice the IQ of this Casanova for the poor, but when we are on the war path, I prefer him to command," he used to say in moments of honesty.

Theo took a whole beef liver out of the bag in a foil bag. He unpacked it and threw to Oggy.

"Enjoy your meal, baby."

Oggy grabbed a chunk of raw material in the air and bit her teeth smugly into it.

"We also need to eat."

"Is there a time and place for that?" Gerard looked at Fronda doubtfully.

"Believe me, we need to eat before the meeting. After that, there may be no more time, and as for the place, it is better to hunt in the suburbs than in the center. Today is Saturday, people party until morning, it's hard to find this little intimacy while eating."

Theo spoke cheerfully and lightly, only Never felt that there was something behind his words. However, he decided not to pursue the topic for the time being. Anyway, he was already feeling a little hungry and willingly hunted with the others.

Indeed, the streets of Paris were still full of people - ordinary passers-by, tourists and city residents, eager to have fun after a whole week of work. Brightly lit streets gave a sense of security, but nevertheless did not weaken your vigilance for a moment. While the behavior of the Vanhelsingers could be predicted with great accuracy, the Rasts were characterized by dangerous spontaneity and could even hit in the middle of the crowd. It was better to be on your guard than to regret it later.

After a short consultation, they left the rented car on the plot and took the metro to the center. As far as they could see, no one followed them and no one paid any attention to them.

Only Never was accosted by some drunk man near Abbesses station, who, seeing his hair braided as usual, took him for a gay. He did not want to leave the handsome Indian alone until Gerard, having an overwhelming burst of laughter, pulled the man aside and silently explained something to him. The stranger, an amateur of male charms, finally let himself be convinced and left, disappearing into the crowd.

"What did you say him?" Never asked as the actor, still chuckling, returned to his friends.

"What only I could in such a situation. That you are my wife and this is our honeymoon."

"Oh?!"

Never's indignation knew no bounds. His keeping up with modernity did not extend to sex, or at least not entirely. He disgusted homosexuality, surprising to someone so old and, in addition, brought up in a country where moral standards differed from those of the West. Even Fronda was less radical on this point, and some medieval prejudices were to be expected soonest from him. Being "picked up" by a representative of his own gender, he usually reacted with amusement, while Rajah was regularly furious.

"Come on, I had to convince the guy that there is nothing to try with you, because he would never leave us," Gerard patted him on the back.

"Don't even tell me such things," Never growled furiously.

"Leave him alone," Theo advised, "we'll be there in a minute, let him not spoil everything with his sorrows. Oggy, make sure Lily Ann doesn't get lost."

"No worries, I can take care of myself and never get lost," the blind girl gripped her cane tighter.

"We know, we know. However, you don't know this city so don't protest. Think to yourself that this is an army and you are a soldier and you must obey your commander. Otherwise you will get a reprimand with an entry in the files or three days of arrest in the garrison," Fronda firmly took her arm and led her to the platform.

The Theater des Champs Elysee was brightly lit. It was the last show and the door should theoretically be locked, but the ticket clerk was easily persuaded by a few bills.

"You know this place," Theo said to Gerard once they were inside, "do you know how to get out on the roof?"

"Of course. If they didn't rebuild something here," the actor led them backstage. "I wasn't here for a long time, you know..."

They quietly passed the dressing rooms and found themselves in an emergency technical aisle from which a winding staircase led up. They climbed them all the way to the fifth floor, where the normal steps were replaced by clamps hammered into the wall of the shaft leading to the roof. The hatch was padlocked, but one of the Fronda's lockpicks dealt with it quickly.

They found themselves on a flat roof overlooking Paris at night, flickering with thousands of lights.

"I hope nobody bothers us here," Never muttered. "They would have us like on the fork."

"Don't worry," Fronda reassured him and looked around. "Beautiful panorama, isn't it? In my day, even at best, shit would be visible from a roof like this. And literally, because the chamber pots spilled right on the street."

"You're so romantic."

"Come on? That's the truth. People do not realize now how clean times they live and how well they are."

Gerard looked around too. He knew the building well, but it was not on its top yet. He felt insecure here, especially when he realized that in the event of trouble it would be difficult to escape. Unless to the roof of the neighboring house... But all these roofs end somewhere and then what?

"Someone should wait for us?" he asked.

"Not altogether. We are to wait. He'll be here any minute."

"Who exactly?"

Fronda sat on the ledge of the wall. He sat Lily down next to him, putting his arm around her protectively.

"He's from the local Menagerie," he said, "don't be scared when you see him."

"Do you really think something else might scare us?" Never raised his eyebrows in a sarcastic grimace.

The term "Menagerie" was used to describe all strange creatures that inhabited a given place, usually without human knowledge. In some cities there were surprisingly many of them. They avoided vampires as carefully as humans, and so far Rajah team had little to do with them. But they had seen, as he rightly pointed out, much worse cases.

Fronda pointed casually at one of the nearby rooftops.

"It's him."

They turned in the direction indicated and froze in surprise. At first they even thought Theo was making fun of them, as was his habit, but after a while they rejected the possibility. The creature they saw only appeared to be ordinary.

At first, they thought it was an ordinary cat, only slightly larger than the average moggy.

The animal ran along the edges of the roofs, efficiently jumping the spaces between the houses.

He was clearly limping on the front paw, which, however, seemed to be not disturbing at all.

He moved with the agility of a glider, hopping precisely from tree to tree, although the distance between the roofs was sometimes a few meters.

They stared at him, fascinated, until he was on the roof of the theater. Only now they could get a closer look at him.

Having jumped with the last, long leap on the roof of the Theater des Champs Elysee, the creature first of all straightened and grew visibly, and at the same time assumed a roughly human form.

It was rather short and slender, with relatively short limbs. In an upright position, it moved not so much as a human, but rather like a squirrel jumping on two legs.

One could be under the illusion that each leg had two oppositely bent knee joints, because they retained the proportions of cat's paws.

The creature was tiptoe and so did these animals. It was all covered with very short, delicate fur in a shade of pure anthracite, from the end of the long, flexible tail to the tips of the ears. Still, there was no cat in front of them.

His hands were decidedly human now, with long fingers ending in flat nails and an opposing thumb. Likewise, the outline of the torso and neck were human. The small, flat skull had rather catlike proportions, but still the face belonged to a human - somewhat triangular, covered with the same smooth hair as the rest of the body, but with undoubtedly human features.

"Hello, Fronda," the newcomer greeted in a low, soft voice.

"Hi, Lasalle," Theo said, "I'm glad you came."

The creature perched on the roof framing in a cat pose, wrapping a pliable, fluffy tail around its legs.

"The situation is unique," he said. "And you know perfectly well why."

"I know," Fronda agreed. The others listened carefully without saying a word.

Lasalle's ears pinched slightly, placing them back against him. He studied Lily for a moment, then shook his head disapprovingly.

"You have exceeded all limits. But that's your problem after all."

"Certainly not yours."

"I've been dealing with mine on my own for so many centuries that I don't even remember them. Now let's focus on what we're here for." The weird creature looked around slightly, penetrating the surroundings with golden eyes like Never. "So, my dear, you are looking for the leader of the Rast organization, right?"

"Oh, yes."

"So, I will advise you one thing: get away."

"What?" He couldn't believe.

"I'm serious. All the Vampire Hunters so far have been human, and very intelligent at that, because you are not easy to track, and even harder to trap.

I'm not talking about morons digging up coffins to see if the deceased looks too fresh, because, as the saying goes, the ignorant people will belive everything.

There was even no point in educating such people. These primitive ghoul specialists worked for themselves, and the honest Hunters worked for themselves.

Times were changing, people were wiser, and there was less and less superstition. Finally, only the latter remained, such as the Vanhelsingers, who approached vampirism from a strictly scientific standpoint.

And here three trends emerged. Some treated vampirism as a treatable disease and tried to find a cure for it. Others decided that there was no point in trying to be treated, but there was a need to find a universal remedy for the extermination of bloodsuckers.

And finally, the third one, which wants, above all, to tear away the mystery of immortality from you. These lasted the longest, but they too eventually disappeared from the world as a result of a change of generations.

People lacked faith that you existed at all. Or to put it another way: the belief that vampires are representatives of the Goth subculture has spread. Ordinary people who put on extended veneers on their canines at the dentist dress up in stylish clothes, i.e. capes with a red lining, cylinders, lace shirts and so on, paint their eyes black and drink animal blood on their orgies, bought by liters at butcher."

Never grunted.

"It's very interesting, but what does it have to do with us?" he asked.

"It has one thing. Nobody is chasing you anymore for scientific purposes, because almost nobody believes in you. Now the sect is doing it, for reasons of a religious nature, and they may survive the next centuries without dying so easily.

As a representative of the Indian people, you are more familiar with religions than anyone else, and you know well how they affect entire generations. The spiritual leader of the Rasts knows this too, and that is why he formed his group.

He took those rastafari who held more radical views than the rest and organized them into a separate sect with the goal of cleansing humanity. Among other things, from vampires, but also from people who help them. With their mortal lovers and friends."

"We know it, cat."

Lasalle nodded.

"You know. But you have no idea who specifically directs the Rasts and where their obsession comes from, and what power they have. You have to realize what you are facing."

"So, with what?" Gerard was obviously getting sick of this conversation. Their interlocutor did not make an impression on him, but the necessity to stay on this roof - yes. He didn't like heights, unlike Theo, who often wandered the rooftops at night as if he were a cat himself.

Lasalle looked at him with his almond eyes, now glowing ruby red in the darkness.

"With an extermination machine," he replied emphatically, "once set in motion, it cannot be stopped. Even if you catch up with the Rast leader, another one will be found shortly. This is how the sects work, and this particular one was founded for one purpose only. To destroy vampires. And it works effectively so far."

"Are you sure that... so successful?" Fronda squeezed the hand of his silent companion reassuringly. Even he succumbed to a mood of horror that slipped imperceptibly between them.

The creature smiled with subtle irony.

"People have always been determined and effective in the subject of killing. Since they were ape-men. If they set a goal, they won't be persuaded soon enough.

I wouldn't be surprised if you were already some of the last representatives of your species in the world. So far you have been very lucky after all. Hunters were few and they wasted a great deal of time on their research experiments. This made them less effective. Rasts act primitively, with blind brutality, and even with the latest technological marvels at their disposal, they are savages, ready to use a microscope as a club. All in the name of their religion, although it's by definition absolutely peaceful. They are not the first to distort the original message. I have seen a lot of such before, I tried to help once, but with time I realized that my interference brings more misfortune than good. Since then, I have remained a passive observer, as have every deity of humanity who wants to at least... not harm. After all, they are no crueler than a man made in their image and likeness. A fragile and transient creature, but monstrous, like the worst of the demons he brings to life in his stories."

He meowed unexpectedly until everyone started.

"Who are you?" Oggy asked hoarsely, "About people, that's understandable, but how do you know so much about these... deities?"

"None of them exist," muttered Gerard firmly.

Lasalle laughed.

"People would love it, I assure you. What a wonderful life it would be, without fear of the consequences of vile deeds, of the invisible doom that punishes you for your bad deeds.

I must worry you, the long gone star. Nothing in the world is as materialists would like, although the human perception of the nature of the retribution they can receive is infinitely naive.

Probably the closest to the truth is the theory that not so much a higher being punishes a man for what he does, but the man himself prepares a whip on his back all his life.

That with each deed he adds or subtracts the weight of the chain that once tied it, as it was beautifully expressed by Charles Dickens, a great one in a pen, but poor in spirit..."

"Nonsense!" Gerard raised his voice inadvertently, irritated by the argument. "How do you know about this?"

The creature raised his hand gracefully, setting it flat in the air. A ball of fire appeared above the human, though furry hand. It swirled for a moment, then exploded. In the glow of disintegrating sparks, the friends saw the image of thousands of demonic images from all over the world changing rapidly like in a kaleidoscope.

"I myself was a god, a human oracle, a messenger of witches, called Behemoth..." Lasalle hummed with a bloodcurdling smile.

"Stop these tricks!" the actor could not stand it and finally exploded like a safety grenade. "We did not come here to watch the circus performances!

I may be a vampire now, but that doesn't mean I have to become an idiot and believe in some medieval witchcraft! Don't expect that from me. I've seen better tricks in my life. I've seen freaks like you before, too, and one more won't make me change my mind."

There was a brief silence after this statement. Friends subconsciously expected something terrible to happen now, but nothing like that happened.

Multi-colored sparks rose to the sky and went out, leaving them in the previous twilight, lit only by the lights of the big city.

"Don't mind him," said Fronda at last. "He doesn't believe in a half of what he sees, let alone something he cannot see. I hope you not insulted. Cheetah sometimes talks a lot, just to talk, he certainly doesn't want to offend you."

Lasalle yawned and stretched lazily like a cat in front of the fireplace. He didn't look offended or even agitated.

"It's irrelevant anyway," he said dismissively, "you've known me for a long time. It's not easy to impress me. Looking at people's windows is my favorite pastime. I observe the world, mainly at night, because I never sleep. I naturally hear and see a lot, and I know what to expect from whom."

"Exactly... That's why I asked for a meeting. We really need advice because we don't know what to do anymore."

Theo looked at Lasalle pleadingly. Others were silent, afraid to even sigh.

"I've already given you advice, use it as soon as possible," replied the creature of the night calmly, "and trust no one along the way."

"Are you sure that's all we can do?"

"Yes. This is what I am sure of."

"Sorry," Never said. "You said yourself that you weren't getting involved in anything. So how do you know what's best for us? You know a lot about people, because you have been associated with them for millennia, but do you also know about us? After all, you probably didn't look in our windows, we would have noticed something."

Lasalle scratched thoughtfully behind his left ear, then flicked it as the animal.

"You're human too. Diet has nothing to do with your humanity, just like a slightly longer life.

Neither gods nor demons of you. I became interested in your fight for survival because you are outsiders, just like me and others.

Ordinary people hated you, although you are only slightly different from them, and they don't believe in you now, but they make you look like stars. A new art trend, literature and vampire movie in which you are romantic lovers, sometimes straight and sometimes homosexual. I was even surprised that there were still some Hunters somewhere, but in the end, there had to be some who did not succumb to fashionable trends. They passed on knowledge to each other and hunted. Some of them fell victim to more warlike vampires or other creatures, the rest were unlucky and ended up in prisons or psychiatrists. Not without your interference. The action of letting the police attack the Hunters was really well thought out. Either way, they're gone. But the Rasts are, and I must worry you, they will stay."

"Can we put them... also in a straitjacket?" Oggy asked helplessly.

Lasalle looked at her and pursed his lips slightly in a predatory grimace. He now looked as if it was about to bristle and hiss like any cat when it sees a dog. However, he mastered himself.

"No. They are protected by rights relating to the freedom of religious practice. This is your current problem. The most powerful weapon you had in this fight was thrown out of your hand."

"So what do you advise?" Fronda decided to make it clear.

The night creature bowed his head.

"As I said, run away," he replied, "that's the only thing you can do. You are not going to win this war."

"We have nowhere to go," Lily whispered. It was the first time she had spoken since the beginning of this conversation. She wasn't scared. She was simply stating a fact.

"It's true," Lasalle agreed. "You have not. Especially you. However, as long as you are in constant motion, they will have less chance of catching you. Fortunately for you, you can travel with almost no hassle, make the most of it and don't stay anywhere longer than you have to. If you know any ordinary people, cut off all contact with them immediately. This is the only advice I can give you."

His spine arched and he leapt over to one of the rooftops below with a long leap, signaling the end of the discussion.

"Wait!" Theo called after him. "At least tell me, who are we fighting? Who is in charge of the Rasts?"

"Move your head and search in the past!" Lasalle shouted back to him. "And remember that in this particular case everything is quite obvious!"

He meowed loudly, shrank a bit and limped on his front paw and ran along the decorative ledge, disappearing from his friends' sight.

"My word. We found out a lot..." Never looked at Fronda. "What now?"

"Nothing. I mean, we are going back to the ruin where we are staying. We have to confer. How do you feel?"

This unexpected question drew friends' attention to something that should have alerted them earlier. They all felt a strong weakness and a strange emptiness, as if they had not eaten for several days.

"What's up?"

"That's why I insisted on hunting before we got here. Lasalle is not one of us, but he has something to do with us. He is, as it were, an energy vampire. He absorbs someone else's life energy like a sponge."

"Nice," Gerard said, irritated again, "you could have warned us!"

Fronda shrugged.

"Let's get out of here better."

They descended from the roof as carefully as they could, passed the technical aisle and mingled with the crowd of people just leaving the theater. They had to keep a tight grip because everyone was hungry, especially Lily, who was at the very height of vampire voracity. The least of the problem was with Oggy - they walked into the night shop for a while and bought her some foil-wrapped steaks. However, they had to wait with their appetite satisfied. They dared to do it only in the vicinity of the North Railway Station. They deliberately plunged into the most forbidden places, where even the police were afraid to enter recently, and they did not have to wait long for potential victims to be found.

This was their favorite hunting method - provoking a few scum to attack and then relishing their blood, often flavored with cheap alcohol or drugs.

Lily liked it very much. From the very first day, as Fronda told, she liked to provoke rapists, tempted by easy prey, a delicate girl with a white cane, alone in an empty alley.

More than one pervert has already paid with his life trying to indulge his desires, because Lily did not leave such an attacker a drop of blood in his veins. Blindness did not bother her at all from such ambushes. She played her part with such passion and skill that even Never felt an amateur with her.

"She is the most terrifying of us all," he said to his friends, witnessing her hunting for the first time, and there was undeniable something in it.

After drinking blood copiously, they finally decided to return to the temporary shelter, until no Rast had discovered their trail yet. Meeting Lasalle not only weakened them physically, but also made them nervous. They had no doubt that the strange, half-mythical creature was speaking sincerely. There was no reason for him to lie. Even so, they couldn't believe what he was saying and avoided talking about it for a while. Only when they got off at the Bobigny station and continued on foot they speak freely.

"Don't be angry, Frondi, but this friend of yours is terrible," said Gerard openly. "Where did you get him from?"

Theo shrugged slightly.

"You know I like to sit on the roof at night sometimes, and that's always been the case. He just came up to me once. I started stroking him, because you understand, I love animals... And at one point he sat down next to me and started a conversation. Oh, a whim. Sorry, I thought he would really help us."

"Well, he gave the best advice he could have," Lily put in.

"I don't know," Theo shook his head. "He cannot be called omniscient or infallible. However, he's very old indeed, and was old when the pyramids were built."

"Because he told you so?" Gerard asked ironically.

Fronda kicked some pebble. The actor's disbelief got on his nerves at times, and he preferred to pour out himself on a dead object before slapping his friend.

"He said," he admitted, "but I believe him. He speaks all languages. He knows and is able to explain all the secrets that annoy archaeologists and historians.

He can read hieroglyphs, petroglyphs, Sumerian cuneiform and Incan kipu. His image appears on the Babylonian gate of Ishtar and on the cylindrical seals of the Hittites.

He was worshiped in Egypt as the goddess Bastet, and in South America as the divine jaguar. The funniest thing is that Lasalle never really had any divine aspirations.

He's just an observer, he's fascinated by people, and he's a great source of emotional energy that he feeds on. At times, he exaggerated his greed and did harm. The Africans who took his toll in his time called him "wobo" and were scared stiff. It's the reason why people do not trust cats."

"Not all of them," Oggy protested. Though she was half a dog, she loved cats and it hurts her that they were afraid of her and would run away as soon as she got close.

"That's true," Theo smiled, "there are those who love them, and even those who subconsciously know about the existence of Lasalle and worship the good buzzards for his sake. Sometimes he befriends them on a whim, you know, when he's curious about somebody's mental potential. He inspired many writers, for example, Mikhail Bulgakov and Edgar Allan Poe. For Alfred van Vogt, he was the prototype of Coeurl, an intelligent alien killer who massacred interstellar travelers. For Lovecraft, the vivid concept of the Cats of Saturn. He is also Lewis Caroll's Cheshire Cat. Aslan C.S. Lewis, although he is actually closer to Ginger. Thanks to his acquaintance with him, Bulat Okudzhava wrote one of his best works. I could keep counting for a long time, but that's not the point. I don't know who he really is, but I'm far from a scientist who has to break everything down into its component parts and catalog, otherwise he'll go crazy. I just recognize his existence."

They walked in silence for a while. There was no living soul around, the sounds of the big city were left somewhere on the side, they could feel safe, but nevertheless something was tormenting them.

"Do you think you really are the last one?" Oggy asked softly at last.

Never shook himself violently.

"Spit the words out! It's impossible. I spoke to Octavio myself recently, and Theo had just driven Dean to Poland, and he saw nothing strange. Anyway, the "oysters" probably still exist, since Bell visited us. He was as much alive as possible."

"That's true," Fronda admitted. "And yet none of our friends are answering the phone anymore. Neither Octavio nor Dea nor Conan. I cannot call Lenor either."

"There is definitely some simple explanation..." Never raised his voice in nervousness, but then fell silent. His sensitive hearing suddenly caught in the distance the characteristic siren sound.

"Fire department," muttered the werewolf, who had been hearing it for a few seconds.

Lily tightened her hand on her shoulder. She heard the sound, too, and sensed something else.

"Sniffle," she said, "do you smell the smoke?"

"Something is on fire somewhere," Oggy agreed, sniffing eagerly.

Alarmed by the noise of the engine, they jumped to the side of the road, among sparse trees. Fire truck passed at full speed. It traveled another mile, then the sirens stopped.

"It's... close," Theo whispered, pointing. They all thought the same and exchanged terrified glances.

"Impossible..."

Hiding among the trees, they approached the villa they occupied cautiously.

The sight that showed them confirmed their worst fears. The hut was on fire and the car in the yard was on fire. Firefighters fought the fire, there was also a gendarmerie unit on the spot.

"Run," Never ordered, whispering for some reason. In the confusion, no one outside would hear him anyway.

*****

"We are homeless again, broke... All our movable property is lost. All we still have are our teeth and what's on the back. Anyone have any idea?" Gerard asked as they found a temporary shelter with no little difficulty in the temporarily closed construction site.

Having ripped off a rusty padlock, they hid in a tool container, hoping that no one would look at it for now. It would be an extremely unfortunate coincidence if the workers returned to work that day. Friends hoped that this would not happen. Lily, like her mentor, was undeniably a "moth" and sunlight could seriously harm her, especially since she was just beginning her nightlife.

"To the point. Who has what?" Never asked matter-of-factly.

It turned out that the losses were not that serious. According to the procedures developed over the centuries, when they left their place of temporary stay, they took with them a complete set of documents, their secondary weapons (if they had a local permit for it) and all the money they had at their disposal.

Each of them - apart from Oggy - had a similar bag like Fronda, slung over the shoulder on a long strap, in which, just for storing the most necessary trinkets, the victims of the fire were mainly spare clothes and small electronics, plus a rental dodge. The only blow that was more severe was the loss of an iron supply of canned blood, but there was nothing that could be done about it.

"We've had much less," concluded Fronda carelessly.

"The basic question is: accident or arson?" Oggy mechanically nibbled on her tail, simultaneously trying to contain the urge to completely transform into a dog. "If the latter, it all points to a role for Bell."

"You didn't like him from the beginning," Lily remarked coldly. She sat quietly in the corner, as still as the marble statue. It was doubtful that anything would throw her off balance.

"Because he smelled like fear! And I felt a lie in his voice... Something was wrong with him, but I thought he was just afraid of the Rasts..."

"He definitely was scared of someone and probably not us. Lasalle was right to say that we must not trust anyone now. "Oysters" have always been honest and loyal, if they changed, everything could be done. But what next?" Never looked around. The faint smudge of light under the barricaded door of the container clearly said that the day had already risen. "We will not come up with anything today. We need to rest. I take first watch, second Oggy, third Cheetah. After dusk we will consider our next steps."

Fronda yawned nervously.

"You're probably right. I'm exhausted. In the evening we will talk and prepare a sensible action plan. As long as it is possible at all."

He lay down on the pile of bags in the corner, hugging Lily against him. Oggy curled up at their feet, covering her face with her tail. Gerard shrugged and followed their example.

Despite his earlier declaration, Never did not wake anyone up in the end. He did not feel like sleeping.

He never needed much sleep, and many years of training at the temple of the goddess Kali had taught him to manage his needs.

In case of extreme need, he might not go to bed even for a week, but then he actually had to rest for several hours. One night's watch posed no challenge to him.

As soon as the sun went down, the friends began to wake up spontaneously and by the time it got dark, they were already on their feet. They left the construction site hurriedly on their way downtown. If the headquarters of the Rasts was in Paris, they must have been there too until they found him. Lasalle advised them to escape, but even Gerard, who was undeniably the weakest link in their team, rejected the possibility.

"I've thought it over," Never said on the way. In my opinion, only someone who knows us very well can be involved. He knows where to look and knows all the weak points. And so..."

"One of us," Fronda finished.

"Lasalle said, "Seek in the past". That would suggest we know him. All indications are that he made it to the "oysters" and somehow intimidated Bell. I don't know about you, only one person comes to mind."

"Me too."

"Who are you talking about?" Lily asked. She walks alongside the men, one hand on Oggy's shoulder and the other holding his cane. It hit the ground lightly, almost imperceptibly.

"A guy named Gusto Vanderbelt," Gerard replied grimly.

"Maybe it's Amargo Lorca?" Fronda suggested uncertainly. Even though so many years had passed and so much had happened, he still hoped to salvage something from his former friendship.

Never shook his head decisively.

"Amargo, even if he did survive that blast, is too crazy to lead anyone. He's always acted alone, and I don't think that could change in any situation. Everything points to Gusto. He was thoroughly brainwashed at the Van Helsing Institute... but something's off here. If it is what I think it is, why did it start acting alone? Why did he turn against the vanhelsingers, attacked Medlab, and then organized his own group?"

"Wait a minute," Fronda paused, "Do you think he is the one behind the spread of IVH and Medlab? Where did this idea come from?"

"Call it a hunch if you like, but I just did a detailed analysis of what we know. Everything fits together for me."

"Well, let's say," Theo was rather unconvinced. "So how do you find him?"

"First of all, it would be good to know what the gendarmes discovered about the arson situation in the villa in which we were staying. Maybe they found something that could be useful to us?"

The friends looked at each other.

"Good idea," admitted Gerard, "but how to implement it? Do you think the gendarmes will tell everything to the first person who asks them about the investigation? I don't think so."

"You need to have good touch," Never agreed with him.

The actor shrugged and looked at his commander with pity.

"What am I going to change into when all our rags burned? Alternatively, I can make a leaf loincloth and pretend to be Tarzan."

Fronda laughed.

"With your look? You're kidding, rather a shipwrecked man on a desert island. You're skinny as if you were freshly released from the death camp. Tarzan had muscles to look at, he was a bull not a man, look at Johnny Weissmuller."

"I'll go," Lily interrupted a nascent quarrel.

The men looked at her confused.

"You?"

"Yes. I'll go to the police station, tell some teary stories and tell the truth," the girl smiled sweetly. "The blind are very well perceived by public service officials. I can assure you, they are never suspected of anything, not even an innocent lie."

"Hmmm," Theo scratched his head, not entirely convinced, "I'd rather not let go of you alone now."

"Why alone?" Lily opened her haversack and took out what looked like a coil of webbing straps. "Oggy, I need you now in doggy form."

"What's that?" Never asked.

"Harness. Souvenir. I once had a guide dog."

"What happened to him?"

Lily paused, the harness in her hand, and pressed her lips together for a moment.

"Someone poisoned him. Apparently, the neighbors were bothered by barking."

"Motherfuckers!" Fronda could not stand it. Gerard, too, looked as if he wanted to say a heavier word, but managed to keep quiet.

"Regardless of the country, people are different," Lily muttered. "I lived between not very pleasant ones, so it turned out. Does not matter. Oggy, come over here."

The girl eagerly threw off her dress, transforming into a sheepdog. She shook herself, barked happily and ran to her friend, who deftly fastened the harness on her and straightened up. She put on the large, dark glasses that she didn't usually wear, and made a helpless face.

"Well, I would be fooled," admitted Gerard honestly, after examining both of them carefully.

"Well then," agreed Never, though not very willingly. "We lurk at the station to be close just in case. You never know."

"It's unnecessary, but thank you." Lily felt the guide by the harness and took it in her hand. "I'll talk to the gendarmes, it's gonna take a while, so don't go crazy. Nothing will happen to me. Even if one of the Rasts followed us, he would not attack us at the police station. Anyway, you'll spot him sooner than he will spot me."

"How do you want to play it?" Fronda asked.

"Let me say I know about the fire. That my partner had seen a couple of Gypsies with a small child on this property the day before. That he doesn't want to get involved in anything, but I can't stop thinking about it. And I will ask if no one has died for sure. And could it be arson? Not everyone likes the Gypsies in the neighborhood."

Gerard smiled approvingly. His artistic soul was able to appreciate the invention of his new friend and her undeniable acting skills.

"Remember not to fall out of the role even for a moment,'" he warned her just in case. "You gotta put that bull on them right. They may ask many questions, such as where are you from and where do you live, something like that. You'll have to improvise."

"No worries. I can handle."

It had to be admitted that the calm self-confidence that is characteristic of this girl is impressive, especially considering her disability. She had a decidedly strong personality and was able to impose her point of view on others. Even Never, who would normally never let go of the "jailbait" for independent action. It had to be admitted, however, that the situation was far from normal, even to which he and his friends had grown accustomed for centuries.

Fate was on their side - near the gendarmerie station responsible for this quiet, generally suburban quarter, there was a small vacancy, not yet completely finished. It was built as a shop, but it did not yet have the necessary safeguards. They got inside easily. From there, they had a good view of the nearby houses, streets, expressway, and especially of the station illuminated by two lanterns.

"Go," Never turned to Lily and the werewolf after briefly examining the area. "If something goes wrong, make Oggy howl twice like a wolf. We will hear you easily."

The girl nodded briefly, adjusted her glasses and went to the street. They watched her for a moment as she walked confidently, holding the harness of a sheepdog trotting beside her in one hand and a white cane in the other.

From a distance she looked so harmless, so gentle that no one would believe how dangerous she was.

The impression of fragility and defenselessness was enhanced by an airy ankle-length skirt and a loose blouse with long sleeves, matched to the color.

Loose blonde hair blew in the light breeze, falling over Lily Ann's back like a waterfall of liquid gold.

"Stop staring like that." Never nudged Fronda in the side. "Take a cell phone and call ours. Here's the phone book. Do you remember the code?"

"Yes. Yes of course."

"Then sit in the corner and call. To each three times. Maybe you can connect with someone. We will be careful if nothing happens."

Theo nodded absentmindedly, picked up the notebook he had been given, and walked away to the corner. Never's notes were always encrypted in a way that he made up - he used phonetic

Sanskrit, written in Glagolitic characters. Only a few people around the world knew this system and could read the notes made with it, and even fewer knew that it had a second bottom.

So Fronda was hopelessly against the wall, patiently tapping out the numbers and listening to the signal that was trying to say "No one is home" as clearly as he could.

In desperation, he finally called the unlisted number of the military base in Klewki, where he and his friends lived for some time. The call was answered by a man who understood neither English nor French, and finally cursed Fronda in Polish, then breaking the call. It all looked rather suspicious indeed.

"It does not make sense. They couldn't all change numbers at one time, including those junks from the base. Was Lasalle right in saying we might be the last of our blood?" he said finally, lowering his hand helplessly with the phone.

"That Lasalle is a pessimist," Never said over his shoulder. "Perhaps someone gave the generalized termination of contacts slogan in the press announcement, as we are used to. Could it happen? It could. Will you swear that not? We haven't read the newspapers lately, because we had something else on our minds, so we don't know what was in the small ads columns."

"I suppose so..." Theo looked unconvinced.

"Don't be a child. In the past, there were no telephones at all, then you had to fly to the post office or to a telephone booth to call someone, and we still lived somehow.

Now everyone is crazy that when someone does not answer the phone, he probably is dead."

Fronda listened to his friend's arguments with one ear and turned the phone in his fingers at the same time, watching it with a certain disgust.

"They could reduce this stuff somehow," he murmured finally, "big and heavy, it doesn't fit in a pocket..."

"You see. You're used to making things easier and you grimace that it's not bigger," Gerard pointed out, "and you know that the first such phone was described by a certain Erich Kastner in a children's book?"

"Who cares?"

"Shut up," Never silenced them. "Lily just left the station."

All three went to the window.

"Where is she going?" Theo was surprised.

"She knows what she's doing. Unlike you, she has a lot of reason. She knows she can be watched. We follow her, only carefully. That just wasn't enough for the cops to get on our backs."

They circled the area in a wide arc and sneaked past several semi-detached houses, then crossing the street just in front of Lily and her companion approaching from the police station. Oggy barked cheerfully at the sight of them and wagged her tail. Never silenced his friend by placing a finger on her nose and pointing to a nearby park, empty at this time. There you could talk in peace.

"Did you learn anything?" he asked nervously as they reached the children's playground in the middle of the park.

Lily, led by her guide to a stand with a swing suspended, felt for a swing hanging on thick ropes and sat on it, setting the device in a slight motion.

"Nothing specific, actually. They confirm deliberate arson, they used barbecue lighter and probably homemade thermite or black powder, they don't know exactly," she brushed her hair away from her face. "Nothing else they can say so far. They collected a lot of material for the laboratory, but today is Sunday, no one has come for it yet. Everything they found is still in the back. Of course, we wouldn't be allowed in there, but you can deal with it. I talked to the gendarmes and Oggy went there and sniffed exactly what she could. Anyway, even I felt a burn from these finds..."

She grimaced in disgust and rocked back on the swing.

"A nasty stench."

"They questioned someone?" Never asked.

"Yes, all of the neighborhood houses. Nobody saw anything until the fire started burning for good. However, everyone confirms that they heard the singing before. According to them, it was like humming without words. They thought they were some tourists and didn't pay attention to it then."

Theo crouched next to the werewolf, stroked her head, and took the harness off her.

"Come on, baby, be polite and show what you can," he encouraged, "become a girl."

You could see Oggy was trying to obey him, but her efforts had failed.

"Leave her," Gerard advised, "she's in the same troubles as before, only now we can't count on Vandis to help. You wouldn't even know where to look for him."

"Come on," Theo shook himself at the mention of Winger. "Better let him not help us anymore. It's because of him that Never is possessed now, like Annieliese Michel."

"Somehow I don't see that it bothers him, so it shouldn't be for us either."

Never's ghoulish companion initially depressed them all, even Gerard, who didn't really believe in any possession. Finally they just got used to it. They called this strange entity "Partner" for their own use, and after a while they stopped paying attention to its external manifestations, quite rare, by the way.

"But they didn't find any bodies," Lily continued. "Which is understandable, because these bodies were at that time meeting with Lasall. However, it seems to me that someone may not have known about it... or even be convinced that we are inside."

"Yes... The car behind the house could even tell them about it. Bell betrayed, we don't know, voluntarily or under duress. According to the rules of art, we should find him now and punish him, but I honestly don't see the point," Never said glumly. "He's a pawn. We have to find the one who rules it. Him and the entire Rast organization."

He scratched his head. He had some idea - that fire, the sudden silence of the whole world-wide community, the intimidation of "oysters" and all the rest somehow did not fit "Saint Obadiah," whoever he was. He began to suspect that they had made a serious mistake when looking for an Old Testament sect. Plus, something told him that the name was the key to solving the mystery of Rast effectiveness. He looked at Oggy, panting with her tongue hanging out.

"Well, our little girl? Try a little harder," he asked. "We're gonna need your human abilities."

"I'm afraid it's impossible," Theo muttered.

"Shit... I'll have to take care of this myself."

"I guess you can? As far as I remember, your IQ is well over two hundred points, you are better than we are, schmendricks," Gerard sneered. He wasn't really in the mood for jokes, but he wanted to cover the obvious fact that he felt like a duck on fire when the hunters were invisible and were always a few steps ahead of them. "It's strange how rarely you use it."

Never took the challenge. Perhaps he had not even realized what the former actor, and now one of his closest friends, was saying, because his thoughts were occupied with something else.

"Let's get out of here. We have to get to the center, I have an emergency den there."

"How much emergency?" Theo asked distrustfully.

"As far as I know, no one knows it. I never even told you. Just in case."

"Yeah. You don't know what you don't know, and you never know."

"It's good that you understand that, knight. Let's go, before any unauthorized person spots us."

The "Emergency Den" turned out to be an authentic painter's atelier in the Montparnasse district from the time of Modigliani, entered in the register of monuments and therefore untouched. It was unlikely that anyone would want to live there. It was located in the attic of an old, carefully renovated tenement house, but the workers did not move the room with the sign "Here lived and created..." The name meant nothing to the friends, but neither of them was an art connoisseur. The atelier was dusty and littered. The only source of daylight was once a dormer window, now boarded up. There were empty bottles everywhere, crumpled papers, and here and there - judging by the smell - dead mice. In the center of the room stood a rotten, crumbling easel and a low table with a set of stone-dried paints.

"Picturesque interior, so to speak. It's not the Dracula's Palace," said Gerard, looking around the studio.

"Well, it is not," Rajah agreed with him, "but it has its advantages. Look here."

He walked over to the part-wood wall, stuck his finger in a knot-hole in one of the planks, and swung it open like a hinge.

"If so, this is where the road leads to the roof, and from there to other roofs. They are close enough to each other that you can jump without fear. There are firefighters stuck in the wall leading from a few houses downstairs. But I hope you don't have to use this escape route. As I already mentioned, I never told anyone about this place. We'll get some sleep and move on at dusk."

"Move on?" Theo looked at him with some disappointment. He was already arranging this place in his mind to make it more comfortable.

"We cannot stay anywhere longer now. I'm beginning to understand what Lasalle was trying to tell us. And I don't like it at all."

Fronda led Lily to a still looking quite solid chest, wiped it with a spare t-shirt, taken from the bag, and helped the girl sit up comfortably.

"It's a bit spartan here," he said, looking around for anything that, with a little imagination, might be considered a bed. "Let's make it clear right away: are we supposed to sleep on the floor? This floor?"

"Exactly," Never opened the second chest, from the lid of which rose a cloud of dust immediately. From inside he took out, one by one, neatly wrapped in nylon, brand new military blankets, at which the expressions of his friends' expressions instantly brightened.

He glanced at them with a smile.

"I can prepare myself for all possible contingencies," he reached into the crate once more. This time he took a small bundle out of it, which turned out to be a wallet full of hundred-dollar bills.

"Forewarned is forearmed."

His friends whistled in admiration and applauded him. Never divided the money fairly into four pieces, handed each of them except for Oggy, who was still a dog, and put the wallet in his pocket.

"I used to have more of these "hollows", he confessed, "but most were found by the Hunters and appropriated what they contained. Okay, we spread the blankets and sleep. Who's on first watch? I pass today, I'm terribly tired. I need to sleep."

Fronda looked at Gerard.

"Do you have a coin?"

"No, only bills."

"Then we'll play some game. Even or Odd?"

"Even."

The first watch fell on the Fronda. He spent it sitting against the wall, trying not to fall asleep from boredom.

Oggy gasped in her sleep, curled at his feet, clearly happy in the dream. Lily Ann lay on the blanket to the right, also asleep so peacefully as if nothing special was happening.

At one after midnight, Theo woke Gerard and lay down on his own next to Lily, falling asleep almost immediately.

At dusk they left the studio, taking their blankets after a brief consultation. Since they were living as the homeless tramps now, they could be useful to them, especially since they were not ordinary rugs. Their specific cut made it possible to use them as a cloak with a hood or a large bag, and when folded and fastened with straps sewn to them, they made a handy package, slung over the shoulder like a backpack.

First of all, they had to hunt. They had no canned blood, and they were all hungry. Only after they had satiated it, could they think what to do next.

"I think we need to find Bell after all," Theo said after they finished their hunt. It took a little longer than it should have been because Lily, being a very young vampire, needed far more food than the rest.

"It will not be that difficult, we all know where to look for "fossils"," Never took a tissue from the haversack and put it in Lily's hand. The girl carefully wiped the remnants of blood from her mouth. Contrary to the image promoted by horror movies, a typical bloodsucker after a "meal" is not dressed in red at all. Only complete beginners are unable to draw blood from their victims so as not to get dirty, but they quickly learn moderation and neatness while eating and strictly observe it. This helps to avoid suspicion and, consequently, detection.

"Yeah... just, you know, don't hit them right between the eyes. I think Bell was forced to cooperate, so let's treat them, you know, empathetic."

"If it is possible, knight," Rajah assuredly promised. "Where do we start?"

Theo looked thoughtful.

"Oysters tend to linger in the poorest neighborhoods where the corruption is the worst. They feel safe there. There, everyone watches his nose and has more trouble than the appearance or habits of the neighbors, as long as they do not concern him. Personally, I would look around Rue Saint Denise."

"Do you know it well?" Gerard asked. He did not admit that he had been there himself - out of curiosity.

"Sure. When I was hunted once, it was before the last war, I lived there for six months, with fleas, lice and prostitutes. I know all the nooks and crannies, and I know where to hide so that even the tracking dogs won't find you."

"Come on then."

Rue de Saint Denis has never had a good reputation, and is now known mainly for the sex business that occupies its front seats.

Despite various improvements, the street's character has not changed. In the back, where no one is looking, all kinds of social scum nests in the old days, just like taken out of Emil Zola's novel "L'assommoir".

Of course, asking anyone for anything would be pointless here. Normally friends would use psycholocation, but "oysters" can disguise themselves from it, and they usually do.

It was possible to assume that they would do it all the more now. Fortunately, they were not helpless. They had Oggy with them, who remembered Bell's scent well.

She was catching him with her nose in various places now, but she would not stop there because it was cold. Bell had been to those places, but had left them a while ago, so there was no point in checking them out.

Only where he seemed to be stronger did they stop for a moment, trying to find something specific. It was almost 3 am when the sniffing werewolf finally found a stronger and fresher trail that led her and her companions to the most unexpected place - the Church of Saint-Leu-Saint-Gilles.

"Are you sure?" asked Theo in surprise, contemplating the monumental structure.

Vampires generally avoid sacred buildings because of the unique aura that prevails there, which causes them almost physical pain. The reason for this is their extraordinary sensitivity - and it does not matter whether it is a Christian, Judaic or Muslim temple, or some other one.

Oggy barked, clearly insisting on hers.

"Here we go," Never sighed. "Lily, hold her tight, let them think she's your guide."

"No one will be there at this time anyway. In France, churches are not well attended, to say the least. Even I know that," Lily took off her usual dark glasses on the street and put them in her haversack.

"Indeed, there is no one in Notre Dame at night, let alone here," Gerard agreed.

Despite these words, they were extremely careful. Fortunately, they did not have to enter the temple itself - Oggy led them to the back, where the entrance to the dungeon was located. They were not even fair catacombs, but simply cellars, serving as a storehouse of various rubbish. In the last one, they finally saw Bell. He was lying against the wall, curled up in a fetal position, and had obviously been dead for a good twenty-four hours. His hair was white as snow, and his clothes were splashed profusely with the frozen blood.

"What a misfortune," Never muttered. He knelt beside the body and began examining it diligently.

"No visible injuries," he said finally, "strange thing. Traces of massive bleeding from the mouth. And here..."

He barely opened Bell's fingers, clutching the crumpled piece of paper. He straightened up and, in the light of the flashlight, read aloud the scribbles spreading out in all directions, forming one word "Preserve". It ended in a completely illegible zigzag, giving the impression that Bell wanted to write much more.

"He was poisoned," Theo understood. "Oysters eat mostly canned food, usually they don't hunt, lest they attract attention. Someone must have poisoned their stuff."

"Not someone, but Gusto Vanderbelt," Never put the paper in his pocket. "Stop hiding your head in the sand, the matter is clear. We are dealing with a perfidy to which no one has gone before."

"Bell knew we would look for him and find him," whispered Gerard in horror.

"So it seems. He warned us with the last of his strength."

Until now, they always brought "canned food" with them, but for several years none of them even touched it. They no longer liked it, they even felt bad about it, although they had not had such problems before. It was not just their whim, it seemed, but their sense of danger.

"What now?" Lily asked. Even she succumbed to a mood of horror, though she could not, for obvious reasons, see the dead Bell.

Rajah tweaked his fingers on his lower lip, as he always did when he was thinking hard about something.

"We need to find shelter for the day," he said after a while, "here is a closed church cemetery nearby. There will probably be something there, or rather nobody is there. Such cemeteries were closed a long time ago, they exist only as a relic of old times, and because it would be stupid to plow them up."

"Yes," said Theo, "I've spent my days on these more than once. The living one does not go there, and the dead will not do any harm."

"Then let's go."

The cemetery adjacent to the church was indeed shut off, which they handled easily. The area was overgrown with shrubs that had not been trimmed for a long time, among which the graves strewn with dead leaves could hardly be seen. In the center they found a small mausoleum - as the half-obliterated plaque proclaimed, members of the Fibi family were resting there. Inside, it was pleasantly dark and cool. Knowing that you are sleeping on someone else's grave is not pleasant, but this time no one paid much attention to it. The situation became so dangerous that it was better not to freak out.

"The first watch is for Fronda," Never said. "Then Cheetah. I have to sleep. In the afternoon I will go looking for a place with internet access.

I have a few things to check. Until my return you don't move a step from here, okay?"

They nodded to him without objection. They spread the blankets on the stone floor and lay down on them, trying to fall asleep as soon as possible and not think about where they were.

As promised, Never got up in the afternoon. He wrapped himself up a bit, exchanged a few words with Gerard, who was on watch with Oggy dozing at his feet, then left. He hoped to find an internet cafe near Galieni Station, only half a mile away. These types of facilities were just beginning to become popular, although Never, well versed in the dynamics of technology development, predicted that they might soon be as common as regular cafes.

It turned out that a lonely stroll through the Rue Saint Denis is quite dangerous for a young, handsome and well-dressed man with a dark complexion and hair braided. After the fourth aggression by a passer-by eager for male charms, Never capitulated and entered the first hairdressing salon he encountered.

"What hairstyle do you want?" asked with a polite smile a scissor-master with an almost feminine beauty and such a voice, slightly painted and in a slightly exaggerated way smelling of a floral composition.

"I trust you," the Indian muttered, taking his place on the armchair.

The man removed the ruby clasp from his braid, then undid it, brushed it and examined it for a moment.

"You have really beautiful, healthy hair, which is rarely seen today. Would you be interested..."

"Definitely not!"

"...donating them to the Cancer Foundation? For a wig for chemotherapy patients?"

"Oh, if that's it, please," Never breathed a sigh of relief, which the barber took with discreet amusement.

He washed his head, braided his hair again, cut it as short as possible against the skin, and only then began to model the client's hair into a fashionable hairstyle, selected from a catalog bound in half-leather. He dried it with a dryer, fixed it with a bit of strong gel, and seemed very pleased with the result of his efforts.

Never's new image may not have made him ignored, but the amount of harassment has dropped. He made his way to the station, where - as predicted - he found an internet cafe. After paying the appropriate fee, he could sit in the cabin in front of the computer. Not as good at navigating the internet as Oggy, but he was doing well enough to slowly find what he was looking for.

"A wonderful tool," he muttered to himself, finally studying his handwritten notes, "to have the power, um, um, carry something with you that would connect to the network without having to use an access point like this... there is nothing to be lacking for a person to be happy."

The development of technology has always fascinated him, but recently it has accelerated so much that he has difficulty keeping up with it. Oggy was definitely doing better with it, only it didn't matter now. It was not known how long it would remain in canine form, and even if it would ever assume human form again. As a dog, she retained a great deal of typically human intelligence, but could not operate a computer. Also, not to write, or even to speak, because the dog's vocal apparatus is not suitable for making articulated sounds. They had to fend for themselves without her help, at least on that point.

He reread what he noted. It made sense, and he was pretty sure he had solved at least some of the mystery.

He knew where to find Gusto Vanderbelt and what name he was using now. He guessed what he had done.

He just didn't know why. What was driving him. How far can it go and whether it must go even further at all.

He put the notebook in his breast pocket and left the cafe. Midnight had long since passed, although the traffic on the street did not seem to be so. Paris was awake. He played, worked, loved and hated, in a word, he was boiling with life, like most of the world's metropolises at this time. Progress blurred the differences between races and nations, between man and woman, and even between day and night, disrupting the eternal order of nature. Not surprisingly, the "creatures of the dark" now stayed out of the cities for the most part - there the darkness had been chained and subdued, no longer able to cover them effectively. But they were not the threats now.

"It's not good," Never sighed aloud.

As he approached the Church of Saint-Leu-Saint-Gilles, he suddenly realized that he was becoming increasingly apprehensive. His ghostly companion must have felt it too, for he woke up and began to vibrate restlessly under his host's skin.

He quickened his pace and almost ran into the church grounds. His entire figure was already surrounded by a halo, like the moon on a foggy day, except that it was not bright, but dark. Maybe thanks to the influence of the Partner, sooner than Never was able to understand what was happening, his hands flashed up by themselves, covering his ears tightly.

The whole cemetery was filled with monotonous, speechless singing from many throats. By the wall of the Fibi family mausoleum, Never saw his friends huddled together in a motionless group.

They looked hypnotized or drugged. About a dozen human figures loomed in the darkness around them.

They swayed to the rhythm of the choral melody, the faint moonlight shone on the metal ornaments woven into their dreadlocks and objects held in their hands - silver-wrapped wooden spears, canisters and something else.

There was a strong gasoline smell in the air. Never rushed forward, realizing in a split second that there was not a moment to waste. Breaking the circle, he covered his friends with himself, and, turning in place, facing the Rasts, let out a shrill scream.

He rarely used this extraordinary skill. It was a great weapon against the overwhelming force of the enemy, but it cost him too much. A scream acting like a deafening blow, causing physical trauma and striking the human mind with an unmanageable fear, was capable of tearing his lungs out, and certainly seriously damaging them. It was painful and exhausting for Never to make that sound, but sometimes, like now, there was no way out.

He managed to drown out the singing of the Rasts. Thrown out of the magical trance, people dropped what was holding and almost simultaneously grabbed their heads.

Never with horror noticed that, unlike the victims of his "secret weapon" so far, they stayed on their feet. Though they shook like electrocuted, none of them fell, some even made an attempt to pick up a dropped weapon.

Whatever put them in a trance, it had to be very strong. He screamed again, raising his voice to registers he had never reached before. He couldn't see the ghostly tentacles rising above his head and shoulders, acting like tuning forks.

Their vibrations amplified the screaming effect, forcing the Rasts to flee at last.

Only then did the Indian turn to his friends. They were just regaining their orientation and, not understanding anything, looked around, gasping for air. They weren't fully conscious yet, but he didn't have time to wait. He knew they were in danger of falling into shock for a change, and - for now at least - he couldn't let that happen.

"Take your luggage and follow me!" he exclaimed in order, "come on, get your asses up!"

In this situation, they could not afford to lose the rest of their property. They could mean "to be or not to be," so you had to waste a few precious seconds rolling up the blankets and taking the haversacks.

Then it was just a run through streets, alleys and squares, until they found a boarded-up shop that was closed. Tearing off one of the planks, they slipped inside and masked the entrance behind them. Never lit an adjustable flashlight, twisted it to the minimum and placed it on a hook near the ceiling, thus obtaining a kind of dim lamp. Only now could his team allow itself to finally lose their temper.

Pale as death, Fronda hugged the hysterical Lily, from whom all stoicism had evaporated in one moment. Gerard was trembling like a malaria bout, his teeth were snapping constantly, and he couldn't even light a cigarette stuck in his fingers. Oggy whimpered and growled alternately, and the bristled fur made it look like a huge chimney sweep. Their leader also felt bad. He was still trying to contain his dread, and the sharp pain behind the sternum of screaming was almost unbearable at this point. Still, he just had to be the strong one now.

"Get a grip now!" he demanded sharply, "because I will hit you on the heads. There is no time for lamentation, we must quickly come up with a sensible plan of action.

As you have seen for yourself, the danger is exactly as serious as Lasalle said. And it was not for nothing that he advised us to run away instead of fight."

He coughed and rubbed his hand over his throat. He felt like he was swallowing razor blades.

"What did you find out?" Gerard muttered vaguely.

His teeth were still chattering, though he did his best. He sat down on an overturned crate and managed to finally light a cigarette. Oggy pressed against his knees, her body still trembling.

"Give it to me too," Never reached out to him.

The actor handed him a pack of Gaulouis and a lighter. Rajah lit a cigarette, took a few puffs, and only then did he begin to speak.

"There is no Saint Obadiah. Someone like that never existed. It's not even a name, just a proper name. In the Old Testament it means "one who obeys God in all things"."

"But it could have been named as a name..." Fronda interjected without conviction.

"Again, there is no such saint or prophet. Instead, there is Sauti Obeah, primal, deadly magic straight from the Dark Continent, which uses so-called intonations to manipulate the human mind. Misunderstanding due to phonetic convergence, or perhaps deliberately misleading the uninitiated. Cults, even a little Christian or based on the Mosaic religion, are less frightening, and therefore less cautious.

"Holy smoke, man, don't make me believe in some witchcraft now, old devil!" Gerard interrupted abruptly. "What magic? Circus tricks and that's it!"

"Now you say that when we nearly died because of the damn thing?" Theo tapped his forehead eloquently.

The Indian sighed desperately. He did not know how to explain to the unbeliever something he had come across in his early youth and which he had learned to take as part of his life.

"That's how we usually define something we just don't understand," he said finally.

"Okay, but what does this have to do with the Rasts? What have they done to us? I'm just begging you, no fairy tales or sorcerers."

"Okay," Never agreed, for the sake of peace. "Let me put it differently. Hypnosis was once considered magic, but today we know that it is not.

And what the Rasts used is akin to hypnosis. Influencing the brain with appropriately modulated sound. They mastered this skill masterfully, which you had the opportunity to test on your own skin."

Fronda shuddered. He still felt the dread and dizziness.

"If you hadn't started screaming like only you can, they would have burned us alive," he whispered hoarsely. Lily huddled against him sobbed more violently than ever before, and finally fell silent.

"What does this have to do with Rastafarianism?" Gerard asked. His demonstrative self-confidence, despite his acting skills, was now so artificial that he would not even fool a child.

Rajah shook his head.

"Don't use that term. They find them offensive, as do anything that ends in -ism. According to them, it hurts people and perpetuates divisions. They even have a saying "no ism, no schism"."

"Never mind. What's in common?"

"Just like I thought before. Nothing. The Rasts are merely hooking up to the rastafari movement in order to deceive the public and the authorities and be able to act calmly. Some of them actually come from there, but they broke with all traditions when our mysterious persecutor picked them up, I'm sorry, Fronda, but it really all points to Gusto."

Theo shrugged resignedly.

"Okay, so Gusto. What's next?"

Never looked at him sympathetically. He knew his friend's weaknesses well, and one of them was truly chivalrous loyalty. He stuck to it even when the situation became completely clear.

"We have to find him, and quickly," he said, "next time we may not be as lucky as we are today."

"How?"

The Indian ran his fingers through his shortened hair. Some of the gel was left on his fingers, he wiped them automatically on his pants.

"Personally, I only see one way," he said. "Remember Vandis's "angelic triangulation"?"

His friends nodded without conviction.

"Do you want to do it again?" Theo asked. "Like to strengthen our targeting skills? How can you be sure that it will work?"

"Do you have a better idea? Triangulation enhancement of psycholocation... even then I thought that something like this could work, but there was no opportunity to try it out."

There was silence. Fronda helped Lily sit on the crate next to Gerard and lit a cigarette himself, which he never did. He wanted to hide at all costs how upset he was about what had happened to them.

"Okay, let's do it," he said after a long moment, brushing ashes on the floor, "but there are only five of us, including a blind woman and a dog. In addition, Rasts can always find us as if we had a bug with us. I don't really see how we could win this fight."

"Wait, what did you say? A bug?" The Indian jumped up, as stabbed. "Put what you have from your pockets and bags. Immediately!"

He moved the second box to the center, right under the flashlight hanging from the ceiling.

After a while, on the improvised table there was a pile of trinkets - utensils, souvenirs and small amulets. As it turned out, even Gerard, the unrepentant materialist, had them. He never took each object individually in his fingers, felt it and examined it carefully. What consisted of several elements, he would take apart and put back together. He was particularly interested in items acquired relatively recently, although the existence of a hidden transmitter in one of the older ones could not be ruled out either. The "bug" was finally found in a lighter, actually bought on arrival in France. Now everyone remembered how at the airport someone accidentally - as it had seemed then - knocked the old one out of the actor's hand, and then stepped on it. Now they couldn't even remember what that someone looked like. In any case, he apologized for a long time, then "bought" this useful item in the duty free zone, choosing a beautiful, decorative model. As it turned out, not without hidden intention.

"If it weren't for your hideous addiction..." Theo grunted, squinting angrily at his friend.

"They would have found another way," interrupted Rajah. He tossed the tiny transmitter onto the concrete floor and squashed it under his heel.

"We were followed and opportunities were looked for. Not this one, it would have been different. They noticed that Cheetah had a habit of playing with the lighter to keep his hands occupied, then they stuffed a bug into this thing. The rest is probably clean and so far no one will surprise us. We are safe for now, so let's rest after these ordeals.

"I wonder why they didn't track us down on the roof of the theater," thought Gerard.

"There is interference from antennas and transmitters. Luckily we were safe as in the eye of the storm."

"I'm hungry," Lily moaned.

"Too bad, suffer a little. We will hunt in the evening and spend the day here. They portend a cloudless sky and heat, so we better not stick our nose out until the sun goes down."

****

They didn't quite remember the "power triangulation" principles Vandis had once briefed them.

Nevertheless, after several attempts, they managed to find the right layout and the optimal distance from each other, so that the psycholocation abilities of the three participants could be accumulated into one.

They did not know the mechanism of this trick, they could only guess it, but in the ensuing situation, they were not interested in anyway.

It was important if it would work, not how. For the experiment, they chose the already known roof of the Theater de Champs Elisee - as it turned out, it was possible to get to it from the outside, as long as you showed some dexterity.

It was enough to climb onto the roof of one of the adjoining tenement houses by means of staples hammered into the wall, which could be made almost open, and jump further from there. An ordinary human would probably have a hard time making such evolutions, but they didn't have much trouble with it. Only Oggy had to be brought in, which Fronda had done. They didn't even have to jump - the coatings were undergoing renovation on both roofs, and workers had built a makeshift bridge to make their work easier.

Having discovered the correct proportions, they could finally concentrate and strain their psycholocation sense.

It worked. At first they felt like a slight jerk, as if they were struck by a small electric charge, then their sensations were intensified almost painfully.

The rush of visions and sounds became unbearable, yet they remained fused together for as long as they could. Finally they broke the connection and, panting heavily, leaned against what they could.

"What and what?" Lily asked anxiously, staying on the sidelines of this experiment.

Oggy squealed softly, as if to let her know she wanted to know something too. Fronda scratched her behind the ears with a trembling hand.

"It's okay, baby."

Never wiped the sweat from his brow.

"Okay. Your impressions?" he asked.

"Chaos," Theo and Gerard replied almost simultaneously.

"I was also confused in my head and I saw, you could say, everything at once," the leader agreed with them. "The method is good, but we do not know how to use it properly. It requires some refinement and practice, and we don't have time for that."

"Maybe it's just a matter of interpretation?" Lily clearly had her doubts.

Rajah shook his head, forgetting that the girl couldn't see it.

"Probably not. As you are attacked from all sides by images of different places, it is rather difficult to interpret. Look, I didn't really tell you anything, but I located the Parisian "temple" of the Rasts. They wrote about it on the web."

"Then why didn't you tell?!" Gerard shouted angrily

"Exactly because they write about it. It's an official temple, or rather a meetinghouse. I already know you, you would go there right away and nothing would come of it, only embarrassment."

Lily coughed lightly to get attention again.

"Boys, I have a suggestion: take the cards and have each of you write down the places you have seen or felt. Then compare the records, maybe something will overlap?"

They looked at her in surprise. The idea was simple and at the same time accurate, it seemed strange that they did not come up with it themselves.

"There is something to it," Never agreed after a moment. He ripped two pages from his notebook, handed each of his friend's one and a miniature pen, which he had recently bought a whole packet, along with other useful knick-knacks.

They sat cross-legged and went to work while Lily cut her waiting time by brushing Oggy's tangled hair.

In her indispensable haversack, she carried a scraper, also a memento of the guide dog, which she had lost before getting to know Fronda. Oggy submitted to her treatments with obvious pleasure, sighing deeply from time to time.

When the notes were compared, it turned out that they mainly contain descriptions, not names of specific places.

"It's even logical," Never admitted, comparing the pages. "It's like a flight over some area, hard to expect Boening's passengers to see signs from above that read "South Scottish Moors" or "Finnish Lake District." You have to guess."

"Guess then, I'm too stupid for that," Theo grumbled.

"Nothing new."

Rajah took another page out of his notebook, drew three interlocking circles on it, and began to write something into them.

"What are you doing?" Fronda asked after a moment. He couldn't help but look around carefully, though his instincts told him that this place was really safe. Otherwise Lasalle would not have scheduled a meeting for them here.

"I assigned each of the places we mentioned a specific symbol. Now I'm dividing the data into subsets and looking where they intersect. A simple mathematical operation in which a finite number of subsets, which together form a set, simultaneously forms another subset with joint forces, containing some data common to all basic subsets. De Morgan's set theory of law, does that tell you something?"

"Nothing at all."

"I thought so too."

"Don't be a pig!"

The Indian laughed involuntarily. Theo, a mathematical anti-talent, sometimes struggled with up to four actions, and any higher algebra was far beyond his capabilities.

"Relax, knight, you don't have to know everything. You have your talents and I have mine."

He finished his work and tapped the paper with his pen.

"It seems that one place was stubbornly recurring in all of us' visions. I marked them with the E symbol. Each of us described them in the same way: a lot of people, especially children, big wheels, bizarre buildings, colors and models of fairy-tale creatures. In one place crowded castles, ships, a town on the prairie and a space rocket. Does that tell you something?"

"Disneyland," Lily said.

"Is there one here?" Gerard was surprised. He still had a tendency to think of Paris as the city of his stardom.

"It is," the Polish woman assured him, "I have heard about it."

"Are you absolutely sure? I associate it more with America."

"Yes, I'm sure. I have an eidetic memory, I remember everything I hear and touch. It was built quite recently, but not in the city itself, just... let me think," she rubbed her forehead with the back of her hand. "In Marne-la-Vallée. Yes, that's what the place is called. Over eighty hectares of pure entertainment."

"You think Gusto and his murderers are hiding there?" Theo clearly had his doubts. "But if this is a playground, there are kids!"

"That's what it's all about, silly. Gusto assumed that no one would be looking for him there."

"What an idea to build a monument to the American entertainment mogul near Paris," Gerard's thoughts continued to revolve around another aspect of the matter and he was rather disgusted.

"Disney was Norman and his real name was d'Insigny," Never reminded him. "He's an American like you and me. But it doesn't matter now anyway. What matters now is what we have."

He thought, mechanically nibbling at the end of his pen.

"It makes sense," he said after a moment, "there's always a lot of fancy dress and weirdos in places like Disneyland, and all kinds of things happen. Sometimes a person does not know if this is reality or some kind of artistic improvisation. If you want to know my opinion, I would choose such a place myself if I were Gusto."

"So what do we do?" Fronda asked.

Before his friend could answer him, something hummed in the air. Everyone jumped up from their seats when a large creature landed on the roof near them, at first glance resembling a monstrous bat.

But when he got up and straightened, they saw a young girl in front of them, covered with membranous wings like something like a long coat.

The newcomer had incredibly thick black hair that covered her hips, a chalk white face, full vermillion lips, and enormous eyes that gleamed like polished agate.

"Hello," she said calmly, as if she had met them in the most ordinary way, somewhere in the street.

"What the hell?" Fronda, usually extremely sensitive to the fair sex, this time he was not charmed at all, but he immediately took a defensive stance. "Who are you?"

"My name is Athalie," the girl replied, "Lasalle told me where to find you."

"All right," Theo persisted. He took a step forward, taking his place between the strange flier and Lily.

"Do we know each other?" Never joined him, unconsciously assuming an aggressive tone.

"No," Athalie pushed her hair away from her face. "But you knew my mother. And my foster father."

It took a while for them to match up all the facts.

"You are the daughter of the harpy!" Gerard exclaimed, raising his voice involuntarily.

"Who died because of you," she added.

"We did not want it," Rajah whispered. There was genuine guilt in his voice now. "She killed young women and ate their brains. We were asked for help. We didn't want to kill her. If she only tried to talk, instead of attacking us right away..."

The girl waved her hand. Her hand, pretty and girly in itself, ended in long bird claws curved like sickles.

"I know. And I did not come here to seek revenge for the death of my mother and unborn sister."

"Then what for?"

She came closer.

"The Rasts killed my foster father and his friends. It is them that I want to avenge. I hardly knew my mother, and they were my family. I want to go with you."

Never backed away slightly.

"Let's say," he said carefully, "let's say I believe you. However, you yourself understand that not entirely. If I were in your place, I would seek vengeance on both of them. Either way, we are responsible that you became an orphan, even though we did not want to hurt you."

The young harpy's eyes glittered even brighter, red flickered in its pupils.

"My poor mother shouldn't have killed those women. I know why she did it, but she still shouldn't.

You didn't hunt her like the Hunters. You tried to help the police who were looking for a serial killer.

You didn't even know who you were really dealing with, and most importantly, you weren't shooting at her.

You could say that if she showed a little understanding, tried to coact with you, everything would have ended differently. And if the police had not interfered... Too bad, it happened and that's it."

"And that's all?" Gerard dared to ask. Somehow he couldn't believe the goodwill of this winged creature, beautiful and formidable at the same time. He remembered too well what her mother could do.

She looked at him for a long time.

"It would be an exaggeration to say that I have no grudge against you... or that I somehow love you madly... but at least for the moment I'm chasing someone else."

"That sounds quite ambiguous," Lily said coolly. She knew the story of her encounter with the harpy only by hearing, but she knew it and was as distrustful as the men.

Oggy nodded her short snarl. Athalie sighed and bowed her head.

"I can be useful to you. You don't know where to find our common enemy."

"Imagine that we know," blurted Fronda.

"What?"

"That he's at Disneyland."

"Really? And more specifically? This is not your average funfair! These are two separate complexes and hundreds of buildings. If you start rummaging around, they'll track you down. Psycholocation will be useless to you, because at such a short distance it works both ways, and they will be in a stronger position. Am I wrong?"

Never shook his head in apparent desperation.

"I need a drink," he muttered.

Theo without a word took a flat bottle with a measuring cup cap from his bag and handed it to him. The Indian took a long sip and coughed involuntarily.

"What the hell is this? Sulfuric acid?"

"Chacha. The original, sixty percent, Georgian grape vodka. I bought in Poland."

"You could have warned me," Rajah handed him back the bottle and wiped his mouth with the sleeve of his shirt.

"Molly," Fronda drank himself.

"Give me a shot, too," Gerard held out his hand. A friend poured him some liquor into the cap. "Strong as hell indeed. Lily Ann, do you want?"

"No thank you. I'm abstinent. Back to the point, how are you going to help us?" The girl moved out from behind Fronda and turned to the young harpy, as if taking over the negotiations."

Athalie looked questioningly first at Never, who only shrugged, then at Lily.

"I know exactly where the Rast leader made his nest," she said finally, "I've been following him since he murdered Bruce and his companions. If I haven't taken any action yet, it's because I'm not a suicide woman. There are always five well-armed acolytes with him. I thought about planting an explosive, but even if I could do it undetected, there could be many casualties. Together, however, we have a chance. My mere presence will block the possibility of psychic discovery, so we can strike it unexpectedly."

Theo rubbed a hand over his chin.

"These acolytes... ordinary people?"

"Probably not. In my opinion, he preserved them. Of course I can be wrong, but everything points to it."

Rajah decided that he had to sit down.

"Does that mean Gusto created a vampire commando to hunt other vampires?"

"I don't think so. Rather, it's his personal protection. The hunting is done by ordinary Rasts, who are under his religious influence. I've been to their temple, they say regular prayers and burn a lot of incense which I think contains psychoactive additives. It's a sect, but it's a peculiar one."

"Why?"

"I watched them. Neither of them have a family. No children, no one outside the sect to contact. As I found out, if one of the women becomes pregnant, they cause an artificial miscarriage. Not only this. If any of them are mutilated or become ill with something incurable, they commit ritual suicide with the help of fellow believers. There is no place in their circle for children, for the disabled or for people who need care at all."

"They definitely have nothing to do with real Rastafari," Never muttered in disgust.

"No, no."

Athalie flicked her left wing, the smaller one. She had four of them - the larger ones formed a cloak on her back, the smaller ones formed a neat cape around her shoulders. In flight, it must have looked more like a ghostly butterfly than a bird or a bat.

"What do you decide?"

"I would advise to get things done tonight," said Fronda, taking another scoop of Georgian vodka for the courage. "And before you say something, Rajah, we have nothing left to lose. We're practically dead anyway."

"Don't be so dramatic!" Never bridled.

"Yes? So please, take a phone, look for one of your old friends and good luck. Do they, in your opinion, all of them are a mere nobody? They had their hands to dangle them like sausages?"

"What do you mean?!"

"Rajah, it's time to face the truth. They are dead, they were murdered by the Rasts! Do you think they didn't defend themselves? That they didn't fight?" he wiped his face with his sleeve. "They died and we will die."

"You know what?" Never firmly took the bottle from him. "You better not drink anymore. Even if you are right, which is not said at all, it still does not mean that we will be killed. Athalie, we accept your help."

The harpy looked at Lily and the she-wolf at her leg.

"And she?" she asked, "I don't go into how she handles it on a daily basis, but she's unlikely to be of any use in combat. She might even put us all at risk."

Oggy snarled again. Lily placed a reassuring hand on her head.

"She is right. Blindness doesn't bother me in many ways, but in ranged combat it is an insurmountable obstacle.

Even if Oggy helps me, I won't be of any use."

"We have to accommodate you in a good hotel, one with a security guard on every floor," Never said after some thought. "You will wait for us there."

"And... what if you don't come back?"

"Then you'll be on your own."

Lily's lips twitched. Theo hugged her and hugged her tightly.

"Listen, honey: Oggy had been doing for years all by herself when she didn't know us. If anything happened to us, she will take care of you."

"I don't want anything to happen to you."

"We don't want that either. And I can assure you that they will not get us easily. Have a little faith. We are the lucky ones. We've come out alive from all sorts of oppressions and now we won't lose."

It was evident that the girl is trying very hard to believe him, but it was difficult for her.

"Take her to the Hotel de Penisula in the sixteenth arrondissement," the harpy said.

"Just like that, in the middle of the night, like to go to some cheap hostel for ten francs a bed?" Gerard, well versed in hotel realities, had doubts.

"Yes. I will go there with you. I can influence people... their minds and their perception of reality. They will be convinced that they are hosting a famous artist who wants to be incognito and will accept her with all possible honors."

The men exchanged glances.

"Well, we have no choice but to continue," Rajah decided after a while, "but why there? There are different ones, after all."

Athalie smiled for the first time since they had met her. She had sharp teeth with clearly defined fangs.

"There is now an Englishman, a famous musician, visiting... a good friend of mine."

"Friend? In the sense of friend-friend or friend-lover?"

"Both. He is currently married but did not bring her with him. We're still in touch. He is not quite human himself, and who I am affects him like an aphrodisiac."

"Save us the details. Can you trust him?"

"Absolutely not. But in this case, it will be helpful. If we die, only he will help them two to leave the country. He'll know what to do."

"If you say so..." Theo was rather unconvinced.

"Believe me, I know what I'm saying. If the Rasts knew his identity, he would be in danger himself. He became an avant-garde artist, because this was the easiest way for him to hide his otherness, but he probably went too far, because for my taste he is too well known and one day it may take revenge on him."

"A vampire?"

"No. Completely something else. If we survive, I will introduce you to him. For now, however, there is no time for this."

Never glanced at his watch.

"Indeed, we'd better hurry up because this night won't last forever. We'd better get it all over with."

*****

Disneyland seemed to be the last place Vampire Hunters might be hiding and, paradoxically, perfect for the purpose. Well guarded, monitored day and night... where to hide, if not there?

"The one you were looking for is the Tower of Terror," Athalie explained fully, pointing the direction with her claw.

"He got into the Walt Disney Studio Replica as an administrative clerk or something. He and his acolytes take care of the facility and the attractions assigned to it, so they can stay there 24/7 and no one is surprised."

"How will we get there? Usually, the alarms disabled Oggy." Theo took the military binoculars away from his eyes and looked questioningly at Never.

"Do you know where they have a video surveillance center here?" the Indian asked Athalie. She nodded.

"Always a few security guards staring at the cameras. They guard the area day and night, and there is also a physical security there. I'll try to do something about it."

"How?" Gerard looked at her with interest. Knowing the harpies' abilities, he had expected the answer to be interesting.

Athalie licked her lips with the tip of her tongue.

"I've never tried to manipulate consciousness on this scale, but I can try. If we succeed, we'll have some time."

"How much?"

"I don't know. We'll see. Give me a minute."

She moved away from her friends and spread both pairs of wings wide. For a moment she remained as concentrated as possible. Watching her, the men watched with fascination as the wings contracted and retracted into the back, and the sparrowhawk claws on the harpy' hands diminished into normal fingernails. After a while they were faced with a fascinating but quite ordinary-looking girl in a tight black leather studded outfit and high wedge heels.

"Follow me now, but don't speak, and be quiet. I don't control the sounds as well as what is visible. And don't step aside, we'd better be a tight group."

"What you want to do?" Never asked suspiciously.

"We have to neutralize security. I'll do it myself, because they're just ordinary people, but I need your company in case something goes wrong," she explained. "Not everything is predictable. I can unintentionally mess something up, then I'll need your intervention."

"Okay..." Rajah again had the unpleasant feeling that he was losing the leading role in the team to the woman, but decided that this was not the right time to argue about the principles.

The video surveillance point was located outside the proper boundary of Disneyland, in a small brick house equipped with a system of electronic locks.

Friends watched Athalie's actions, curious how she would deal with such an advanced obstacle, but it turned out that the girl had no intention of dealing with her at all.

She just stood in front of the door and stared at it, concentrating as much as she could. After a long moment, electronic bolts clicked and the door swung open.

The man in the black uniform standing behind them looked hypnotized or under the influence of a strong drug. Athalie stepped inside freely. The rest of the bodyguards rose from their seats at the sight of her and stood against the wall like mannequins.

"I..." muttered Fronda with admiration, and fell silent, remembering the harpies' warning.

Meanwhile, Athalie had turned on the microphone and, in a deep male voice, made the announcement:

"Physical security will report urgently to the monitoring station."

"Man, she's brilliant," Gerard said.

The bodyguards against the wall shifted as they regained consciousness. The harpy turned quickly from the lectern and made a strange noise, like a broken page.

It echoed under the skull of each of the friends who instinctively clenched their hands over their ears. As if on command, people rolled their eyes at the same time and slumped slowly to the floor, freezing.

"They'll sleep for a few hours," Athalie explained calmly, "I told you to be silent, yes or no? Now step back into the corner."

They obeyed her order without a word of objection, shocked by the girl's abilities. Field security guards began to descend into the room, and anyone who crossed the threshold stood behind him like a pillar of salt, immobilized by Athalie's gaze.

The harpy didn't do anything special, just stood and watched, and yet none of the armed men could make the slightest movement under her gaze. Soon all Disneyland security lay unconscious in the indoor monitoring room.

Now Theo has started to act. He took a screwdriver from his locket wallet, opened the panel of the desk, and with a few decisive movements tore out the cables and switches there. Then the friends left the building and closed it carefully. They didn't even need to talk anymore, everyone knew what their next step would be.

The building, called the Tower of Terror, was in fact a hotel, equipped only with additional attractions, known from the films of the studio. Approaching him, everyone sensed a kind of dark emanation, which unmistakably indicated the presence of one or more vampires inside. Even without using psycholocation, they could register it with their sublime senses.

"They are in the part closed to visitors," Athalie whispered, who also felt it. "As I said before, the leader and the acolytes. How do you want to do it?"

"Good question," Theo remarked, "we're not likely to get in through the front door. Gusto must have fortified himself, that is, he prepared some traps and trained his "heavies" well.

We sense them, they probably sense us too. If they also have silver knives, and I bet they do, they'll chop us up faster than we can say "Goodbye, beautiful world"."

"Probably," Never looked around. "Hey, sidekicks, what can drive the average vampire out of his hiding place?"

They looked at him, puzzled.

"Same as extraordinary," Theo said after a moment.

"Exactly... There's a firework depot somewhere. We could use them."

"Ridiculous idea. Pull yourself together! After all, there are smoke detectors everywhere! In less than two minutes, we'd have the fire brigade and the gendarmerie on our backs," Gerard protested vigorously.

"Shit, right," Fronda worried. "So how...?"

"Athalie can manipulate consciousness. She has already shown what she can do. Maybe she will try now? What you say, girl? Would you tell the acolytes there's fire?"

The harpy hesitated.

"I could try... But then I would have to take the veil off all of us. They'll sense us. And we have to come closer."

"Tough! Let's take a risk. Since we have come this far..." agreed Rajah. He felt clearly stupid for not taking into account the smoke detectors and their connection to the nearest fire station himself. "When the door opens, you and Cheetah pull away the acolytes and make sure they do not disturb us. Me and Fronda will take care of our Gusto."

"Why is that?" Gerard was not satisfied with this division of tasks.

"Because I'm in charge here. Don't behave like a diva now, there's no time for that."

Circling the building, they approached the rear door, marked with a sign that reads "Business Entry. Unauthorized Entry Denied".

"Prepare yourselves." Athalie touched her fingers and closed her eyes, concentrating as much as possible. Wings reappeared on her back, nails replaced claws, and her hair rose as if blown by a gust of wind.

Seconds later, there was a sound of scuffling feet and frightened voices deep in the building. The door burst open and four men and a woman ran out, all clearly panicked.

"Calm down! It's an illusion!" someone from inside shouted, but they ignored him.

It was only outside that the acolytes realized that they had been deluded and turned back, but it was too late. The harpy leapt at them, wings spread wide and claws spread out, hissing like an enraged snake. Her eyes flashed red, her face stretched into a toothy muzzle. The most terrifying change, however, was the long, segmented tail that suddenly sprouted from one half of her back - mobile and flexible, ending in a thickening and solid spike like a scorpion's. It soon turned out that it plays a similar role. The acolyte, smacked by it, fell and stiffened like an electric shock.

Gerard was not idle either. He started to fight, waving a piece of iron tube lifted from the ground. Training for years under the watchful eye of Fronda, he gained skill in fighting with everything he had at hand, and although he did not match his friends in physical strength, he made up for it with agility and speed.

Meanwhile, Theo and Never were already inside, knowing well who they were looking for, they expected either a research lab or - given the current activity - a temple-styled interior, but instead found themselves in a maze of corridors lined with mirrors, like in a cheesy movie sensational.

For a moment they didn't know where to turn, then their psycholocation sense told them the direction. One of the corridors led to interior rooms. They tried to be careful, but nothing suspicious happened. There were no trapdoors, no poison darts sprinkled on the walls - everything around them, except for the mirrors, and was perfectly normal.

Gusto Vanderbelt was waiting for them in the last room, which looked like a bourgeois parlor. He was standing with his arms folded on his chest and he didn't think to run away.

"Hello," he said, "I knew you'd be here sooner or later."

All his posture and expression made it clear that he had prepared himself well for this confrontation.

The friends looked around, tense, ready to flee or defend at any moment, but still could see no typical trap. As if there weren't any. After a while, they realized that even someone as smart as Gusto could not stealthily install something unapproved by the chief architect and engineers. Any major manipulation would have to attract someone's attention, and in a facility such as this construction supervision was conducted very carefully.

"Have you been waiting for us?" Theo broke the silence. Emboldened, he took a step forward. Gusto didn't even move.

"Oh, yeah. You guys are crazy enough to crawl into any lion cave. I'm just curious what you're looking for here. Death, mine or maybe yours?"

"No," Theo shook his head and waved to hold Never back. "I mean, it's hard for me to speak for others, but I don't care about your head."

"So, what do you want?"

"Answers."

"Which ones?"

"What's all this for? Why?"

Rajah was speechless. He stared at his friend with eyes that turned completely round from the long leaves, and he was unable to utter a word.

"Are you crazy?" he choked finally, "are you here for the talks? After all that...?"

"Wait," Fronda put a hand on his shoulder, his eyes never leaving Gusto. "Can't you see he's not afraid of us at all? He must have something up his sleeve."

The Austrian laughed out loud and Never shuddered. It was the laugh of a madman who is very comfortable with his insanity and was terrifying.

"Compliments to your suspicious instincts, Knight," Gusto said. He walked over to the sofa against the wall and settled down comfortably on it, crossing his legs. "All right, it will be as you like. Attention, quiet on the set! The scene of the villain's final monologue, take one, action!"

"Holy God... I'm begging you, without such antics..." Fronda sighed.

"Stop! Can't you see he wants to gain time?!"

Gusto laughed again.

"You've always been a mystery to me, Radhjaleah. So intelligent, and you let such a barely literate donkey follow you. Another thing is that his simple mind sometimes hits the nail on the head," he paused for a moment and carefully examined the nails on his right hand, as if nothing more important existed at the moment. "Do you want to know, knight, why I made it a point of honor to eliminate bloodsuckers, among which I ironically belong?"

"Kind of," Theo agreed, wondering in passing what was also going on outside. None of the acolytes tried to sneak up on them from behind, and that was fine, but...?

"You probably think that when I was imprisoned in the Van Helsing Institute, I was brainwashed and turned into a kind of tame wolf, helping to hunt my kin.

You are wrong, completely wrong. I myself went to them together with years of knowledge about modern vampires. Do you want to know why? I had a family.

A wife, two teenage children and a younger brother. I was neglecting them, it is true, but scientific work requires sacrifice... One day when I got home, they were all dead. According to the coroner's report, they had died of blood loss, but no one knew where that blood might have gone. She was nowhere on the floor of the house, and nowhere at all. I did my own investigation and found out a terrible thing. My wife, bored and impatient with the constant absence of her husband, found a lover. From what I found out, he killed her, and our children and Gunnar by the way. I didn't understand how or why... but I found it too. Then I swore to myself that I would destroy all vampires in the world. Okay, but how? I could join the Hunters right away, but what would be the solution? I'd kill one, two, maybe ten. Is that enough? I didn't have a scientific mind for nothing. I decided to develop some kind of global decommissioning method. This, however, required long and extensive research that as an ordinary person I could not have done."

"Jesus Maria... you wanted to be preserved in order to work us out... How you achieved it?" Now Theo was struggling to make a sound, and he was pale and paler.

"Ah, it was easy," Gusto dismissed him with a wave of his hand, "it was harder to bear your company and pretend to be your friend. So many years...

More than once I thought how easy it would be to set fire to the emergency point where we were sleeping, or otherwise... but it would be too little, too little.

Finally, when I thought I knew everything, I went to the vanhelsingers. I had a bit of a problem convincing them to the purity of my intentions, but it worked. Only they turned out to be mollies. Those from Medlab, to whom I turned later, too. Lots of talk, little effect. So I finally started to act on my own and what would you say? I did it!"

Never took a deep breath. He felt a little dizzy and felt stuffy.

"And where did you get your Rasts from?" he asked.

"Oh, it was brilliant in its simplicity. Science is great, but it has a downside because scientists think too much. Religion has proved to be much more useful for my purposes."

"Okay, but why exactly them?"

Gusto shrugged.

"I found them in Africa. I followed you there, thinking that I could nail you in Congo, but I lost my way. And by accident I found an old shaman educating his students in the art of hypnotic singing. Sauti Obeyah. They called it magic, I prefer to call it the brilliant use of the unknown possibilities of influencing the human brain. After all, the fear of the possibilities of African sorcerers did not come out of nowhere. Then I understood what I should do and it turned out to be a bull's eye. Of course, I continued my research. Thanks to them, I discovered a new formula of a blood preservative, which in combination with sodium citrate becomes a poison for vampires, and for humans it's completely harmless. End of eating at the blood donation stations Mesdames et Monsieurs!"

Theo shook his head slowly, never taking his eyes off him.

"You're crazy. More than Amargo Lorca."

"Perhaps, but I also have better results than him. What are you gonna do now? Will you kill me? Go on, try.

Even if you do, you will gain nothing. I have already trained those who will replace me, and not here, but in the whole damn world. Got it? My death, even if you manage to bring it about, will get you nothing. Isn't that a great joke?"

"You mean those pathetic acolytes?"

"Hell, no. They're just my protection. You will not find those, I guarantee you, until it is too late."

Never immediately noticed that the dark fog, which was a manifestation of his ghastly companion, was starting to appear outside. Only when it wrapped his head like a dark, transparent helmet did he regain his clarity of thinking.

"Fronda, back!" he screamed.

Theo lunged instinctively. His body reacted faster with nothing dazed about. Partner's shadow seized him as well, then pulled sharply back down the corridor.

They literally avoided the grating falling from the ceiling, which would trap them together with Gusto - by a hair, as it still managed to catch the sleeve of Fronda's shirt. He tore it off with a strong tug. Surrounded by a thick shadow, they ran out of the building into the fresh air, and only there stopped, gasping for breath.

"What was that?" Theo groaned.

"He sprayed some filth. He must have taken the antidote himself earlier," Never staggered, but he regained his balance immediately. "He's well prepared, son of a bitch. If not for the Partner, it would be end of us."

"He'll probably bring you to hell anyway."

"I don't care. I have hell while I'm alive. Where are ours?"

They looked for enemies, but Gerard and Athalie were already there.

"They are all lying," reported the actor. He was visibly excited, his green eyes glittered, and his usual pale face was flushed. "Look, she's absolutely gorgeous...!"

He was interrupted by the whir of an oncoming pickup truck, from which at least ten Rasts spilled out, armed with long-barreled rifles and two types of knives - metal and wooden.

"Oh shit..."

"Can you scream?" Theo asked, assessing his opponents with a skilled eye and figuring it wasn't looking good.

"Not now. Because of the stuff we both inhale, I can barely speak."

"At least they don't have flamethrowers," said Gerard, gripping the metal tube tighter in his hand.

"They can't use them now because they could hurt themselves, but I bet they have," Never enlightened him. "On three."

They broke apart in lightning speed, attacking the Rasts from all sides with their tried and tested tactics to smash the enemy's smaller forces. The idea was that they could not use their potentially deadliest weapon, their rifles, without risking hurting one of "theirs". The still darkness certainly did not make the task easier for the Rasts, although the pickup driver initially tried to illuminate the battlefield with headlights. Never and Fronda quickly tried to eliminate light sources, which tipped the scales in their favor. Though the Rasts were still outnumbered, they fared worse in the dark than their opponents. However, not bad enough for it to make a definite difference. In addition, the pickup driver quickly dealt with the inconvenience, illuminating the area from the inside with powerful flashlights.

When shots were fired, the first reaction was surprise. Instead of the expected roar, the friends heard only a thud, like a bottle of champagne being opened.

None of them were successfully hit, and after a while the mystery was solved. Everyone smelled the faint scent of bitter almonds in the air.

"Carefully! These are veterinary rifles!" Never cried.

"They shoot cyanide, motherfuckers," said Fronda.

Not all poisons are dangerous to vampires, but cyanide, due to its ability to block oxygen metabolism within cells, is one of them. No wonder Gusto Vanderbelt provided his soldiers with this very poison, the possession of which is, ironically, perfectly legal in most countries.

There was only one thing that worked to the benefit of friends at this point, that veterinary rifles were not multi-shot. It was, however, little consolation.

The military group they faced now looked highly trained, and not even the sight of the furious harpy made her feel as expected. They were all wearing thick coveralls, reinforced with some inserts so resistant that Athalie's sting could not handle them.

It had to aim at parts that were covered or, as a last resort, less shielded, and this significantly worsened its effectiveness. So far, she had only managed to bite one of the Rasts, on the wrist, just above the cuff of the glove. The men had no less problems, and if they could not move much faster than an ordinary human, they would have lost this clash from the very beginning. The situation began to look hopeless very quickly, especially when the Hunters chanted their song. Being prepared for its hypnotic influence, they knew how to counter it, but they did not know how long they would be able to resist and remain fully aware. The Rasts went on the defensive, clearly waiting for their opponents to weaken.

In the heat of the fight, no one noticed the slender Ferrari that appeared near the pickup truck. It pulled up on the lights off and stopped, and three figures sprang out: a wolf-like creature, a large cat, and a thin, fair-haired man.

The three of them attacked the Rasts from the side where they would have expected support - the one where their car was standing.

The newcomers turned out to be a powerful support. The werewolf, who assumed his combat form, broke the Rasts ranks immediately upon falling into the enemy's rear. Lasalle, clinging to the ground, darted between the fighters' legs, neatly cutting the Hunters' knees. Their secret companion, however, acted as planned, although he did not use any physical violence. He only stood to the side and began to sing out loud in a language unknown to anyone. The sound of his voice immediately broke Sauti Obeyah's influence and clearly confused the Rasts. Their movements lost their initial coordination, while the friends regained their full potential and began a regular slaughter.

Silver and wooden knives, which were actually stakes with a handle, were of little use to the Hunters if they failed to hold down a potential prey and drive the blades through the heart. So far, neither of them has succeeded in shooting their opponent with a cyanide dart.

It soon became clear that fanatical hunters, unless they were given extra reinforcements, would not be able to cope with those they hunted this time around.

A bizarre song chanted by a stranger clearly gave the friends strength and spirit, and - what was already disturbing - deprived them of scruples.

Even the usually gentle Gerard began, as the Americans say, to "see everything in red" and his worst instincts woke up in him. The fact that the light that had been disseminated so far from the pickup was gone only made the situation of the Rasts worse. And when most of them were on the ground, there was something else to think about.

Never waited for Fronda to be beside him and patted him on the shoulder. As he turned around, he pointed his thumb at the Tower of Terror. Theo nodded.

Two of them have always been able to communicate without words and sometimes used it before considering what their behavior would look like to others. And what can they think about him.

"Wait, where you want to go?!" Athalie shouted, twirling in place.

Out of the corner of his eye, Gerard noticed that one of the Rasts was reaching for a dropped rifle at a speed he would not have expected from someone he had thought stunned a second earlier. He reacted more instinctively than deliberately, lunging for the girl, but only had time to shove her shoulder to the side. At first he didn't even realize what had happened, only as the sudden pain gripped his chest did he notice the arrow in his arm. He sank to the ground, gasping for air.

The harpy was with him in one second. She tore the sleeve of his shirt, tore the dart from his body, and slapped her talons, tearing the man's skin and muscles apart. Then she pressed her lips to the wound and began to suck, spitting the sucked blood out onto the side of the road. Fronda fell to them, terrified.

"What's up?"

"They hit him with cyanide," she said, almost continuing to work. "Clench his arm above the wound! Tightly!"

Busy saving their friend, they didn't even notice that the fair-haired singer took the initiative, so quickly that his movements were almost impossible to notice. He acted strangely, to say the least, but was surprisingly effective. Under the light touch of his fingers, one of the last Rasts still on his feet went limp and fell as if he had been struck by lightning. Lasalle jumped on the neck of the second, getting ready to attack, knife raised, and Oggy knocked the third to the ground, knocked the rifle out of his hands and bared bloody teeth straight in the eyes.

"Don't let him die!" the artist exclaimed commandingly, and disappeared between the buildings.

"It's easy to say..." Theo pulled the primitive tourniquet as tight as he could.

Gerard gasped for breath with increasing difficulty and become paler and paler.

"It hurts," he whispered.

"Hold on. Show that you are a tough guy."

"I'm not."

"Yes, you are. Otherwise you wouldn't stay with us that long."

The stranger came back running, carrying a plastic cup filled with some liquid. He pushed Fronda aside and knelt beside the actor himself. He tilted the cup to his lips.

"Drink," he said imperiously.

Gerard dutifully swallowed the liquid he had been given, and had difficulty suppressing his gag reflex.

"What is this?"

"Antidote. You drink too, you could poison yourself," the singer handed the mug to Athalie. She drank obediently and made a face.

"Seriously, what is this nasty stuff?"

"Fixer. I took it from the photo machine. What's up? Sodium thiosulfate is an antidote to cyanide."

Theo whistled in admiration.

"How do you know?"

"I know all kinds of things. Anyway, I saw it in one movie. Believe it, it's the only way."

Fronda nodded appreciatively and looked at the musician, examining his inconspicuous form and gentle, thin, boyish face. "A typical Englishman indeed," he thought and decided that he liked him after all. He held out his hand.

"Dideric de Janville."

"Duke Jareth," the singer shook his hand friendlily, "we have the same initials. Funny isn't it?"

They both looked towards the pickup truck, alarmed by the clang of the door opening. Lilly Ann stepped carefully out of the car, wiping her mouth as she went.

"Are you okay?" she asked.

"Yes," Duke replied. "Did you get the driver?"

"Of course. It took me a while because he wasn't alone. But they are both not dangerous anymore," the girl unhooked the folding stick from her belt and pulled it apart with the push of a button. With this help, she easily passed the lying people and approached her friends. "So I was useful after all. How are you?"

"Cheetah was hit, but he will survive. The rest is fine."

It wasn't entirely true. They all took more or less damage in this fight, not only Gerard, who was slowly recovering. Fronda had been stabbed several times with a silver knife, Athalie was bleeding from her nose and mouth, Oggy had a torn ear and was limping on one leg. However, the fact was that they had won and were safe for the time being.

Theo kissed Lily on her upturned cheek, then efficiently bound the hunter, lying and not daring to twitch, with Lasalle still sitting on top of his head. The cat creature wagged its tail and mewed maliciously, pressing its forepaws into the sand. The fight seemed to be a real pleasure for him.

"All right, you can let him go," Fronda said to him.

"I think so." Lasalle jumped gracefully to the ground and stretched delightfully.

As a second one, Theo released Oggy, still guarding her captive. While he was restraining the semiconscious, bitten man, the werewolf shook itself unexpectedly and turned into a human. It was clearer now that she had sustained a few wounds in the fight, maybe not too serious, but certainly painful.

A friend threw her his shirt, torn and bloodied, but better than nothing in this situation. She put it on hastily.

"It's over now?" she asked not very clearly. She has recently become unaccustomed to using articulate speech, spending most of her time in canine form.

"It would be too good... but this fight is behind us."

Never ran out of the Tower of Terror.

"Gusto escaped. We better get out of here, too, until the police or somebody else will come here. I bet this son of a bitch called for help."

With difficulty, they all fit into the Jareth's Ferrari. They could have used the Rast pickup, but they preferred not to risk it.

It was only on the way, when the tension eased, that they began to feel how much they had suffered in the fight. Duke had a first aid kit in his car, but its contents were not sufficient to heal all his friends' wounds. He had to stop the car at the nearest gas station, where there was a pharmacy department, and buy additional dressings.

"You're so lucky," said Lasalle. He reduced his dimensions as much as he could and lay down on the back of the passenger seat, wrapping his tail caressingly around Lily's neck.

"It could have been worse," Never tightened the bandage on Oggy's chest, which turned out to have broken two ribs in a fight. And that you have come to the rescue. "Their overconfidence had lost, and we were saved by the fact that we stuck together. Otherwise they would have turned us into chopped liver."

Lasalle meowed and thoughtfully licked the top of his human, though smooth-furred hand, now reduced to the size of a child's.

"Admittedly, you asked for it," he said, "and I knew you weren't going to take good advice. As a rule, I don't get involved in anything, but this time I decided to make an exception to the rule. And I admit I had a lot of fun."

"Good thing at least you," muttered Gerard sourly, "if someone tells me again that death from cyanide is quick and painless, I'll laugh in his face."

"Enjoy your life."

"If it weren't for Athalie, I would be dead as a stump," he looked at the girl hugging his shoulder with obvious affection. She smiled back at him fondly.

Duke returned from the station and tossed the Indian a packet of bandages.

"Where can I drop you off?" he asked, slamming the car door.

For someone who had four vampires in his car, a werewolf, a harpy, and a creature that didn't even have a name, he was remarkably calm, so to speak, impassive."

"First to some night market with clothes," Never answered him. "Then... I think to the airport."

"Why not?"

"How is that?" Fronda was surprised angrily.

"Just because, knight. I'm afraid that despite our victory in this battle, we generally lost. It'll be better if we hide somewhere, rest and coolly develop a further plan of action."

"I advised it," Lasalle reminded casually, "Hey, slow down a bit! I'll jump out right here."

The driver slowed down and opened the door. The big cat flashed to the side of the road and disappeared between the outbuildings of the suburbs.

"Peculiar guy," Duke added the gas again.

"You're a fine one to talk! You tour all over the world and people don't even know who they are applauding." Athalie snorted and winced slightly as she touched her broken nose.

"Well, they better not know."

"Right. Who are you exactly?" Never was interested. "Your singing is hypnotizing, and very much, which can be explained scientifically in the end. But touch? I saw what you do to that Rast."

Jareth shrugged.

"It's such a trick. It works if I use it very rarely. I need this skill every time, so to speak, it takes even several weeks, so I hide it for a special occasion. Now it has happened."

"Haven't heard anyone do that."

"Because you can't do it, you have it."

He paused for a moment and became serious. A signal from several ambulances came from afar. They passed them quite a distance, heading towards Disneyland.

"We run from there just in time," muttered Fronda with an involuntary shiver.

"It looks like," Duke agreed. His friends could see his pale eyes in the driver's mirror and still couldn't guess what color they were, blue, gray, or hazel.

Gerard hugged Athalie protectively.

"What will happen to you now?" he asked warmly.

"I don't know... I have no idea or even the strength to think."

Nobody had. They felt like beaten dogs, and the taste of failure was reaching them more and more clearly. True, they saved their lives - again this time. But they also gained nothing, and their situation was still unenviable.

Duke glanced back.

"I have a suggestion," he said. "In this state, you'd better not pack on the plane. You need to rest and recover, preferably in a safe place."

"You know one?"

"Sort of. My apartment is big, you can accommodate."

"Are you serious?" Never shifted in his seat and grunted involuntarily. "We doesn't want to bother you...?"

"Absolutely not. I'm starting tomorrow a series of concerts and will rarely be in a hotel. I'll check-in you as a technical team that will be working on the material from the recordings in my absence, and no one will ask."

"He's right, Rajah," said Fronda. "I didn't want to come over as a crybaby, but I feel like a scrap. And we all look like the proverbial sour apple marmalade. We really need at least a few days of peace."

"I don't deny it..." Never was not entirely convinced. "Duje, and it will not threaten you? The Rasts don't stick around, and they've seen your face, not to mention your voice, which is, so to speak, quite recognizable."

The musician laughed merrily.

"No worries. They will forget about everything. They won't even know I was there."

"Do you manipulate people's memory too?"

"Only what concerns me. I can't do anything else, I tried. It is a pity, I would help you."

"You're helping anyway, you don't have to... Why, exactly, do you have any interest in it?" Oggy asked distrustfully, wrapping herself tighter in Fronda's shirt.

"That's not nice," Lily scolded her gently. She was the only one who hadn't suffered any injuries, but a few blood stains stained her blouse as well.

Duke didn't seem offended.

"Not at all... It's just that we freaks have to stick together," he replied lightly. "One of us, one of us, gooble-gobble, gooble-gobble"

He whistled a short tune.

"He's right," sighed Fronda. "We won't get far in this state. And we'd better trust him. After all, he helped us a lot."

"We can trust him," the harpy said, touching her nose again, "I should probably go see some doctor."

"I'll take care of you at the hotel," Never promised her.

"And everything will be like in a Disney fairy tale," finished Duke humorously, slowing down a bit.

They had already joined the normal traffic, and you had to be careful not to get a ticket in the end.

*****

They didn't have much. They never burdened themselves with unnecessary baggage, but now they were poorer than ever. Had it not been for Jareth's help, they wouldn't even have had enough tickets, and they would have had to have them.

The set of new documents also cost. After the deliberation, they decided to go to a place where no sect could act with impunity, legally or even in secret - to China.

Their hearts advised them differently, rather to look for survivors in the world, to determine the actual extent of the defeat, but reason dictated a better solution.

They needed peace and security to be able to develop any plan of action, a plan for the next life. They had never been so anxious to live, and they were determined to do whatever it took to prevent any Hunter from reaching them.

"Come with us," Gerard asked Athalie, tearing his mouth away from hers.

They both did not know why or how a strong, insurmountable feeling overwhelmed them. Perhaps it was the effect of the action at Disneyland that one saved another's life there, or maybe love came by itself, uninvited.

"You think I can?" The girl looked hesitantly at Never. In her new dress, with hidden wings and beige nail polish, she looked almost like a model, not the monster of legends she really was. Only her friends were aware of her true identity, but they did not mind. Especially Gerard.

"If you are not afraid," the Indian gave the impression that he did not care. "You had a sample of what can happen to you with us. As for me, do as you see fit."

The young harpy was still hesitating, looking at Gerard, then Rajah, then looking at the airport gate.

"What's happening?" Lily asked softly. She was standing at Fronda's side, one hand resting on the shoulder of Oggy clinging to her, the other clutching her folding cane.

"Athalie is flying with us," Theo explained, grinning from ear to ear. He loved happy endings, even those small ones.

"Avion à destination de Shaghai décollage prévu dans une heure. Les voyageurs sont demandés de se réunir devant la porte 42," the loudspeaker screeched.

The Harpy waved her hand.

"What the heck," she said brightly, "you only live once. Please kidnap me, brave Chevalier. And then we will see."

"One of us," Fronda said.

Gerard hugged her warmly. It had been a long time since he had felt so calm and happy, despite everything.

"Here we go," he said. "There must be a place for us somewhere. Some kind of our own piece of the world."